THE CUPID CAPER

PRAISE FOR LARISSA REINHART

The Finley Goodhart Crime Caper series

"This is as fun a novel as it is moving and at times heart-breaking, never the more so when the final page comes and readers are only left wanting more."

CYNTHIA CHOW, *KING'S RIVER LIFE MAGAZINE* ON THE
CUPID CAPER

"Another great mystery by Larissa Reinhart. Con artists, murder, a cast of sinister characters, and some laughs along the way. Loved it."

TERRI L. AUSTIN, AUTHOR OF THE *ROSE STRICKLAND
MYSTERIES* ON THE CUPID CAPER

The Maizie Albright Star Detective Series

"The mystery and detective cases drive the story, but Larissa Reinhart's characters steal the show every time."

THE GIRL WITH BOOK LUNGS ON NC-17

"NC-17 is simply fabulous. Fans of cozy mysteries, southern chick lit, hick lit, crime capers, and humorous mysteries will love it."

JANE READS ON NC-17

"If you love southern settings with plenty of sweet tea and eccentric characters, the meet up of these two heroines is epic."

"Maizie's missteps make each of her successes an absolute joy, and I encourage readers to delve into this lively, funny, and genuinely satisfying series."

"With visually descriptive narrative, humorous quips, witty repartee and a quirky cast of characters, this was a such a fun book to read."

"Larissa writes a delightful book. Suspense, romance, and some funny situations. [Maizie's] a teen star grown up to new possibilities."

"I love Larissa Reinhart's books because they are funny but they also show the big heart of the protagonist."

"Hollywood glitz meets backwoods grit in this fast-paced ride on D-list celeb Maizie Albright's waning star. Sassy, sexy, and fun, 15 Minutes is hours of enjoyment—and a wonderful start to a fun new series from the charmingly Southern-fried Reinhart."

PHOEBE FOX, AUTHOR OF *THE BREAKUP DOCTOR* SERIES ON 15 MINUTES

"Maizie Albright is the kind of fresh, fun, and feisty 'star detective' I love spending time with, a kind of Nancy Drew meets Lucy Ricardo. Move over, Janet Evanovich. Reinhart is my new "star mystery writer!"

PENNY WARNER, AUTHOR OF *DEATH OF A CHOCOLATE CHEATER* AND *THE CODE BUSTERS CLUB* ON 15 MINUTES

"Child star and hilarious hot mess Maizie Albright trades Hollywood for the backwoods of Georgia and pure delight ensues. Maizie's my new favorite escape from reality."

— GRETCHEN ARCHER, *USA TODAY* BESTSELLING AUTHOR OF THE *DAVIS WAY CRIME CAPER* SERIES ON 15 MINUTES

The Cherry Tucker Mystery Series

"Anytime artist Cherry Tucker has what she calls a Matlock moment, can investigating a murder be far behind? A Composition in Murder is a rollicking good time."

TERRIE FARLEY MORAN, AGATHA AWARD-WINNING AUTHOR OF *READ TO DEATH* ON A COMPOSITION IN MURDER

"This is a winning series that continues to grow stronger and never fails to entertain with laughs, a little snark, and a ton of heart."

"Cherry Tucker is a strong, sassy, Southern sleuth who keeps you on the edge of your seat."

"Because of Cherry's experiences, she knows that—Super Swine notwithstanding—man has always been the most dangerous game, making her the perfect protagonist for this giggle-inducing, down-home fun."

"The perfect blend of funny, intriguing, and sexy! Another must-read masterpiece from the hilarious Cherry Tucker Mystery Series."

"Artist and accidental detective Cherry Tucker goes back to high school and finds plenty of trouble and skeletons...Reinhart's charming, sweet-tea flavored series keeps getting better!"

"Like front-porch lemonade, Reinhart's cast of characters offer a perfect balance of tart and sweet."

"Reinhart manages to braid a complicated plot into a tight and funny tale. The reader grows to love Cherry and her quirky worldview, her sometimes misguided judgment, and the eccentric characters that populate the country of Halo, Georgia. Cozy fans will love this latest Cherry Tucker mystery."

"Reinhart's country-fried mystery is as much fun as a ride on the tilt-a-whirl at a state fair. Readers who like a little small-town charm with their mysteries will enjoy Reinhart's series."

"This mystery keeps you laughing and guessing from the first page to the last. A whole-hearted five stars."

"*Portrait of a Dead Guy* is an entertaining mystery full of quirky characters and solid plotting...Highly recommended for anyone who likes their mysteries strong and their mint juleps stronger!"

"Reinhart is a truly talented author and this book was one of the best cozy mysteries we reviewed this year."

"It takes a rare talent to successfully portray a beer-and-hormone-addled artist as a sympathetic and worthy heroine, but Reinhart pulls it off with tongue-in-cheek panache. Cherry is a lovable riot, whether drooling over the town's hunky males, defending her dysfunctional family's honor, or snooping around murder scenes."

THE CUPID CAPER

A FINLEY GOODHART CRIME CAPER
BOOK 1

LARISSA REINHART

Past Perfect Press

THE CUPID CAPER

A Finley Goodhart Crime Caper #1

Copyright © 2018 by Larissa Reinhart

Author photograph by Scott Asano

Cover Design by The Killion Group, Inc.

Library of Congress control number: 2018934576

ISBN: 978-0-9985484-8-7; 978-0-9985484-7-0; 978-0-9985484-9-4

Past Perfect Press

This is a work of fiction. Names, characters, places, and incidents are either the products of the author's imagination or are used fictitiously, and any resemblance to actual persons, living or dead, business establishments, events, or locales is purely coincidental.

Printed in the USA

BOOKS BY LARISSA REINHART

A Cherry Tucker Mystery Series

A CHRISTMAS QUICK SKETCH (prequel)

PORTRAIT OF A DEAD GUY (#1)

STILL LIFE IN BRUNSWICK STEW (#2)

HIJACK IN ABSTRACT (#3)

THE VIGILANTE VIGNETTE (#3.5)

DEATH IN PERSPECTIVE (#4)

THE BODY IN THE LANDSCAPE (#5)

A VIEW TO A CHILL (#6)

A COMPOSITION IN MURDER (#7)

A MOTHERLODE OF TROUBLE (#8.5)

Audio

PORTRAIT OF A DEAD GUY

STILL LIFE IN BRUNSWICK STEW

HIJACK IN ABSTRACT

DEATH IN PERSPECTIVE

THE BODY IN THE LANDSCAPE

A VIEW TO A CHILL in CRIMES MOST MERRY AND ALBRIGHT

A COMPOSITION IN MURDER

Box Set

CHERRY TUCKER MYSTERIES 1-3

Maizie Albright Star Detective Series

15 MINUTES

16 MILLIMETERS

NC-17

A VIEW TO A CHILL

17.5 CARTRIDGES IN A PEAR TREE

18 CALIBER

18 1/2 DISGUISES

19 CRIMINALS

20 CARATS

Audio

15 MINUTES

16 MILLIMETERS

NC-17

18 CALIBER

18 1/2 DISGUISES

CRIMES MOST MERRY AND ALBRIGHT

Box Set

#WANNABEDETECTIVE, MAIZIE ALBRIGHT 1-3

CRIMES MOST MERRY AND ALBRIGHT

A Finley Goodhart Crime Caper Series

PIG'N A POKE (prequel, short story)

THE CUPID CAPER

THE PONY PREDICAMENT (coming soon!)

THE HEIR AFFAIR (coming soon!)

ACKNOWLEDGMENTS

Thanks to the wonderful people at The Page Turner Awards for all the work you put into the international awards ceremony.

Eleanor Cawood Jones, thank you for your patience with me. Also for editing what turned out NOT to be a short novella. Kim Killion of The Killion Group for the awesome cover (once again!).

A big hug to Atlanta, Newnan, Griffin, and Woodstock. And a big thanks to the trustees at Oakland Cemetery for all they do in maintaining its historic preservation. Please continue with awesome events like Malts and Vaults! Also to great Atlanta restaurants like Noodle, Flying Biscuit, Chick-Fil-A, and Octane Coffee. All delicious!

Terri L Austin for being such an awesome critique partner and friend. For Ritter Ames for all your knowledge and assistance. Gretchen Archer, thank you for your sense of humor.

Dru Ann Love for your continued encouragement, and all the great things you do for writers. Plus for being such a sweet friend.

The Mystery Minions, thank you so much for your incredible support, friendship, and goat videos. xoxo

Special thanks to Mary Ann Forbes for letting me borrow her nickname!

My Rockin' Review Team! You are such a huge help in each of my releases. Thanks so much for all your support.

As always — Trey, Soph, Lu, Diana, Erich, Irma, and Mark. Thanks for hanging out in Oakland Cemetery with me! Love you so much! Gina, Bill, & Mom — thank you for all your support!

For my readers who asked for more Finley Goodhart. Thanks so much for all your encouragement. xoxo

"The first and worst of all frauds is to cheat one's self. All sin is easy after that." — Pearl Bailey

---

Whoever is faithful in small matters will be faithful in large ones; whoever is dishonest in small matters will be dishonest in large ones. Luke 16:10

1

THE APPROACH

WEDNESDAYS OFTEN BROUGHT the college boys to Jello's Pool Hall. Particularly in the winter. I'd call it cabin fever, except we were in Georgia. Still, too cold to drink on their frat house front porch rocking chairs. Too early in the week to host a party. The non-heathens would be attending Wednesday night church. The good students would be in class or the library.

But the bad boys would bring money to places like Jello's. Which was why I was there.

And how Lex knew to find me.

I had just racked a fresh round. Satisfied with the smooth lift of the triangle. No balls escaped. Feeling good about the roll of twenties tucked into the front pocket of my jeans. That gratification disappeared upon sensing a male presence behind me. The scent of his aftershave cut through the pervading smell of beer, stale smoke, and old fryer oil. I sniffed once. Recognized the spicy scent of his cologne. Rested the cue stick on the table.

"Wanna make a wager? I'm having a lucky night." I bent over the table to place the cue ball. Angled the stick. Shot it backward. And turned to face him.

"Hello, love." Lex grabbed the stick. "Watch yourself. I'd like to remain a baritone, if you don't mind."

"Sorry." I didn't sound sorry. Didn't even get close. "Careful where you stand next time. Another town, maybe?"

He pushed the stick away. Grinned. Sidled forward. "Don't want me too deep in your pocket?"

I rolled my eyes, then studied the man. His thick, sandy hair had been trimmed to maintain an artful dishevelment. Smiling blue eyes. Sensuous lips held a relaxed smile. His boy-next-door good looks never revealed anything but indolent charm and false promises. A real ace. Too careful and too practiced to show anything else.

"You look tired." I took a careful step to the side. Rested my hip against the table. "Tinge of blue beneath your eyes."

"Too many lonely nights."

"I bet. They have medicine for that, you know."

"Not the cure I seek. You're looking fit, though." His gaze traveled the room. "How'd you do tonight?"

"What do you want, Lex?" My hand reached for the cue ball. I rolled it beneath my palm.

His eyes snapped back to me and told me what I already knew. I narrowed mine. His mouth quirked.

"Relax," he said. "Gave you my word I'd leave you alone, didn't I?"

"Your word isn't worth much. And you just proved it, seeing as how you're here and all."

"When have I ever lied to you?"

I gripped the cue ball.

He raised his hand. "Right. But I am here out of the goodness of my heart. Thought I should see you about Penny Forbes."

"What about Penny?" I frowned. "Are you working together? Not interested."

"You haven't heard?" The mask fell. His face tightened and he appeared older, matured. "Fin, we should go somewhere private."

"Why?" I didn't like the mask, but I didn't like what he'd replaced it with either. He looked worried. Lex never worried. The carefree charisma wasn't just an act. I was the worrier. "You know I'm on the square now. If you and Penny have gotten yourself into a mess, y'all just get yourselves out of it."

"On the level, but still dodgy enough to plunder these wankers," he muttered. "Finley, I'm serious. I don't want to tell you here."

"You're never serious." I turned. Settled the white ball. Chalked the cue tip. Moved to the side and leaned over the table. Sighted the ball. Placed the stick between my thumb and fingers.

Lex leaned over me, close enough for his words to buzz in my ear. "She's dead, Fin. Penny's dead." A hand fell on my shoulder. "I'm sorry. I didn't want to tell you like this. Finley, come with me."

I pulled in a breath. Ignored his hand and the clamor ringing between my ears. Gritting my teeth, I lowered my head. Centered my gaze on the space between the second and fourth racked ball. Brought the stick back and let it glide. The break rang. Two solids slammed into the back and corner right pockets.

Lex's hand shot forward. Caught a stripe as it raced toward the front left. "Sloppy. That's a scratch."

"Hey." I turned, swinging the stick with me.

He caught the stick again, pushed it aside, and grabbed my arm. "Love, did you hear me? I'm sorry. I didn't want to be the bearer, but God knows I can't... I had to see you. News like this. I cocked it up." He shook his head. "Fin. Are you all right? What can I do, love?"

"Nothing." I shook my arm free and fixed my eyes to a point on the wall behind him. I hadn't seen Penny for months. She'd been busy. I'd been hiding. But dead? She was too young—mid-twenties, like me. Car accident? Cripes, I hoped she didn't get sick. The fatal illnesses I knew that struck Penny's age bracket weren't pretty.

I sucked in a deep breath. Let it out. Hated how shaky it sounded. "How'd she die?"

"Let's talk somewhere else." He paused. Sighed. "Right. Drug overdose. Heroin, is what I heard."

My eyes flew to his face. The blue eyes watched me. Soberly, with a hint of pity. I despised that look even more than the worry.

"No way on God's green earth. Penny's momma was a junkie. Crooked as she could get, Penny wouldn't touch a substance stronger than champagne. You heard wrong, Lex."

He shrugged. "I'm sorry, love."

"Stop calling me that." I felt my throat tighten and forced a swallow. "Don't call me that anymore."

"Can't help myself." His head tilted, the pitying expression deepening. "Let me at least buy you a drink. We should toast Penny. You've known her since, when? First time on the street?"

He reached for me, but I sidestepped. "I'm not drinking to that lie. She didn't overdose."

"Fin, it's hard to hear, but it's true. Heard it from Dot, then checked myself."

"Who found her?" I gripped my cue stick. My chest felt like it was going to cave in. "Police? Which one? County? City? The heroin could have been planted, Lex. You know she's on *his* list because of me. It's not beneath him to do something like that just to make her look bad. He's got the county coroner in his pocket. John Prince is a drunk and a gambler—"

"What would be the point in that? Penny was taken to the hospital, love. Wasn't a bust or anything like that. Your da—"

I held up a finger.

"Right. Come on." Lex glanced around. Spotted my cue case under a nearby chair. Pulled it out. Took the stick from me. Unscrewed the shaft from the butt, flipped the top open on the hard case, and slipped the sticks inside. Slinging the long case strap over his shoulder, he cupped my elbow.

I had stuck on the word *hospital*, rooted to the floor. Absently, I'd reached for the ring hanging from the chain around my neck. At Lex's touch, I shook off my daze and dropped the ring.

"Where are you staying?" said Lex.

"Nowhere." My stomach squeezed. I allowed him to walk me to the door. "Motel on Thirty-Four."

"You're coming to my place." He glanced at me. "Don't worry, love. You can trust me."

"No, I can't." I could feel the tears forming. I swallowed hard. "I can't go home with you. I should talk to Dot."

"Let me go with you."

I shook my head. Before I could speak, a voice hollered from the rear of the hall. The shouting intensified. We turned. A young man jogged forward, followed by a small herd of beefy minions. The insults thrown in my direction did nothing to faze the other patrons. Nothing new for Jello's. Behind the bar, Jello called out, demanding payment of the young man's tab. Jello didn't care about fights as long as his end was covered.

"Did you take him?" whispered Lex. "Of course you did." He spun us back toward the door. Hurried our pace.

"Wasn't much of a hustle," I said. "He saw me beat the pants off his friend first. He's drunk."

"Drunk, stupid, and big. Not a good combination." Lex handed me the cue case.

"He practically begged me to—" The obscenity the guy shouted caught me off guard. "Vile boy. Guess he's worked himself into a lather about it at the bar. I am a mere female, you know. A blow to his pride. Took him three large before he gave up."

"Right. Blighter. He's going to catch us in the parking lot. Student, yes?"

Before the doors, Lex stopped. Pivoted. Retraced his steps toward the ape. Lex put out a hand as if to shake, then used it to steady the gorilla. "Hey, mate. Couldn't help but hear you. Let me correct the situation."

Behind him, the man's friends—an indistinguishable line of baseball hats, college-branded hoodies, and beards—blundered to a halt, confused by Lex's friendly voice and relaxed candor.

"What?" bellowed the man. He shook a fist in my direction.

"Were you carrying her stick? She friggin' has her own cue? What the f—"

Lex cut off his drunken cursing. "Sorry, mate. Didn't catch your name. Drew, was it?"

"Yes, how—?"

"Your friend mentioned it." Lex jerked his chin toward the line of monkeys behind Drew. They shifted, widening the circle. One twisted away to wander back to the bar.

"Listen, Drew. She took you for a ride, did she? Are you upset that this young girl beat you in pool?" Lex's voice rose while seeming to drop. "You know, she's a brilliant mathematician. Really. It's all in the angles. Trajectories. That sort of thing. Her father's a professor. Maybe you had him. Physics. Genius, really. Doctor—"

"Williams?" offered Drew.

"You know him? You might know me as well."

"You're British."

"Accent gave it away, did it?" Lex smiled. "Yes, a doctoral student. I work for Williams. Unfortunate situation, his daughter." He gave a nod in my direction.

Leaning against the door, I shrugged. Gave Drew an apologetic smile.

"A bit touched. Explains the maths, yes? Can't help herself, you know what I mean?"

"What?" said Drew. "She seemed normal."

"We won't speak the words. Minor's right to privacy. So hard to tell sixteen from twenty-one these days."

Drew's eyes widened. "She's sixteen?"

"And Jello," Lex continued, "as all you students know, looks the other way on such things. Fake IDs and the lot. Probably why you and your friends are here. I trotted over to find her. Mission for Dr. Williams. Campus Police are on their way."

"Security? They're not cops."

"No, but they report criminal incidents to the police. Under the Clery Act, I believe. Campus police is not mall security, Drew. The actual police will be just behind them. Nothing they love more than a fake ID bust. Identity theft and the like is a serious concern these days."

As Drew swayed, Lex dropped an arm around his shoulder and steered him toward a table.

"Let's chat, Drew. Dr. Williams has a protocol for these things." Lex pulled out a chair.

Drew sank into it. His remaining friends drifted toward the pool tables.

Hovering above Drew, Lex crooked a finger at me and raised his voice. "Miss Williams, we need to settle this. If you could join us, please."

I slunk to their table, doing my best imitation of sixteen-going-on-twenty-something.

Lex cupped a hand around his mouth and raised his voice. "Jello, how much does he owe you?"

"Fifty," called Jello.

Drew blanched.

"Heavy night for three-dollar beer," said Lex. "All right, Drew. Let's pay Jello first. Jello only takes cash. Doesn't like to pay those pesky credit card service fees."

Or taxes, but I kept that thought to myself.

"Can't." Drew pointed at me. "She took all my money. I told Jello she'd have to pay."

"You lost your bet," I said. "Bets, rather. All six of them. After the first three times, you might have realized the odds were against you. Really, after losing the first two, it's sixty percent in favor of losing. A betting man should know these things."

"Miss Williams, what have we told you about speaking so bluntly? People perceive that as rude." Lex shook his head. "Sorry, Drew. Looks like I got here just in time."

He presented a clip of cash. Palmed the clip. Counted off what appeared to be fifty. Handed the folded notes to me. "Miss Williams, pay Jello. And tip him well."

I nodded meekly. Trotted to Jello and delivered the fold. "Payment for young Drew."

Jello scooped the bills into a meaty fist and dropped them in his till. "You're going to catch it one of these days, Fin."

"Not if they catch it first." I winked. "Drew had an extra Benjamin for you. Gratis. Also in case the others don't reconcile. These rich kids are the worst at paying their debts. Money spilling out of their pockets, yet too cheap to pay a tab."

"And too dumb not to see it fall out of their pockets and into your hands. I thought you went straight, hon."

"I did," I said. "Can I help it if these boys won't let themselves believe what's right in front of their eyes? If I don't hide my skill, it's not a hustle."

"This is Lex's money then?" Jello's smile stretched, making his chins wobble.

"I didn't say that. Lex would never short you, any more than I would. But Lex would rather have Drew pay his own bill. As he should." I leaned forward. "Jello, what did you hear about Penny Forbes dying?"

"Thought you knew, hon." Jello's chins quivered with a mournful shake. "Can't believe it. She was engaged, too, did you know that? Found a way up."

"Up?"

"Rich guy. Didn't surprise me too much. That Penny. Gorgeous and smart. A legend."

"Hold on." I checked on Lex. While drawing out a story with one hand, he slipped the money clip back into Drew's pocket. Typical Lex. Let Drew think he'd blown his cash when he woke hung over and broke.

I turned back to Jello. "Penny was engaged to a rich guy and OD'd on heroin? Doesn't add up, Jello. She didn't use and she'd never pimp out. She was a good roper, but never let herself get too dirty."

"I reckoned the same. After her momma—" His chins shook again.

"Exactly. The rich guy, was he a mark? Or legit?"

"Dunno, hon." Jello fixed his piggy eyes over my shoulder. "Lex is wrapping up."

I turned, catching the exuberant expression lighting Lex's face. He could be mistaken for a young doctoral student. A highlighted lock had fallen over his forehead. His lean physique gave the impression of slightness. I knew the wiry strength that hid beneath his designer button-down. He just needed a pair of wire-rims to complete the picture of a slightly nerdy but cute grad student. Not that Lex had ever set foot in a college classroom. No more than I had.

At least I didn't think so. You could never be sure with Lex.

I wouldn't put it past him to audit the classes that interested him. And it wouldn't surprise me if he had somehow obtained a diploma. He was good at that sort of thing. Got his kicks from pitting his wiles against bureaucratic quagmires. Anything that frustrated a normal person, Lex loved to unravel and beat.

Including trying to lure me back into his questionable operations. And other areas of his life.

Catching my eye, Lex gave me a slight nod. I slunk back to the table, seemingly chastened.

"Thanks for covering my tab," Drew said. "And if I see her in here again, I'll leave her alone."

"Do that, young man. Although I'd give Jello's a wide berth, if I were you. He overlooks anything but paying your bill, which you almost didn't do. But if you risk Jello's wrath and do see Miss Williams, give Mr. Jello the word that you've spotted this young sociopath. He'll escort her out the door. Likely you as well. Jello hates rats even more than scarpers. I think it's a cattle prod he uses."

Lex's smile quirked as he peered down his nose at me. "You heard that, Miss Williams? It's for your own good. Respectable young women don't hang out in pool halls."

I pursed my lips. Lex was really pushing it.

He grasped my elbow. "Past your bedtime, Miss Williams. Time to go home. Your father will be sorry to hear about this."

"He certainly would," I said dryly. My father was always sorry to hear about me and any sort of hustle—imagined or real. Particularly since my father was a cop.

And more crooked than any swindler I'd ever met.

2

THE HANDLER

"I DON'T NEED A RIDE." Those were my only words in the parking lot. Yet I still found myself in Lex's ridiculously orange Camaro. Not because he was that good. Skipping the ride would have been my way of punishing him. Lex knew that's how I'd see it. In my view, a punishment meant that I still cared about his feelings, so I had to be purposeful in not consciously punishing him.

Stupid as it sounds.

But then he probably knew that, too, so the whole point was moot anyway. Which was just one of the countlessly frustrating things about Lex Leopold.

I wasn't even sure if that was his real name. Another frustration. And another reason to steer clear of Lex.

As we zipped down local highways toward the outskirts of Atlanta, I said, "I didn't need your help with Drew."

"Of course you didn't, love. I've seen you handle plenty of Drews."

"That's why I carry a hard pool case and not a soft one."

"Right."

"And I don't need you to take me to Dot's."

"Moral support. That's what I am."

"Moral." I snorted. "That's a good one."

"Going down that road, are we?" Lex quirked a brow. "Still beating yourself up? Guilt doesn't solve problems, love. Just clouds judgement."

"Guilt has given me clarity."

"No, it hasn't. Clarity comes before guilt. Guilt just makes you wallow in self-loathing. Does you no good whatsoever."

"How would you know?" I said. "You never feel guilty."

"Because it's a fruitless emotion. If I believe I did something wrong, I seek to rectify it. That's not guilt. It's restitution."

"You never think you do anything wrong."

"Not true, love." He cast me a long, heated glance.

I held my breath for a second, forcing my stuttering heart to slow and my expression to remain calm.

"Just drop me off at Dot's." I turned to look out the passenger window, but the dark, tree-lined road showed only his dashboard light reflection. Lex faced the dark stretch of highway, but I knew his eyes were dancing.

Cripes.

"I have business with Dot as well," he said.

I let out an exasperated sigh.

"That's a fruitless emotion, too, love."

"Shut up, Lex."

His reflection grinned, then sobered. "I *am* sorry about Penny."

I caught my own image and melancholy expression. Remembered a time when Penny had given me a similar lesson on remorse. She'd given up guilt long before I met her, even at seventeen. Penny said we couldn't afford guilt, only survival. But she'd been alone much longer. She never had a real family—not one she could rely on—other than the kind she occasionally cobbled together.

At least I'd had a family once. Maybe that made guilt harder to expunge.

Bright lights swallowed the darkness, disrupting our reflections. The trees gave way to gas stations, fast food, and dollar stores. The car slowed to halt at a stop light. People milled in front of a taqueria bodega. Three doors down, more folks spilled from a hot wing joint. Across the street, young punks loitered before the Quik Mart. A patrol car rolled by and the punks scattered.

"Jello said Penny was engaged," I said. "To a rich guy."

"Legit?" said Lex.

"Jello didn't know."

The light changed. The Camaro sped forward. Lex turned off the highway onto a side street. Bright storefronts were replaced by dark warehouses, busted parking lights, and broken concrete. We turned again, passing a fortune teller's house. A neon hand blinked in the window. He slowed. In this neighborhood, people walked more than they drove. Driveways with pickups and old Cadillacs. Squat brick apartments. Weeds grew taller. Chain link grew rustier.

Lex turned again, honked, and waited for a gate to open in front of a car repair shop. No sign marked it as such. Just a lot filled with rusting heaps of uninteresting vintages and cheap models. Stacked, balding tires created a fence of sorts, hiding a real metal fence topped with circles of razor wire.

The gate opened and closed behind us as we drove through. Lex waited again while a garage bay door slowly lifted. We pulled inside. I clambered out before Lex could open my door. Held my breath against the stench of old oil, grease, and rubber. It masked the more exotic merchandise that hid within the connected office and supply rooms. I avoided those rooms, not wanting to know more than I needed. My appearance at Dot's upstairs apartment was rare enough.

Thankfully.

"Leave your case in the car, love," said Lex, climbing out his side. "You know how Dot feels about weapons."

"She called me a two-bit hustler, not a gangster. Anyway, Dot knows I'm on the level, right? You told her?"

"And I told you what could happen if that got out." He moved around the car and leaned his back against my door. "I'm trying to protect you."

"No, you're not. You just want to use me. I'm only here to get information about Penny."

"Wouldn't do you any good to tell Dot tonight. You need information. Dot isn't going to share unless there's something in it for her. And if you're on the square..."

"I get it."

I stepped away, but his hand snaked out and hooked a loop in my jeans. He reeled me back. I returned to my spot but resisted letting him pull me closer.

"Fin, love. This"—he waved his hand between us—"is no good. We need a resolution. We can't go into the dragon's lair like this."

"I gave you a resolution." I crossed my arms. "No more partnership. No more us."

"And I rejected it. Therefore, not resolved." Lex shook his head. "You're going to need my help in there. I'm not the only one who knows Dot scares you."

"I'm not—" It was true. Dot the Jamaican scared the bejesus out of me. But she scared the bejesus out of everyone. Dot was six foot five. An indeterminable age. Almost indeterminable sex. Nobody knew if she was really even Jamaican. Hands like catcher's mitts. If Dot cocked her head and squinted at you, you felt like committing hari-kari. "Why aren't you scared of her?"

A smile curled Lex's lips. He raised his brows. "Who said I'm not? Fear is a useful emotion, as long as you keep it in check. And don't show it."

I glared at him.

"Anger, on the other hand, is not useful." Lex laughed and drew me closer until I stopped between his open legs. His expression grew somber. He gently swept my long, brown hair from my face. The bright eyes roved over me, rested on my lips for a beat, then caught my gaze and held it. "I miss you, Fin. We were good, you and me. And when we're good, we're very, very good."

"And when we're bad, we're terrible." I clenched the sides of my thighs to keep my hands from reaching for him. "I don't want this life anymore, Lex. And you need it."

"Maybe I just need you." His eyes dropped back to my mouth.

I licked my lips, then caught myself. If only. "I can't give you the same kick. And boredom doesn't suit you." I backed up slowly, then turned. "Come on. Dot doesn't like to wait. She knows we're here."

DOT CAMPBELL LIVED above the garage, although occupied was a better term for it. Her surroundings were sumptuous but sparse. The reinforced concrete walls were left bare but for a mega flat screen and an even bigger portrait of Dot, done in a frenzied style with bombastic colors. The furniture was glass, metal, and leather. Modern discomfort. Except for Dot's throne, a plush leather recliner facing the flat screen.

It was rumored that Dot didn't own a bed because she never slept. True or not, appointments with Dot happened at any time of the day or night. And she always wore a black silk bathrobe over a track suit, adding to the mystery.

We found Dot standing before a long row of cabinets, housing various aquariums and terrariums. Dot's pets. Not a mammal among them. All lethal. Likely illegal. Glancing over her shoulder, she gave us a nod and returned her attention to a glass case of tiny neon frogs.

"Hello, Dot," said Lex. "Feeding time at the zoo?"

"I'm rearranging. Previously…" She grunted, hefting the terrarium of frogs to an empty space. "They were by genus. I'm switching to a more geographic-type arrangement. I'm curious to see their reactions to their neighbors."

"Fascinating." Lex grimaced. "I've got Fin with me."

"Saw her. Heard she lost her vehicle. She should stick to pool instead of poker. Or get better at counting cards."

I felt the twin burns of humiliation and temper crawl up my neck.

"'Course," continued Dot. She picked up a smaller terrarium and turned it slowly before placing it on top of the frogs. "Goodhart ain't just along for the ride, now is she?"

"Yes, well, she has some questions about our mutual acquaintance, Penny Forbes," said Lex. "About her death, actually."

Dot shot him a look over her shoulder. "What am I? A funeral director? Finley's not part of the business we're discussing tonight, Leopold."

"Listen, Dot," I said. "I'll wait in the car while you discuss business—"

"You know the rules, Goodhart. No one waits downstairs."

"I'm already here, Dot," I said. "Penny and I were tight. You know that."

"If y'all were so tight, then what'd you need me for?"

"I didn't know… I've been busy—"

Dot turned to face us, her robe swirling out behind her. Crossed her arms and cocked her head, studying me.

I shuffled my feet. Knew that wasn't a good move. Raised my chin and met her eye.

"You've been hiding, Finley Goodhart. From him." She nodded toward Lex. "Or me or someone else. Maybe check all those boxes. I don't trust people who hide. 'Specially some two-bit country hustler."

I pulled in a breath but let it out low and slow. Felt my cheeks flame. Told myself to chill.

Dot's eyebrow rose. "Anyways, you ain't here to find out where to send flowers. What's the issue? Penny didn't get it from any associate of mine. You looking for a fight, country girl? You want to tussle with Dot? You that stupid, Finley Goodhart?"

"By 'it,' you mean the heroin?" I kept my voice level. "Penny didn't use. There's no way she died of an overdose."

"I think the hospital that declared her dead would disagree with you."

I felt my flinch before I could control it. "Who was this man she was engaged to? When did she get engaged?"

"I wonder what you're thinking? She shot up with her fiancé? Or he shot her up for some nefarious motive?" Dot was fond of five-dollar words.

"I don't know what to think," I said. "That's why I'm here. You're the thinker. I'm just the country hustler, right?"

She strode to her chair, robe whipping out behind her like a cape. Dropping into the thick leather, Dot popped the handle to kick back. Her Adidas high tops knocked together. She steepled her hands on her chest.

I gave Lex a look. Followed Dot to stand before the throne. Heard Lex move, glanced behind me, and saw him standing before the zoo. He was listening but giving me space.

He knew I wasn't pleased with the way he took over at Jello's.

"Don't tap the glass," called Dot to Lex. "If they spit poison at you, it's a helluva mess to clean off that glass."

She turned her attention to me. "Let's see. You and me both know Penny loved some racket but didn't get over-involved much with the real stuff. And she did get engaged. Some rich dude. So I was surprised, myself, to tell you the honest truth."

I nodded, thankful my words had assuaged her. I'd learned to walk on eggshells the hard way. I'd talked Lex out of dealing with Dot in a number of projects. She hadn't taken it kindly. Lex had a talent for analysis and planning. Reading situations and people. An inside man. Dot was a handler; she put together crews. More Fagin than Corleone. She knew everyone and everything. Plus she was a fixer. She knew the law's enforcers and protectors.

Particularly the ones who could be greased.

When she'd found out Lex had turned down jobs because of me, Dot sent one of her human pets to pick me up. They brought me in for a come-to-Jesus meeting. Laid it down that I was holding Lex back from "higher purposes" and "greater financial reward." I'd better "rethink my relationship parameters" with Lex Leopold. Dot would "do the thinking" for me.

"Or what?" I'd stupidly asked.

She had given me a taste of the "or what." Cuffed me with a mammoth paw. Slammed me to the ground. Almost knocked out my tooth.

"You think I don't know where you are at all times? You think I don't know who your daddy is? Who your momma was? I know you, Finley Goodhart. Have your relationship or what-have-you with Lex Leopold, but keep your damn mouth out of my business."

I turned my thoughts from my teeth and back to Dot's current state of mind. I needed her mellow.

"You're right. Penny kept a good head. She made careful choices," I said. Not always legal or ethical choices. But Penny fended for herself. "I want to know about this fiancé."

"Don't know him. I heard she met him at some hookup."

"Hookup? Like on Tinder?"

"You think a rich man needs Tinder?" She reconsidered. "Not for finding a wife, anyway. No, like a match service. But not online. They meet in person because they're serious. Like on those reality shows, but it's not a reality show. High level business-types. Those folks who don't have time to meet a date and aren't so good at dating anyway, so the service creates opportunities for them to hook up."

"How would Penny get into a service like that? They must screen."

Dot chuckled. "Depends who's running it."

"What do you mean?" My voice had sharpened. I caught myself. "The dating service is a front?" That sounded more like Penny.

"You got to wonder, don't you, how a face like Penny got into some millionaire matchmaking digs."

"Penny was good looking, young, and smart. She played the face well. Maybe she wasn't really engaged. Maybe she was working and got in some trouble."

"That's what you think."

"That's what I'm wondering."

"I know a guy who knows a dude." Dot never dropped names. "Dude likes his Korean BBQ. You know up in Doraville-Chamblee? Buford Highway."

"There's a lot of Korean BBQ in Chamblee. Along with every other kind of Asian cuisine."

"That's his normal hangout." Dot nodded. "But there's a few Asian places in Midtown, too. Where these techie dudes like to eat."

"Your dude knows Penny's fiancé? From a restaurant?"

"He's not my dude. I know somebody who knows him. And he might be an outside man. If the match place is a hustle. Which I'm not saying it is."

"Right," I said. "A Korean guy? You think he'll meet with me?"

Dot shrugged "I don't know where his grandpa was born. He likes Korean food is all. It's good stuff. You know the Bibimbap? I like it spicy. They got this chili paste that'll rip through your sinuses."

I swallowed the urge to lose my patience. "If I wanted to meet this man, where should I go and when?"

"I'll let you know." Dot smiled wide. Her even, white teeth gleamed. "But that's a favor now, ain't it."

I bit the inside of my cheek.

"You know, Dot." Lex edged next to me. "I'm doing you a favor as well. Perhaps my favor for Fin's would be a fair exchange. What do you say?"

"Forget it." I wasn't owing somebody like Dot, and I didn't want Lex's favors on my conscience. I'd finally freed myself from the grift. I wasn't going down that road again. "I'll figure this out myself."

"What you going to do?" Dot chuckled. "Visit every Korean restaurant, hoping you run into the right dude? You gonna offend someone, Finley."

I pressed my lips together. I'd go to the funeral, talk to the fiancé myself. But I didn't want Dot muscling in. Or Lex.

Lex's eyebrows quivered, but he remained silent.

"Thank you for your time and information," I said. "If you open the gate, I'll mosey on home. Y'all tend to your business."

Dot laughed. "Suit yourself, country girl. You wanna walk in this neighborhood, help yourself."

3

THE FOUNDATION

I MADE it to a bus stop without incident. I'd learned a thing or two since running away at seventeen. Understanding the Atlanta bus network was more difficult than walking through rough neighborhoods, but I'd gotten it down. Knew where to change. Knew where to grab a lift without costing me an arm and a leg.

Finding the funeral would be trickier. People like Penny didn't have funerals. Likely why it hadn't occurred to Dot. If the fiancé was legit, he'd probably do something. But what was I going to do? Call every funeral home in the Atlanta telephone directory? Exactly. And I didn't want Lex tracing my Googling. I wasn't sure if he could, but it seemed like something he would do.

Luckily, I knew some people, too. Real people. People who knew about funerals.

Bev Talmadge had worked the ER at Grady Memorial Hospital with Mom. Downtown Atlanta. I grew up listening to stories about gunshot wounds, tail lights, and full-moon crazies. Now Bev had an easier job at one of the local Piedmont Hospitals. Bev knew my deal. Knew what had happened. Didn't blame me too much. She'd know how to find a funeral.

Plus, Bev still liked the graveyard shift. Late was never too late.

I put in a call. Got through all the "Fin, honey," questions about my current situation and got down to the heart.

"I have this friend, Penny Forbes. Had, I guess. She was a little twisted, but good people. Brought into a local ER, DOA. Heroin overdose. She wasn't a user, so that's my concern."

"Fin, honey. I'm sorry," said Bev. "You just don't know about some people. It can happen on the first time, too."

"The thing is, her momma's a junkie. Penny grew up around meth heads and all that. Child Services would yank Penny out, then give her back until they'd find out her momma couldn't stay clean. Got caught in that cycle until she was about fourteen. Penny was smart. Swore up and down she'd never have anything to do with drugs."

Bev sighed. She'd heard those stories plenty of times. And knew the statistics.

"Anyway," I said. "I just heard about Penny. She was engaged. I think there'll be a funeral but don't know where. Can you help?"

"Since we know her name, it shouldn't be that hard to find out which hospital. The funeral might be in the paper."

"I don't know about that," I said. "Who would advertise an overdose?"

Bev snorted. "It's not an ad, Fin, it's a funeral announcement. They don't have to list the cause of death."

"But Penny didn't know the kind of people who attend funerals."

"The funeral is for the bereaved. If there's an announcement, it's for the fiancé's folks. But if I find out which hospital admitted her, I can find out where they took her." Bev paused. "Fin, honey. After this funeral, why don't you come see me? It'd do me some good to see your face. Marian—"

"Sure thing, Bev," I said quickly. "And thanks for checking on this for me."

I got to work, scanning The AJC-Online for funeral announcements. The *Atlanta Journal Constitution* covered Atlanta but also had sections for the metro-area counties. The search didn't take long. Penny was given a three-liner in the Sunday obits. Beloved fiancée. No funeral. A celebration of life at a country club and private interment instead.

Penny had certainly moved on up. Too rich for a funeral.

I WASN'T sure what to wear to a celebration of life. Figured basic black was safe. The country club was on the north side of Atlanta. No bus service, so I had to Uber. Just as well, since I'd Goodwill-shopped for a new dress and heels. I'd pulled my long hair into a chignon. Went heavy on the makeup. Kept on a pair of knock-off sunglasses that even fooled the Fendi sales rep at Nordstrom's.

My diamonds weren't real, either. But my boobs were, so I figured I had one up on most of the gals at this event.

The celebration of life looked a lot like a cocktail party. A blown-up photo of Penny and the fiancé on an easel. A table with flowers and more pictures. I scanned the guest book but didn't sign. Snagged a glass of wine and a cheese straw. Meandered the room. I nibbled and sipped. Smiled and nodded. Ignored the looks from the businessmen. Also from their trophy girls. The business-women didn't cut me a glance. Didn't hear much mention of Penny. But I hadn't found the fiancé yet, either. Seemed most of these folks worked for the same tech company as the fiancé, Mark Davis.

Lots of money in the room. My toes curled in my heels. I could barely contain myself from licking my lips. Money meant greed. Greed meant easy hustles from people who'd be too embarrassed to report the con, since the hustle meant they were willing to bend the law themselves.

That's what I loved about a con. Sticking it to some rich jerk who wanted to pad his wallet the easy way and thought they were important enough to be above the law.

Also, the money. I couldn't pretend I didn't like the money.

And partnering with Lex. He'd made it fun. Lex had turned me out. Elevated the stakes to long cons. Penny had given me my first taste. She taught me the art of hustling pool. Quick-change. Pigeon-drop. Fiddle scam. And our teenage favorite, the bar bill scam. Grifting was as bad as any drug.

But that was all behind me. I was here to find out what happened to Penny, then get out.

A hand palmed my elbow. "Hello, love."

I spun toward the voice and glowered at Lex. "What—" I knew what he was doing here. "I don't need your help, Lex."

"Of course." He gave me an appreciative once-over. "I like the dress. Makes good use of your legs. And you're wearing my diamonds. Feeling sentimental? Or feeling the itch?"

"Just trying to dress for the occasion, you know."

"Dressing the part always came naturally to you. Feels like old times in here, it does." He smoothed a non-existent wrinkle on his Armani jacket. "A celebration of life. Champagne nights and caviar dreams for our Penny. She would have had a right laugh at that."

"Particularly because of the way she died," I said sullenly. "Like a cheap hooker. Not especially caviar worthy."

"Speaking of caviar," said Lex. "There's someone I want you to meet. The fiancé. Mark Davis."

"What else do you know?"

"This is his father's club. But Mark's VP of sales at his firm. High tech."

"How long was he with Penny?"

"Three, four months. Quick engagement."

"Penny knew how to work fast."

"So cynical, Fin. Maybe she found love."

"Right, and then died of an overdose?" I lowered my voice. "I want to know where they met. This matchmaking service. She must have been working on the inside. Penny would never have gone for this." My lip curled at the crowd of bow ties and botox.

"You never know, love. Maybe, like you, Penny got tired of the grift. Wanted to settle down." Lex sounded wistful. I gave him a sharp look and he shrugged. "She'd be on easy street here. That's the dream, right?"

I didn't know what the dream was. Surviving the night with more money than you began, maybe. Didn't take long for the romance to wear off when you're grifting. "I wasn't tired, Lex. Conning people, even rich assholes, is wrong. A scam's a scam."

"Truer words never spoken."

This was old ground. I moved on. "So, Mark Davis. Family's the country club type, he's a sales guy. Young to be VP, so he's been working his tail off or he knew the right people to climb over."

"You got it." Lex circled an arm around my waist and leaned into my ear. "And by the way, his father is on the superior court."

I froze. "He's a judge? Penny was engaged to a guy whose father's a judge?"

"Penny was as convincing as anyone." Lex drew me closer. "Although that's a risk I was surprised she'd take."

"She would have vetted the vic. No way she'd hustle a judge's kid."

"Maybe it's all legit."

I pushed away. "I don't believe it. Let me get a feel for this guy."

"Right." Lex smirked. "What do you say? Elizabeth Ann and Carter?"

"They'll do." Figured he'd choose those roles. Elizabeth Ann and Carter were a couple. Sometimes engaged. Sometimes married. Sometimes recently dating. Whatever we needed for the situation. Elizabeth Ann ran the gamut of hair color and professions. Carter, too. But they were always on the level. Chumps.

Lex turned toward a passing waiter. Placed my glass on his tray. We strolled toward the far end of the room. I kept my stride long, pacing him. Hung a half-step back as we approached a young man. Clean shaven. Bow tie. Impeccably tailored suit. His expression was distant. Suitable for mourning. But also preoccupied. His thoughts elsewhere. Maybe with Penny. Maybe somewhere else.

Could this guy get his hands on heroin? Anybody with money could get their hands on anything. It's all in the connections. Who did he know?

Behind him stood an older couple. He had gone gray. She was still blonde. Both in dark suits. Bow tie and suspenders beneath his jacket. She had on pearls. Watching their son. Watching us. Watching the room.

Not just money. Old Southern money. I could tell by the accessories. I wondered what they thought about the dead fiancée. Lucky break for them?

A judge would know where to obtain heroin. All he needed was a sketchy cop.

Like my father.

I banished that thought. Ran a tongue over my teeth in a lipstick check. Formed a sympathetic smile. Said my "nice to meet you" and "so sorry for your loss."

"Damn shame." Lex could do a Southern accent better than a homegrown Georgian. "So young. Penny was a real sweetheart, wasn't she, Elizabeth Ann?"

"The best. Penny and I were college roommates." I studied Mark Davis's reaction, wondering what he really knew about Penny. "I was hoping to meet you, Mark. Before…"

Mark shoved his hands in his pockets. "Penny would have liked that."

"Penny and I had lost touch until recently." The sadness in my voice was real. "It was my fault. Carter and I have had our ups and downs. Penny knew that. Unfortunately, after our last breakup, I took some time off to gather my thoughts and ignored all my old friends in the process."

"Don't blame yourself, Elizabeth Ann." Lex took my hand and squeezed. "The news about Penny brought us back together. It's certainly helped me to reexamine what's important."

I leveled a look at Lex. "That's sweet of you, Carter."

"Where did y'all meet, Mark?" said Lex. "Elizabeth Ann forgot to tell me."

Mark shifted his stance. Glanced away. "Kind of a Match.com but in person. Platinum Partners."

I filed that away, also noting his body language. Defensive. Nervous. Deflecting. "It's so hard to meet people these days. You shouldn't be embarrassed."

"I guess so." Mark ran a hand over the back of his neck. "I don't know."

"Elizabeth Ann and I met on Facebook," said Lex. "We had mutual friends and kept liking the same memes."

I cut him glance to say, "Really?"

"I can't imagine what you're going through," said Lex. "This memorial is a nice touch. I'm sure Penny would have liked it."

"Is there anything we can do to help you? Maybe with Penny's things? There's a women's shelter, Penny and I both knew... But I'm sure it's too soon to speak of that. I'm sorry." I quieted, watching Mark consider what he was going to do about Penny's belongings.

His mother answered for him. "That would be helpful, Elizabeth Ann." She held out her hand. "I'm Melanie Davis, Mark's mother. What shelter did y'all work with?"

I mentioned one in Hapeville, near the airport, where Penny and I had crashed when we were younger. I still knew the woman who ran it. "I can drop by to pick up anything you'd like to donate. I'm sure Penny would have liked that."

"I had the same thought myself," said Melanie. "It'd be easier on Mark, not to have to deal with that sort of thing."

Mark shuffled his feet. "I don't know, Mom. I was just going to have a service do it."

"Nonsense," said Melanie. "It's better for everything to go to charity. Particularly one that Penny knew. Those women will benefit greatly."

I thought about Penny's real things. She wouldn't have stashed them at Mark's. She'd probably kept them at her apartment. I exchanged phone numbers with Mark's mother. It was possible nothing at Mark's home could tell me anything useful. And if Mark was involved in her death, he would have gotten rid of anything that implicated him. Unless he was really stupid.

"I for one am glad to see Penny represented here," Mark's mother said. "It's such a shame she didn't have any family. I didn't have a chance to really know her. Men don't tend to look into things like old friendships and far-flung relatives, particularly in the first blush of romance. I didn't know who to contact."

Did they even know how she passed? They were treating Penny like she'd died saving kittens from a house fire.

"Penny kept to herself," I said. "Maybe because she didn't have family." Last I heard, Penny's mom was still alive. Somewhere. I watched Mark to see his reaction, but he didn't seem to follow the conversation. The vacant expression had returned.

"I expected more people from her work," said Melanie. "Mark, did you let her office know about today?"

"I left a message with Human Resources. I don't know, Mother."

"What did you say your name was?" The judge shouldered in between Melanie and Mark. He held out his hand. Lex pumped it.

"Carter," said Lex. "Carter Lexington. And this is my—"

"Good friend. Elizabeth Ann Lockhart," I interrupted. "Penny told me you were a judge. That's very impressive."

The judge's hand felt warm and dry. He had a strong grip. "Did she, now? And you've been friends since college? Like my wife said, Penny didn't speak much about old friends. Odd, I thought."

"Well, sir, if you'd known us when we were younger, I'm sure you wouldn't have approved. Maybe that's why Penny didn't mention me."

Lex chuckled and elbowed me. "Now, it's not like y'all were girls gone wild or anything."

"Enough to raise my daddy's eyebrows." I couldn't bring myself to smile. "But Penny was my best friend. She got me through a hard time. And I—"

The words were real. So were the tears and the knot in my throat.

"I'm sorry." I spun away, forcing myself to slow my rush toward the exit.

Behind me, I heard Lex's apologies. A moment later, an arm slipped around my waist. He drew me into his side. "Come on, love. Let's get you home. Harder than I thought, too."

Furious with myself, I shook my head. "I'm fine. I want to go to Penny's."

"If Penny had anything suspect, the Davises would have gotten rid of it. And if Dot thought Penny had another place..." Lex paused to open the front door to the club. "There wouldn't be anything useful for us at Penny's if Dot knew about it."

"Dot doesn't know everything." I sniffed back my tears and hardened my emotions. "And you better not tell her."

WE ALL HAVE OUR HIDEY-HOLES. That's what I call them. Sanctuaries where only a few trusted individuals knew the location. Certain folks knew Dot's because that's where she did business. That and she had the fix with local authorities.

I didn't trust anybody, so I didn't have such a haven. That's why I slept in cheap motels and only kept possessions that fit in a suitcase.

Con artists are transitory. For one, to avoid the heat. For another, you don't get into grifting if you're looking to settle down. For the most part, we avoid violence, although violence sometimes happens when you're ripping off a mark. That's why you have to be smart. But in the underworld, you rub shoulders with those who use violence as a means to an end. That was Lex's problem— one of Lex's problems, anyway. He enjoyed Atlanta way too much. Was getting to be a permanent fixture. And kept rubbing shoulders with people like Dot.

Penny and I stuck around Atlanta because we didn't know

better. But we hid ourselves outside Atlanta because we knew better.

Penny chose an apartment in Newnan, a smaller city southwest of Atlanta. She let me crash there sometimes. As far as I was aware, nobody else knew about her place. Far enough from Atlanta to not attract attention. Close to I-85 so she could easily get to where she wanted. She could also cut northwest to I-20 and drive to Birmingham in less than two hours. Penny really loved those Birmingham dog tracks.

Wasn't hard to figure out why. When her momma wasn't stoned out of her gourd, she'd take little Penny to the races. Greyhound rescue was Penny's dream. When we were kids, Penny would save five percent of her take for the dogs. Rainy day money, we called it. She told me when she had enough rainy days saved, she'd buy a house in the country and take in greyhounds. *101 Dalmatians* was her favorite movie.

In reality, Penny's momma ran dog race numbers between Atlanta and Birmingham. It became one of Penny's first jobs, until the syndicate started having other ideas about how to use "pretty Penny." That's when she cut loose from the organized stuff, met me, and we began the small-time country hustling that wouldn't attract too much attention.

I wondered if Penny had planned on using Mark Davis for that dream. Finally cut out of the racket for good. Play with dogs for the rest of her life. I said as much to Lex as we sped south on I-85 through Atlanta toward Newnan.

"Possible," he said. "You noticed the mother mentioned Penny's office?"

"You think Mark Davis got wise? He said he put in a word with HR about the celebration of life. I couldn't tell if he was lying. It's possible a receptionist took the message without realizing there was no Penny working there."

"Davis wasn't all there, was he? I couldn't read him either. The judge was canny, though." Lex stayed absorbed in thought as we entered the narrow, serpentine track of Atlanta's downtown corridor.

I averted my eyes as we sped by Grady Hospital. "How long did Penny think it would last?"

"What do you mean, love?" Lex cut me a look. "With Mark Davis?"

"Hustle him. Then bug out before the wedding? Or stay married long enough for a settlement?"

Except for a twitch in his jaw, Lex didn't react.

"She couldn't lie to him forever, so it had to be one or the other."

No response.

"What?" I said sharply. "You think she planned on making it work? Bury everything about her true self and become somebody else? It's a house of cards."

"Maybe she wanted marriage. What's her true self anyway? Her history? Or what she believed was her true self?"

"Don't get philosophical on me. I'm talking practical terms. You can't just make up a role and play it for the rest of your life."

"Happens every day, love." His pitying look sickened me. "Look at yourself."

"What are you talking about? This is me. I can play Elizabeth Ann or whoever, but I can't become her for the rest of my life."

"You're more Elizabeth Ann than you give yourself credit for, Fin. You've talked yourself out of being an Elizabeth Ann. You think you're not worthy of being Elizabeth Ann. But if your mum was still—"

"Cut it out."

"Right." Lex covered my hand with his. "Personally, Elizabeth Ann is a no go for me. I wouldn't have met Finley Goodhart if she'd been Elizabeth Ann. And a sorrier bloke you'd never hope to meet."

"Cut that out, too," I said. But I didn't move my hand.

He squeezed my fingers. "We've all got our demons, Fin. And

sometimes the way we deal with those demons is to tell ourselves we're somebody else. Maybe Penny thought she could climb out from under her past by becoming whoever Mark Davis thought she was."

"I guess that's not so bad, considering what Penny lived through." I curled my fingers inside his. "But the past will always come back to bite you. And I'm afraid that's what happened with Penny."

"That's why fear is so useful, love. It keeps us vigilant." The smile he gave me nearly broke my heart all over again.

Good thing fear kept me from giving him my heart. I liked it in one piece.

4

THE HOOK

THE APARTMENT LOOKED like every other new-ish, reasonably priced complex in any small American city. Wood and stone. Balconies in neat rows. An easy place to blend, where nobody notices much.

Penny had given me a key. Lex followed me to the third floor of her building. She had a one-bedroom. The balcony facing the parking lot instead of courtyard, by choice. When the key turned, I let out the air I hadn't known I'd been holding. Afraid Penny had bugged out and not told me.

"Nice digs," said Lex, strolling into the living room.

"It's mostly rented stuff." But I agreed. Penny had a good eye for interior design. Staying at Penny's almost made me feel like a real person in a real home.

"Where'd she keep her stash?"

It felt disloyal, but I pointed at the hall. "Her bedroom has all these dog prints. She usually kept money behind the frames. But her rainy day money is somewhere else."

He didn't move. We weren't there for the cash. Although I should do something with the money. Before someone else found Penny's place. Lex was probably thinking the same thing.

"Did she take notes? Laptop or something?"

I nodded. "She would have erased most of it, though."

His smile was quick and sure. "Not a problem, love. Point me in that direction, and why don't you clean the place, yeah?"

He didn't mean with a mop and broom. I pointed him to the laptop in her bedroom. Watched him break past her password. I began removing dog prints. Five stacks inside the first two frames. The third, featuring a greyhound chasing a rabbit through a field, brought me up short.

"Lex," I said. "Penny was holding markers."

He turned from the desk. Behind him, the laptop ran a scan through some kind of code. He met my eyes. "Do they say who they're from?"

I shook my head. "Chits with the amounts. No names. Different colors."

"Bloody hell." Lex pinched the bridge of his nose. "Was she running numbers again?"

"I don't know." I gulped. "I don't think so. She hasn't done that since we were kids. But I hadn't talked to her since I went straight. I felt embarrassed."

"Never mind that now. Penny would have understood." He gave me a tired smile and pointed at the slips. "What are the amounts?"

I counted. "About fifty large. Give or take."

Lex pushed out of his chair. "How many bills did she have?"

"Five grand. Just walking around money."

We stood side by side, staring at the prints I had flipped over on her bed. The cash was held in place by canvas lattice stapled to the back of the frames. The markers had been paper-clipped to the lattice. Like it was some kind of kid's craft project.

"Lex, I've never known her to hold markers. Even when she was running, she didn't hold them."

"Bloody hell." He ran a hand through his hair. "Where's her— what do you call it?—rainy day money?"

"Inside the dryer. Back panel."

"Be a dear and find me a screwdriver." He strode out of the bedroom.

I snagged a roomy shoulder bag in her closet. Stuffed the money and markers inside. Glanced at the computer, where it continued to run lines of code. Ignored the computer and began searching her desk for a screwdriver.

Found one just as the doorbell chimed.

I RAN TO THE WINDOW. The noise of the dryer being dragged across linoleum had stopped with the doorbell. Lex darted into the bedroom. I turned from the window and motioned Lex over.

"You know him?" I pointed to a big guy peering into Lex's Camaro.

"Bloody hell. Dot sent somebody. Let's slide." He grabbed my hand. "Where're the markers?"

I patted the bag tucked under my shoulder.

"Good girl." He kissed my forehead, then rested his lips there. "Bloody awful timing."

"There's no back door. How are we going to get out?"

"There's a balcony."

"I'm wearing a dress and heels."

"And looking quite dishy, may I add."

I closed my eyes. "What about the rainy day money?"

"Too late for that." His lips slid to my nose and flew off. "But grab the laptop."

We crept out of the bedroom. Behind the front door, metal jangled. Someone fumbling with a ring of keys. I rushed to the balcony and slid open the door. Behind me, Lex closed the vertical blinds and pulled them shut.

"Will the guy in the parking lot see us?" I whispered. I flattened myself against the balcony's side wall.

Lex slid the door closed. "Not much we can do about that now." He moved around me toward the balcony railing. Leaning out, he peered right, left, and down. "Dot must have reported Penny's death to the manager. Got the right paperwork together."

"How did she know we were here, Lex? Dot didn't know about Penny's place. At least, she didn't the last time I saw Penny."

"They've been tailing me since the country club. Wasn't sure, so didn't want to say. Didn't think Dot would waste her time with this. Of course, I had no idea about the markers." He turned and motioned me over. "Come on, Fin. Can't stay here all day."

"Why—" It was a waste of time to ask. I applied myself to the new concern.

Lex had hoisted himself over the balcony railing. He planted his feet against the bottom rail, body jutting out. Held the top railing with his hands.

I tossed my sandals inside the bag. Slipped the bag across my chest. Climbed over the railing next to Lex.

My heart hammered in my throat. "Really? We're really doing this?"

"Easy peasy." He raised his brows, smiled, and slid his hands down the balustrades. Pushed off with his feet. Bowed his body outward, toes pointed. Swung his legs into the balcony below and let go.

Made it look easy.

It wasn't easy.

I dropped, arms flailing. He half-caught me, gripping my waist. Yanked me over the railing and onto the balcony. We hit the floor and rolled. I found myself pinned under Lex.

"Hello, love." He didn't move except to slip the bag to the side and adjust his body more comfortably over mine. "Fun, yeah?"

"No. This is not fun, Lex." I pushed at him. "Get off."

"Give us a kiss first." His eyes glinted.

"You're so annoying. Dot's people are above us and below us. Can't you be serious for once?"

"I'm deadly serious. I'm above you and you're below me. Can't have it more serious than that." He grinned, eyebrows quirking. "Just one kiss. For old time's sake."

"Lex. Someone might open that door any minute and find us."

"You know as well as I, they're not at home." He smiled. "The lady doth protest too much, methinks."

"I'm not protest—"

"Good." He lowered his mouth to mine. His lips brushed mine softly. Hesitated. Waited for me to respond.

And I did. Just like he knew I would.

Lex Leopold made me weak. I hated that about him. And myself.

But Lordy, could he kiss. The second kiss was not a gentle brush. I responded with all the pent-up heat left from months of avoidance. I drank in the scent of his aftershave and the unique blend of masculine tang and spice that was Lex's alone. Wrapped my arms around his neck and dug my fingers into his thick hair.

I missed him. Missed the way we fit together. The way we knew each other's thoughts. The way his fingers brushed my face then curled behind my neck to deepen the kiss. I lost myself in the memory of him and the good memories of us.

When he broke it off, he caressed my cheek and dotted my temples with his lips once more. Rested his cheek against my forehead and breathed in, like he was holding on to my scent. Or maybe the memory of the kiss.

"Ah, Fin," he sighed. "You miss this, admit it."

"I don't and I won't."

I was such a liar. And he knew it.

I shoved him off and stood up. "I don't know if we're technically breaking and entering by making out on this person's balcony, but we need to get out of here."

"Right." Lex hopped to his feet and winked. "I'm sure they'd approve us getting off, though. Vital necessity. Saved my life."

I laughed. "Okay, genius. Are we jumping from here?"

He shook his head and pointed at the apartment. "You mentioned breaking and entering."

I swallowed. "Lex…"

"If Dot's fellow didn't see us swing from Penny's balcony, he's going to see us jump off this one."

"We could just wait until they leave."

"You're no fun." His waggled his brows. "Unless you fancy another snog."

"Breaking and entering it is." I circled Lex and approached the sliding glass door. Tried the handle. Locked. "It's not like we're robbing the place."

"Whatever makes you feel better, love." He stood behind me. "You need any help with the door?"

"No bar, simple latch, and an outside slider. Should be easy."

"Your dad would be proud."

Not so much my mother. I shut that thought out and pulled the screwdriver from Penny's purse.

"Oh, good show, Fin."

"Shut up, Lex." I inserted the screwdriver near the bottom corner, between the door frame and the door. Pried upward. The door tilted up and the latch released from the bracket.

"Bravo." Lex reached around me to grab the door and slid it along the track. "Poor sods. Second floor doesn't make you any safer from robberies."

"Good thing we don't do robberies," I said dryly.

Inside the apartment, we glanced at the ceiling, listening for movement above.

"Did you put the dryer back?"

"Best I could in a hurry." Lex touched my arm. "Let the rainy day fund go, Fin. If Dot gets it, maybe it'll appease her."

"You think Penny was holding Dot's markers."

He shrugged. "You knew Penny better than I did. Whose markers would she have?"

At the moment, I felt like I didn't know Penny at all. I also felt uncomfortable discussing any theories with Lex. Some coincidence, revealing Penny's secret lair when Dot's guys happened to be following Lex.

"I know that look," he said. "Lack of trust. I've failed you again. You think I'm working for Dot."

"You should've told me Dot was tailing you, Lex. That's a big mistake."

"And if I did, what would you have done? Forced me to leave you someplace. And they would have stayed on you. Made you take them to Penny's. And found the markers themselves." He shook his head. "I like you with your teeth in place, Fin."

"But you didn't know Penny had markers, did you, Lex? We were just looking for clues to find out if Mark Davis was legit."

"Such cheek." Lex's eyes followed the footsteps above the kitchen. "It takes no imagination whatsoever—for me, for Dot, or for you—to know Penny had gotten in over her head. No, I wasn't expecting markers. Hoping for something on the judge, actually."

"Hoping. So you could use it yourself?" I folded my arms over the shoulder bag.

"Bugger off, Fin." He turned, his expression pained. "I know I've done a botch job in the past, but I do have respect for you. And for Penny."

Lex was so good, I couldn't tell when he wasn't putting me on. The hardest lessons came from trusting people who lied for a living. It was the reason I ended up on the streets. I had to go with my head and not my heart. As much as I wanted to trust Lex, I couldn't let myself. Everyone worked some kind of angle. I might be on the level, but I wouldn't allow myself to play the chump.

Although I did that when I kissed Lex.

I hardened my expression. Swallowed my misery. "I've got Penny's keys. She kept a car here, too."

"Right." He sighed. "See you later then, is it?"

We looked up, hearing the heavy scrape of the dryer moving.

"Dammit." All Penny's greyhound money now lined Dot's pockets. Thanks to Lex. I blinked fast and sucked in a long, shaky breath. "Yeah, I don't know about that, Lex. I'm not sure where I'm headed once I straighten this out for Penny."

"I see. Be safe, Fin." He didn't move from where he leaned

against the kitchen bar. He wore the charming-boy-next-door mask once again. But his eyes hinted at sadness. "I'll miss you."

"You know me, Lex. I can take care of myself." But I had no idea how I was going to take care of Penny's memory. A lot had changed in the months I'd turned my back on the grift. I was an outsider more than ever.

5

THE HACKER

I DROVE Penny's Honda to a motel I knew in Griffin. Opposite direction of my last place, where I'd left all but my necessities. East on Highway 16 to avoid the interstate, but stayed on Atlanta's south side. I watched my rear view mirror constantly. Took some county roads I knew, just in case. Passed a few country bars where I used to hustle pool and later played matchstick-men games with Lex. Drove around the old whistle-stop town where I grew up.

Where Mom was buried. Daddy lived closer to Atlanta now.

Which suited me fine.

In the motel room, I did my usual check—under the bed, beneath the mattress, loose carpet in the closet, inside and behind the toilet tank—looking for spots missed by housekeepers. Where I knew I could hide money and valuables. The motel was a double-stack with open walkways all the way around. I liked a second floor room near a stairwell. Easier to watch the parking lot. Did a quick check of the stairwell and vending machine area. Felt better.

Then I opened Penny's purse. Pulled out the laptop and set it aside. Removed the stacks, recounted them, shoved them in plastic bags. And hunted for the markers.

"Dammit, Lex." The markers had been paper-clipped together in the bottom of the purse. The purse was inside out, the laptop open and dark. I stared at the polyester-slick bedspread with my neat row of bagged cash, ready to be hidden around the room. "You played me. Lord help this idiot. I kissed him while he picked the markers off me."

What was Lex going to do? Turn the markers over to Dot? Because he was protecting me or to cover some favor?

"Penny, what were you doing with markers?" Whether Penny was using Mark or trying for a new life wasn't important now. Dot had hinted that Platinum Partners might be a front. If a racket owned Platinum, Penny must have worked at Platinum as a shill, an inside accomplice. Maybe the owner had her hold the markers. Platinum could be a front for illegal gambling. Or something else.

I hid my stacks, then woke up the laptop. Skipped the free wifi and tested a few passwords for the motel's private server. Got access on the third try. The code began to run again. I hit escape. A new code box appeared. I didn't know code except for some basics. I wasn't a hacker. I mostly used Google but knew how to wipe it clean.

Type began to march across the screen without me touching the keys. "Elizabeth Ann?"

"You sumbitch," I typed. "You uploaded this to your own server."

"Easier for running tests."

"What do you need tests for? You got what you wanted."

The cursor blinked for a few seconds. "Lose something?"

"My mind, for trusting you in the first place." I looked for a way to shut down the little window. Thought about shutting the laptop. Or throwing it against the wall. But waited. Like a fool.

"I'm sorry," he typed. "It's safer this way."

The memory of lying beneath him—curling my fingers through his hair, feeling his mouth on my skin—flashed through my mind. His weight against me felt solid, safe. I hadn't been safe. I moved my hand to type and realized I'd been clenching a fistful of little black dress. Over my heart. My necklace caught in that twist of dress.

"I've heard that before," I typed. "Much safer for your associate, too."

The cursor began to type, reversed, and began again. "I have information. PP is not with our associate. Another party is involved."

Another organization was connected to Platinum Partners. Unless Dot was being crafty. If that's where Lex was getting his information. He should know better than to trust Dot.

"This has nothing to do with you. She was my friend," I wrote. "Leave it be."

"Keep the money. Stay away from PP. The other party is too dangerous."

"I'm not doing this for money." I shut the laptop.

I needed into Platinum Partners. To see what I could find out about Penny. And get Penny's greyhound money back from that reptile-loving witch.

I DIDN'T KNOW how to find a connected Korean food lover, so I called Bev to see what she had learned about Penny's hospital admittance. Not content to just speak on the phone, Bev met me at a local Chick-Fil-A for breakfast. After getting our chicken biscuits, we sat near the play area. Bev kept up a steady stream of chatter about her grandkids and work. The night shift at her Piedmont ER was a lot tamer than at Grady. Bev and Mom used to tell some hair-raisers back in the day. But night shift was still night shift. Bev, like Mom, fed on that crazy ebb and flow.

While she talked, I half listened, my head whirring through possible Platinum Partners long-con scenarios.

Bev must have noticed my drift. She cut off her flow of chatter, sipped her tea, then laid a hand on mine. "It's been good to get a look at you, Fin. I know Marian would've wanted me to see you. She wouldn't be too happy to know about these circumstances, though."

"I know." I pulled my hand away to push a hash brown around a pool of ketchup. "I'm fixing to work out something better, don't worry. But I need to settle my friend's death first."

"I figured. It's an odd thing."

I looked up. "You found information about Penny?"

Bev avoided my gaze, played with her straw. "I made some calls. She was taken to a hospital DOA, like you thought. The nurse I talked to said it was the weirdest thing. The pronouncement of death was already filled out by a coroner. Her chart said no postmortem needed. Soon after she arrived, she was taken away."

"Maybe GBI took her to the medical examiner's office in Decatur because it was a suspicious death? If the coroner calls the death due to controlled substances, like in Penny's case, the bureau has to do an autopsy."

"I don't think the Georgia Bureau of Investigation had anything to do with it, Finley. The nurse said a crematorium picked her up. After a death is called and no postmortem is needed, they lay out the body in the hospital mortuary until the family decides what to do. It usually doesn't happen that quickly for an unexpected death. Besides, the hospital's not metro. It's up in Woodstock."

The metro-area counties didn't use coroners. They contracted with the state medical examiner. The rest of Georgia allowed any high school graduate over the age of twenty-five, who wasn't a convicted felon, to put their hat in the ring for coroner. Didn't pay much and was a thankless job. Many ran funeral homes—a suitable position. But not all coroners were suitable. In some circumstances, suspicious deaths could easily be covered if the police didn't question the coroner's pronouncement. Was that what had happened here?

I learned this at sixteen. Looked it up when our coroner called mother's murder a suicide. Instead of high school, I applied myself to the study of local crime. Including our coroner's own criminality. And the cops who should have had criminal records but didn't.

Then became a criminal myself. Felt justified somehow. Easier to hide, too. Or so my seventeen-year-old mind thought. But now I regretted not trying to find another way out. Although I didn't regret my friendship with Penny.

My friendship with Lex was another story.

"Did you get a name for the crematorium or the coroner?"

"Sorry, hon." Bev fiddled with her straw. "Did you find out if there was a funeral?"

"I was up there for it yesterday." I skipped the particulars. "Thanks for your help, Miss Bev. "

She gripped my hand again. "You can always stay with us, you know that, Fin? I'm sorry about all the ugliness that happened after Marian died. Your daddy wouldn't—"

"Don't worry about it, Miss Bev." I slipped my hand out. Slid away from the booth. "Water under the bridge. I'm too old to be orphaned. Take care."

I ambled away, then revved up my pace in the parking lot. From Griffin I could easily shoot up I-75 to Atlanta. Platinum Partners didn't have a designated address, but they did have a website. Before Bev had arrived, I used Chick-Fil-A's free internet to examine it. I still didn't trust Lex not to trace me on Penny's laptop. The Platinum Partners pictures showed beautiful people drinking wine and scotch, laughing at each other's jokes. A few wedding pictures. Taken on beachfronts and mountain tops. That sort of thing. Platinum Partners was by invitation only. After you revealed your references, including assets and education. Only the pedigreed need apply.

I could create a pedigree, but I needed an in. And I had just met someone who might be convinced to give me an in, one way or the other.

6

THE DUMP

MRS. DAVIS HAD BEEN SURPRISED to hear from me so soon, but she also agreed to a morning meeting. Late morning. Coffee. A place that roasted their own beans. Her type didn't do early morning breakfast at Chick-Fil-A.

I flew up I-75 until Monday morning rush hour prevented more than stop-and-go on the connector through downtown. Atlanta was a traffic nightmare most times of the day, but I particularly hated the morning. That's what you get for a road system that looked a lot like broken capillaries without many central veins.

I found the coffee place in ten minutes after our meeting time. I'd grabbed my stuff from my original motel before meeting Bev. In the coffee shop bathroom, I changed from the jeans and tee I'd worn for Bev to young, Southern workout prep for Melanie Davis. Complete with a Vineyard Vines ball cap to better hide my features.

"Elizabeth Ann, we'll have to make this short. I've got a lesson in an hour." Mrs. Davis wore a peeved expression with her tennis outfit.

"Sorry, ma'am. I hit the gym first but should have expected the delays. There was an accident." I shook my head. "It just gets worse every day, doesn't it?"

"I don't like to leave my neighborhood," she said. "Thank the stars everyone delivers these days."

Which probably didn't help the traffic situation, as I saw it. But when you live in motels, you don't do much online shopping.

"I spoke to the women's shelter after I left the club yesterday." My voice was full of charitable enthusiasm, then I switched to an apologetic tone. "I'm sorry for getting so emotional with y'all. I feel guilty about not keeping up with Penny after college."

"It happens. And for someone as young as Penny, it's just tragic."

"I never did hear what happened to her…" I watched Melanie Davis over my coffee, taking my time to blow off the heat.

"It's very strange. Her heart arrested. She might have had some condition that she never told Mark about. A little unforgivable, considering they were engaged. Newly engaged, but still. She should have said something."

Mrs. Davis must have noticed the expression that I hadn't been quick enough to squash. "I'm sorry to be so harsh. I'm a mother, thinking about her son. He's in a lot of pain. If Penny had a condition, we might have helped her."

"And if he'd known her heart was weak, you think it'd be easier on him?" I said the words gently, while I mulled over the possible liars in the scenario. The hospital knew Penny had overdosed. Word had hit the streets that Penny had OD'd. Maybe Mark had lied to his parents. Or maybe Mark didn't know. Maybe someone had covered it up for Mark. "Was Mark with her when she passed? It must have been horrific."

"He's not ready to talk about it." She crossed her legs. Drew her coffee mug closer. "But he was the one who found Penny and called the ambulance. My poor little man. What he's been through."

And what Penny must have gone through. I had no doubt

Mark had been dealt a blow. If it turned out he was the vic in the situation, I'd find a way to make it up to him.

But if he had anything to do with Penny's death, I'd find a way to make him pay.

"I understand Penny's already been cremated." I kept my voice somber but friendly. I leaned forward. Touched my heart. "Where's her final resting place going to be?"

"Without a family, Mark didn't know what to do. And of course, Penny was too young to have sorted any of that business out. Cremation seemed the most sensible and expedient thing." Her tone was apologetic. But her neck had stiffened. She held up a palm and waved it before me. Classic defensive stance. "The crematory is holding Penny until Mark decides what to do."

I suppressed a shudder. "It was kind of you to take care of all that."

"She would have been Mark's wife. We take care of family." She touched her diamond teardrop necklace.

I mirrored her, touching my necklace. She smiled.

The conversation drifted toward the logistics of what service would be best to pack and deliver Penny's things. I half paid attention, more attuned to Melanie Davis's body language. She didn't like Penny. Didn't like her son with Penny. That much was obvious. Whenever Penny's name was mentioned, her glance darted away.

I stopped using Penny's name. Kept my suggestions impersonal. Distanced myself from Penny with little gestures and carefully placed words. Switched sides to Melanie's without her knowing.

With the decision made about Penny's belongings, Melanie brushed her hands together, done with the subject. But she leaned forward while thanking me for my help.

"I feel so sorry for Mark." I dropped my bait carefully. I was the Davis friend now, no longer closely associated with Penny. "It'll be hard to move on. I hope he can find someone who makes him happy."

"It's difficult for young people to meet. In my day, you joined the club and the youth social at church. Fraternities and sororities were different in those days, too. Not that my friends ever did the bar thing, but you young people don't even do that, do you? It's all apps and online chats now."

I thought about the bar where Lex had finally introduced himself to me. Maybe I should've tried an app. "That's why Mark went to Platinum Partners. Will he go back?"

"I don't know. I'd feel jaded, but that's me."

I fixed a shocked expression. "Do you think Platinum Partners isn't as careful as they say they are?"

"They certainly sounded careful about appraising their members." Melanie Davis licked her lips. "Mark needed references. I often wondered about Penny's, but I barely got to know her."

"I'm so sorry, ma'am." I chose my words carefully. "Was there something about Penny that I didn't know?"

Her fingers played with her necklace, then dropped to her lap. She shifted to sit taller on the cushy chair. "This may be hard for you. You haven't talked to Penny in a while. But when Mark said he was going to marry Penny, of course, my husband and I wanted to know more about her background. So we just checked on a few things."

They'd hired a private detective. Had Penny known? "I thought the purpose of membership clubs like Platinum Partners was to do a thorough background check so the members wouldn't have to worry about who they're meeting."

"Yes. However, my husband is thorough. Very conscientious. You know, a career in law." Her hand waved away his suspicious inclinations. "It's not that there was anything disturbing in Penny's background. There just wasn't much there."

She paused. Looked to me for an explanation. I didn't offer any, not knowing Penny's setup.

That was the problem with fake identities. If you didn't have a good forger who also knew how to hack, you wouldn't have much of a history. Which made me wonder who had created Penny's narrative for Platinum Partners. Lex would have seeded Penny's backstory in the right websites if he'd be in charge of rigging the front. That meant a certain sloppiness in Platinum's organization. Assuming Platinum was a front. And the markers were connected to Platinum.

There was still so much I didn't know.

Mrs. Davis sighed. "But some people just don't have much of a past, I guess. And Penny had no family. Only child. Parents dead. No extended family. It's just so…unusual."

Judge Davis thought Penny's story didn't jibe. And rightly so.

"It's strange Platinum Partners would have accepted Penny, when y'all didn't find much background on her. I wonder if they would have taken me."

"What do you mean?"

I worked up a blush. "I don't have Penny's bank account, and my beginnings are more humble. I'm from a small town. I only went to school with Penny."

"Emory does offer good scholarships."

So that's where we went. Emory University in Atlanta. Private, exclusive, and expensive. Made sense.

"Yes, ma'am. I'm so curious about this club where Penny and Mark found each other. Sorry I ask so many questions. It must bother you. After all, you did do your own background work, too."

"It does bother me, Elizabeth Ann." Melanie had forgotten I should be defending Penny, not aiding the Davises' suspicions. "I wonder if you could get in. Then I could tell Mark not to bother going back. And warn his friends."

Not insulting at all, Mrs. Davis. As long as I've got you hooked, we can agree I'm not worthy of Platinum Partners.

"Good idea," I said. "I'd hate for Mark to have his heart broken again. Let's see how far I get."

I extracted my phone from my purse. Found the website. Began typing. "This is exciting. I feel like we're spies. But I don't think I'll advance to an interview stage."

"I'd like to know what goes on in the interview. Let's get you there." She looked over my shoulder. "Raise your income, dear. I know that area is considered hip, but give them my address. It's a better neighborhood."

"I'm on to another screen. So far, so good." I grinned at Melanie, then glanced at the phone. "Oh no. I don't want to give them my credit card. They might charge me. Carter would see that for sure. Oh well, we tried."

I set the phone on the coffee table before us. Screen still shining. Cursor blinking. Ready for a credit card number.

Hooked, she picked up the phone. "I'll use mine. If they charge me, I'll just call my credit card company. I do it all the time."

"Oh, it's too much trouble. You don't want to do that. Besides, I used my name, not yours. That'll flag the system."

"Go back and change your name to mine."

I entered her name, while she fished her card from her wallet, then handed her the phone. She typed. I watched.

"It went through," she said. "Now it says you have to wait for an email."

"I'm sure it didn't work. I mean, your name and my email?"

"It's just an email." She handed me the phone. "Check. The website may be automated to automatically send an email."

I'd used one of my dummy Gmail accounts. Opened the dummy account's mailbox in my Chrome app. I was in. Complete with Melanie Davis's name, credit card, and address. And the background I had created earlier.

It'd been almost too easy. And fun.

I told myself to cool it, then showed her the email. "Look at that. I have a possible interview. But I can still get rejected. Like you said, this was all automated. Maybe they do the real sifting before the interview."

"I'm feeling vindicated. I knew Platinum wasn't as exclusive as it said. You can't trust anyone these days." She touched her hair and the necklace. "Thank you. I'll write your references and send them to Platinum."

"But isn't the offer of an interview enough to warn Mark and his friends? You don't really want me to go through with this. What would I tell Carter if he found out I went to a matchmaking service?" I placed a hand on my heart. Tapped it three times. Then slid my phone away.

She took the bait. "You're not going to get matched. And it's more of a club than a service. A club for the right sort of couples to meet. You're just helping me. Carter would understand."

"It was easy to get through, wasn't it? Oh, can you just imagine? I could go incognito. That'd be so much fun. Maybe color my hair blonde or something crazy like that. I'd be so embarrassed if I were rejected. But it's still a hoot."

"You could do blonde. Your skin color is pale enough." Melanie cocked her head. "I for one would like to know if that place isn't on the up-and-up. And what sort of people are attending their parties."

"But we're just being silly," I said. "Mark must have liked the service. He had to have loved Penny if he wanted to marry her. If Platinum wasn't respectable, I'm sure Mark would have figured it out."

"Mark doesn't always think with his head. You knew Penny. She was beautiful. She took Mark's breath away. He wasn't thinking clearly."

I knew Penny. And now I knew a little something about the Davises and Platinum Partners. I just didn't know who was working which angle.

7

THE BIG STORE

THE EMAIL from Platinum Partners said they had an office in Buckhead, in the center of Atlanta. Buckhead was still considered posh, despite some thuggish issues among its nightclubs that sometimes made the papers. The real estate price tag kept it posh. And residential Buckhead—old Buckhead—kept a tight rein on the real estate. And what made the papers.

Besides shopping and eateries, Buckhead had office space. High value. High turnover. Easy to nab for a front, so I didn't pay much attention to the address when I arrived for my interview. However, I didn't park near the office. I didn't know who might recognize Penny's extra set of wheels. I parked at Phipps Plaza— where a few days earlier I'd picked up items I had ordered with Mrs. Davis's card—and took an Uber to the office.

I figured Mrs. Davis would want me to look appropriate for Platinum and probably wouldn't notice an extra charge at Saks. Although she wouldn't approve of what I deemed appropriate: Helmut Lang hoodie, jeans, and boots. Silicon Valley nerd chic. I'd also fixed my face and hair. No longer a small brunette with brown eyes. Not that you could see my blue eyes with the glasses I wore. I'd also grown more than a few inches, and not just in height.

In the office lobby, I took my time checking the company directory. Dentist. Lawyer. Financial advisor. The empty floors were more interesting. Platinum Partners had a nameplate on the directory sign, but all the nameplates were the type that slid into place. Didn't tell me much. Nameplates were easy to obtain and a cinch to switch.

I checked for cameras in the lobby, then in the elevator. Pretended to hit the wrong floor. Got off. Looked around, slightly panicked. The financial advisor's receptionist spotted me through their glass door. I shrugged my shoulders as in, "Oops, I goofed." Opened the glass door and ducked in.

"I'm so sorry," I said. "I'm looking for Platinum Partners. I have an interview, and I'm running late."

"Sorry, not here." She smiled. "Good luck with your interview."

Couldn't tell if she'd heard of Platinum. She and her office looked legit. That didn't mean anything, either.

Got back on the elevator. Went to the correct floor. Took my time casually appraising the area before entering the office. Not a glass door. No receptionist. I hunched my shoulders. Corrected my stride to something more slouched. Approached the empty desk. Scanned it. Did a quick circle, appearing apprehensive while actually checking for cameras. Audibly sighed. Checked my watch. Took a seat.

The reception area was warm wood and cool glass. Abstract art. Low lighting. Ivy league-ish. Charging station instead of magazines on the coffee table. Smelled slightly of pipe tobacco.

Nice touch. I avoided the charging station, which probably siphoned information while it powered up devices. Instead, I pretended to check my email while I examined the wifi names in the building. Platinum had a free guest wifi.

Probably another way to scan my browser history and passwords.

I was not a trusting person. Instead, I chose the financial advisor's wifi and began deducing passwords. Not to hack. Just to kill time. The receptionist had a cat picture placed prominently on her desk. Same cat on her screensaver. And a blocked-out time on her scheduler for "Mr. Fuzzy—vet."

Finally got through on Fuzzylove.

The back office door opened. A young man approached me. Hand out, ready to shake. Nice suit. Urban svelte. Scar on his eyebrow. Man bun. His other hand held a clipboard. "Miss Davis?"

They'd given me enough time to charge or connect my phone and hadn't succeeded. No point making me wait any longer because there were other ways to check me out.

I beamed. Smiled crookedly—literally because I now had an overbite—and rose with my hand extended. "You can call me Ellie. It's short for Melanie. Do you work at Platinum?" My voice rose, hopeful. "Or are you a member?"

"Sorry, not a member. My name is Tony Riggle and I'm going to do your interview." He winked. "Although I don't think you have anything to worry about."

"I'm happy to hear that," I said. "I have a meeting after this and hate to leave the office for long. Which I guess is why I'm here."

"You work for a startup?"

I nodded vigorously. "It's a trading app. Horses. You wouldn't imagine the algorithms for international trade for such a volatile market. So much can change. The data for the genetic pool alone." I shook my head and rolled my eyes. "Took forever to enter the data.

"And the permissions. Man, those horse people are leery. But we got the right certification and it's a hit. We even have a feature that will give you possible breeding outcomes. The Saudis love it. I'm headed to Dubai next week to assist in a presentation. As the developer. Sales does the actual presentation."

I clamped my hands on my cheeks. "I talk way too much about work. I'm sorry."

"It's fine, Ellie." Riggle waved at the loveseat before the coffee table. "This will be more comfortable. Have a seat. We'll just chat. Don't worry. We like to keep these interviews informal."

"I'm so glad." I slumped in the seat. "I hate formal. I was kind of worried. I mean, it's so hard. I have everything I could want, but I just have trouble finding anyone to date. Do you know what I mean? But I figured I'd give you a shot before I tried something more painful."

"Painful?" said Riggle.

I rolled my eyes. "Surgery. That's what Mom thinks I need. But she doesn't get it. I don't have time to date. I don't have time for the gym. I don't have time for anything but coding horse DNA right now. Before that it was candy."

"You coded candy?"

"Not only coded but developed the game." I winked. "I can't name the app because I sold the rights and, you know"—I spun a finger in the air—"confidentiality agreements.

"That was back when I was still in Silicon Valley. What a soul-crushing place that is. My sister's husband got a job here, so Mom moved to Atlanta. And she insisted I move here, too. She hated Silicon Valley even more than I did. We live together. But I was glad to get away from that California hell hole. Plus, oh my God, it's so cheap to live here. Although I miss In-N-Out Burger. So, so much."

"Wow." Riggle smiled. "Don't worry. We're going to find you someone."

"Thank God. I need to get Mom off my back about this dating stuff. How long does it usually take to meet someone?"

"It depends," said Riggle. "We do things the old-fashioned way. That's what makes us unique. Plus, we're very exclusive. I don't want to be insensitive, but our clientele has to be wary of finding a mate who's more interested in their bank account than them."

"Gold diggers." I chuckled. "Yep. They're easy to spot, though."

"How?"

"Come on. I know I'm not Miss America. The woman-to-man ratio in Silicon Valley should have made it easy for me. But the dude developers didn't care about gold diggers as long as the chick was hot. If a guy approached me and didn't look like a reject from *Revenge of the Nerds*, I'd let him buy me a drink. But I didn't let it go anywhere else. I knew he was just looking for a sugar momma. Which is funny since they called me the Candy Crush girl."

"Aha," said Riggle.

"Just a figure of speech. I didn't develop Candy Crush. That's just what they called me."

I winked, then waved my hand holding my phone. Connecting my need for privacy to their lack of information about me.

"So what do you want to know for this interview?" I said. "We should get to the point. I've got a new line of Russian Dons being added to the system. I gotta go back and check on my coders."

"I think we're good," said Riggle. "We just needed to meet you."

"Great. So what's the next step?"

"We put out an invitation to our new members for a cocktail hour. It's a comfortable way to test the waters. Then we'll invite you to a bigger party with other members. There's a Valentine's party in a few weeks. We have different types of events. Some are sports. Game nights. It's really whatever interests the current members. Finding relationships in common hobbies."

My head pumped. "Cool. I love game nights."

"Figured you would. Next Saturday night is a small, private happy hour. Mostly for high-tech execs like yourself."

"Here at this office?"

He shook his head and pointed to my phone. "I'll send you the address in your email invitation. Make sure you have the invite to get in. They're barcoded, and we'll scan them." He winked. "Don't want any party crashers."

"Coolio. You guys have thought of everything." Barcoded so they could scan my phone. I'd print out my invitation and watch them squirm.

We rose together. I stumbled over the laptop bag I had left at my feet. Fell forward and grabbed Riggle's suit jacket for support.

"God. I'm sorry."

"No problem," he said, helping me to straighten. He watched while I tried to shake my foot out of my bag strap. Then he leaned over to help pull my boot free.

I slipped his wallet into a pocket beneath my hoodie while he freed my foot.

He rose and handed me the computer bag.

"I'm such an idiot. You know, I have an emergency room visit almost annually? Once I actually broke my collarbone stepping onto a sidewalk. I mean, who does that?"

"It happens. See you at happy hour."

I schlepped across the room, out the door, and got on the elevator. Waved to Riggle as the doors closed. Hit the button for the dentist's floor. In the dental reception, I found a seat near the door. Behind a magazine, I inventoried Tony Riggle's wallet.

Felt sure the license was fake, although it's hard to tell these days. I left the cash but checked the names on the credit cards. One had an added middle name, the other was slightly misspelled.

What, no library card, Tony Riggle sometimes Riffle?

I smirked. I got into Platinum without Dot's help. Now I needed to learn what Penny was doing with these people who got her engaged and dead in a matter of months. And if those markers were connected.

Between the seams of his wallet, I found a folded piece of paper. Took a picture of the run of numbers and letters written on it. Refolded and slipped it back inside. Shoved the wallet into my waistline and approached the front desk. Glanced at the sign-in sheet and noted the last crossed-out name.

"Hey," I said to the receptionist. "Do you know how long Jennifer's going to be? I need to run down and put more money in the meter."

The receptionist glanced at the time on the sheet and her clock. "At least thirty to forty-five more minutes."

"I parked around the corner. Does this building have a back entrance, too? Even an employee one I could use real quick? I'm sorry; I'm worried about getting a ticket. I thought I'd be late picking up Jennifer and didn't put much money in the meter."

"Sorry, the back door is only an emergency exit. You'll set off an alarm. Everyone uses the front door."

"Thanks." I left the dental office, waited until the elevator reached the first floor, and shook the wallet out of my pants leg. Stepped over it on my way out.

Someone would find it. Eventually.

8

THE PAY-OFF

THE EMAIL CAME SOON after my interview. Saturday night happy hour, the following week. A location more off the beaten track, but near Ponce. Anything near Ponce de Leon—the avenue running east from Atlanta's Midtown through Decatur—made the cool kids happy. Also allowed for more enterprising locations on the organizer's part. A slightly sketchy "off the beaten path" side street would make the cocktail party more hip.

Hipsters needed to worry more about safety and less about cool. But Lex always said I had aged young. I felt ancient at twenty-seven.

Using my ancient wisdom and Mark's address, I tracked down his county coroner in Canton. Mr. Fisher agreed to meet me at his house on Sunday evening. I found that suspicious until I realized his house was the town mortuary. Tending the dead was a twenty-four-seven job.

Mr. Fisher had no idea what I was talking about.

"I never called a heroin overdose. Are you sure you have the right county, hon?" He was a good old boy, but not bad. Looked like somebody's grandpa. "I have deputy coroners in the county, but they would have reported to me."

"Maybe I'm mixed up." Didn't want him calling the local law.

"Does the name Penny Forbes ring a bell?"

He shook his head. "Maybe a hospital called it."

"Yeah, maybe so."

"Check with the local sheriff's office. If it were a heroin over-dose, they would have responded and had an autopsy done. Could have sent her to the Georgia Bureau of Investigation instead of flagging me."

"Yes, sir."

All righty, then. And I certainly wasn't checking with any local sheriff. I'd bet Penny's dog money whoever played the coroner and cop knew what they were doing. And had the right forms to do it.

Either somebody had pulled the wool over Mark's eyes, or he and his family were pulling it over mine.

I called Bev.

"Fin, hon," she said. "Not that I'm not happy to hear from you, but it makes me worry."

"I'm fine." There was my old friend, guilt, knocking on my door again. "It's about my deceased friend, Penny. When a hospital receives a DOA, what happens to the paperwork?"

"If a patient arrives DOA, we automatically fax the EMS chart to the coroner."

"Would the hospital let me see the chart?"

"Oh no. Right to privacy, hon. HIPAA won't let you."

"Bugger."

"What was that?"

I rolled my eyes at my slip into Lex's lexicon. "Nothin', Miss Bev. Sorry to disturb you. I just hit a dead end is all."

"Sometimes it's best to let things pass, Finley. I know you're upset about your friend, but it's not going to bring her back. Certain things are out of our hands. The powers that be and all."

"Yes, ma'am. I understand what you're saying. But shouldn't there be a check on those powers?"

Bev quieted for a moment. "Honey, you're not still after *him*, are you? Because that's a real dead end. It's best to bury your daddy with your momma. He's not worth the pain it'll cause you. Not to mention what he could do to you."

"Don't worry, Bev. I've been avoiding Woody Goodhart for quite a while. I stopped looking for revenge a long time ago." Stopped looking but didn't stop wanting.

"I'm glad to hear it. He'll get his just desserts in the end. Have faith in that, Fin."

Faith. That's what separated me from people like Bev. That and trust. I felt like I saw her world from the other side of a dirty window. Thanks to Sheriff Goodhart, I had learned that faith and trust were for suckers. Which was why I couldn't let this thing with Penny pass.

"I'll talk to you later, Miss Bev."

"Please do, Fin, honey. And there's always the death certificate. That's public record."

"Ma'am?"

"The name of whoever pronounced the death should be on the death certificate."

Now we were getting somewhere. Although knowing how bureaucracy worked, it'd take some time to get the record. I knew someone who loved to bypass bureaucracy. Too bad he wasn't interested in solving a murder.

Filling out forms to acquire a death certificate topped my to-do list. I had more than a few days to kill until the big night. My nerves were juiced. But with no crew and no background on Platinum, there wasn't much I could do. I was breaking a big rule, walking in blind to the Platinum Partners mixer. I checked the area, did more shopping, and prepared my narrative. Called Mrs. Davis to tell her I was officially in, and asked her to warn Mark not to go to the happy hour.

Mostly to see if he would go anyway.

Went back to Platinum Partners. Sure enough, the office was vacant. Furniture still there, but the nameplate had been slipped off the directory sign. A sign on the door said, "Closed for remodeling." I surmised Platinum had someone in real estate on their payroll. My interview hadn't taken long. They likely bulk-loaded their appointments on a single day. Maybe once a month in different locations.

But I was assuming a lot. This was all shot-in-the-dark guess-work. In my earlier hustles, I banked on human emotion. Namely greed, but pride and vanity, too. To understand what emotion to play to, I had to quickly size up my mark and appeal to their inner vice.

How do you size up an organization? I didn't even know what they were getting out of their own scam.

In the evenings, I stuck to country bar hustling. Appearing like I wasn't doing anything unusual. Just in case anyone had an eyeball on me. I half expected to see Lex. Half hoped. Hung out in the bars longer than I should. Waiting. But not waiting.

He didn't show.

"Y'all planning on sleeping here?" Jello had asked the second night. "Or hoping someone's coming for you?"

"Don't know what you're talking about, Jello." I yawned. "And don't see why'd you care, as long as I'm drinking your swill."

"Nursing's more like it." Jello shook his head. "You kicked him to the curb how many times now? A man's got his pride. You're cute enough, but it's not like you've got the kind of beauty to make a man forget he has a pair. What'd you expect, Fin? "

"I never know what to expect with Lex," I snapped. "That's the problem."

When I returned to the motel, I popped open Penny's laptop. The screen remained blank. Again. Just like the other times I'd opened it that week. Baiting Lex with interesting Google searches.

I lay on the bed, watching YouTube videos from the APA World Pool Championship. Wouldn't let myself think about Lex. Or his funny expressions he'd play up to make me laugh. How he liked to cook for me. Especially late at night like this. Sometimes he'd press against my back. Wrap his arms around my waist. Whisper all my favorite foods in different accents. Then I'd turn in his arms...

I wasn't thinking about him.

He could make me forget myself. Forget my past. Sometimes I'd catch some joy. And a sort-of feeling of contentment.

But that kind of feeling was dangerous. Particularly in our line of work. And I shouldn't forget my past. Lex was right. Fear kept you vigilant. But I couldn't let go of my guilt. I sure as hell wasn't a saint. And now that guilt had caught up with me. I had a lot of repenting to do.

Like with Penny. When I decided to fly right, I should've convinced her to get on the wagon with me. Start her greyhound rescue earlier. But it was easier to duck out on both Penny and Lex. I didn't think they'd understand why I'd quit the grift. And I didn't want them to think I was judging them. Not after all I'd done.

"Who's the hypocrite now?" I thought, rolling on to my back to stare at the ceiling. My friend was dead, and I didn't know why. And the only way I knew how to solve that mystery was to pull a con on her last known associates.

Such a bad idea. If Platinum was a front for mobsters, the organizers would kill me if they thought I wanted to bust them. This wouldn't be a slap on the wrist. No loose teeth for acting like a smart ass. I would be dead.

Just like Sheriff Goodhart had warned. And not from the goodness of his black heart.

What if Platinum was Dot's thing? But Platinum Partners didn't feel like Dot. All the gadgetry I thought they used seemed more high tech than Dot's usual racket. Plus she would have had Lex set it up.

Unless Lex had created Platinum Partners. Which was why he'd intercept me at Jello's before I learned Penny had died. Before I'd start looking into Platinum myself.

Which I was doing anyway.

Overthinking could drive a girl crazy. Overthinking was breaking my heart.

THE DAY of the Platinum Partners mixer I was antsy as all hell. I had prepped as much as I could, then driven to Penny's. I wanted to know if Dot still had people watching the place. I also wanted to see if she'd found all of Penny's rainy day fund. The more I'd thought about it, the more I wanted to give Penny's money to a greyhound rescue group. Knowing Penny, she'd have more stashes than the dryer. She couldn't have told me everything.

I wouldn't have trusted me either.

After stalking the apartment complex perimeter, then the area closer to her building, I decided to try my luck. Lex had probably given Dot the markers. There'd be no reason for Dot to stick around.

To be safe, I approached Penny's building from the central courtyard, exiting through a group of townhomes. Did the ball cap and sunglasses bit. Changed my gait to a scrolling-on-my-phone amble. Head down. Eyes up. Checked the stairwell. Climbed quickly. Then shifted to Penny's door.

The key still worked.

I swung the door open, caught it, and closed it quietly. Slipped off my shoes. Shoved them in my bag. Stood for a moment, taking in the chaos. The couch and chair cushions slashed, innards pulled out. Table and chairs flipped. Rug rolled halfway. Pictures tossed on the floor.

My stomach cramped. I crept past the mess toward the kitchen. The kitchen bar facing the living room allowed me to see the cupboards and drawers standing open. Dishes and silverware littered the counters. I stopped before my toes hit the tile. Cereal and coffee had been dumped on the floor. Luckily, Penny didn't cook much.

Not that it mattered now.

I tiptoed around that mess and into the tiny laundry room. The dryer's back panel had been tossed on the floor. Wires and whatnot exposed. Looking as vulnerable as a dryer could get. The washer wasn't much better.

How did they know to check there? Because I had told Lex? Or because he hadn't had time to move it back into place?

This time, my heart cramped.

Ignoring my feelings, I studied the laundry closet. Wondered why Dot's people hadn't dumped the soap like they had the cereal and coffee. Penny had economy-sized jugs of soap and fabric softener sitting on the wire shelf above the washer. The jugs had a spigot spout and a cap. Openings were too small to hide cash. Plus, they were liquid. Not a good place to hide money.

I cocked my head. Why'd that bug me? I looked around for the pods she normally used. Penny wasn't much of a housekeeper any more than she was a cook. She hated doing laundry. Her good stuff went to a dry cleaner—one that worked for Dot and cleaned more than clothes—and Penny tossed everything else into one load. Whites with darks. Delicates with towels.

Drove me crazy. Before I'd hit double digits, Mom had taught me how to separate and use the machines. She needed my help because a nurse, cop, and kid in one house meant a lot of laundry. Penny had learned how to wash clothes earlier than I had, but she'd taught herself at the laundromat. Toss in everything with a little box of soap and turn it on. She didn't even know about fabric softener when I met her.

Hiding money in the dryer was almost a private joke between us. The pod box she'd normally used had been dumped sideways on the floor. The pods had been on top of the washer before it'd been ransacked. I reached for the jug of fabric softener. Shook it. Full. Thought I heard something inside, but it was hard to tell through the thick plastic and the viscous liquid.

Then I heard something else. In the back of the apartment. A thump. Like feet hitting the floor.

My heart pounded in my back. I replaced the fabric softener. Considered my options. There was no hiding in this closet. Couldn't shut the door because the machines were cockeyed and in the way. I tiptoed into the kitchen. Took my time to avoid the pans and the crunch of cereal. Heard a door creak.

My mouth felt as dry as the old Fruit Loops beneath my feet.

I stole a look into the living room. If the intruder was in the bedroom hall, they'd see me in a few seconds. I ducked to a squat beneath the counters, careful not to upset the scattered pots. Swept a hand through the coffee grounds I'd stepped in. Scattered my toe print. Heard the bathroom door open.

Were they coming out or going in?

Opened the double cupboard next to the stove. Everything had been cleared out, except for a narrow shelf. I was small but not a mouse. Tested the shelf. It sat on plastic bumpers. Carefully lifted the shelf off the inset anchors. Set it on the floor of the cupboard, bumping wood against wood.

Sucked in a breath. Listened.

Cripes, he was peeing with the bathroom door open. Sounded like a man, anyway. Or a horse.

I tested my weight on the cupboard floor. Shoved my backpack inside. Then my feet. Curled my legs up and wiggled inside. Shut the door but for a sliver. Couldn't shift, so ducked my head against my knees. Heard the flush. The bathroom door creaked again. No water ran in the sink.

Disgusting. Who was this man?

Shooting pains rocketed from my cricked neck down my arms. What if the guy camped here? How long could I sit in this cupboard, not moving? My arms were numb as it was. Panic sent small tremors through my muscles. I couldn't sit anywhere long. I had ADD. I'd explode.

"Be cool," said Lex's voice from some distant memory. "When fishing, we don't move lest we scare the fish. You're a cool girl, Fin. You can find a way to chill."

Heavy footsteps trod off the carpeted hall and onto the wood in the living room. Judging by the sound, he stopped not far from the open kitchen galley. Although with the size of this apartment, that could be about anywhere.

I snaked my fingers down my leg toward my scrunched back-pack beneath my bent knees. Fingered through the flotsam I always carried. Found my gum pack and drew it toward the hand still holding my knees together. Pulled a piece of Big Red free. Shook off the wrapper. Jammed the cinnamon-flavored gum into my mouth. Gave my jaws something to keep me busy so I wouldn't spasm out of the cupboard like a Jack-in-the-Box.

The floor creaked and something rustled. I caught a whiff of something. With the coffee grounds on my socks, I couldn't make it out.

"Yeah, it's me."

I stopped chewing. Was someone with him? No, he'd paused. Phone. I didn't recognize the voice.

The wood creaked. He was moving away from the kitchen. I heard a click and dragging sound. I chewed, clearing my sinuses with cinnamon fumes. Felt cool air. He was on the balcony. I nudged the cupboard door with my shoulder. The outside air rushed into the small space.

"Still waiting," he said. "Couldn't find anything."

Who was he waiting for? Someone else was coming? I had to get out.

I chomped on the gum. Bit the inside of my cheek. Blinked back tears and felt the hot kick of cinnamon tracking through my nose.

"Maybe one more run-through. Think they cleared it out, though. No computer or tablet. You think they took it?"

Penny's laptop. I had it. And essentially, so did Lex. But we couldn't find any files on it. Or had Lex already taken them?

Dammit, he could have lied to me about that, too. My head jerked back and smacked the top of the cupboard. Above me, a drawer jostled.

"Hang on. Someone might be here."

I shrank against my knees. Footsteps hit the wood. The scent I couldn't catch drifted closer.

Pipe tobacco. Why was tobacco in my recent memory?

_____

9

THE FLY GEE

THE MAN in Penny's apartment opened the front door, not realizing the mouse was in the cupboard. The pipe tobacco drifted, then grew stronger. The door shut.

"Nobody. Probably heard something next door," he said to his caller. "What'd you want me to do? There are other avenues to explore."

Like Ponce, the avenue where I needed to be in a few hours. If I was going to make the Platinum Partners happy hour. Why couldn't I have spent the extra time applying my Ellie Davis makeup and going over my story notes?

The man was still in the living room. I waited, listening for his heavy tread. The tobacco scent receded. More footsteps.

"Here's what I think—" The balcony doors scraped.

I pushed open the cupboard. Placed my hands between the pots, pans, and cereal. Dragged out my legs. Couldn't wait for them to wake up. My numb nerves pricked and stung. Ordered my brain to move my legs regardless. Waddled through the mess and peered around the kitchen bar.

A man stood on the balcony, leaning over the railing. His back to me. Smoke drifted above and around him. He wore jeans, boots, and a button-down. Baseball cap. Could be any man. Big guy. Still talking. One elbow leaned against the railing. Hand holding the phone to his ear. The other hand waved the pipe in the air. He talked with his hands.

I tossed my backpack over my shoulders. Felt confident he'd hold that position for a moment. Confident but not easy. I crawled toward the front door, not wanting him to catch any movement in his peripheral vision. At the door, I hunkered down in the corner to slide on my sneakers.

Watched him and hoped I got the shoes on the right feet. Still talking. A man with many opinions. Liked to be heard. I'd have to remember that. I made mental notes on the sound of his gait. The scent of the tobacco. The way he bent over the railing, enjoying the sunshine. Probably liked being outside. He'd peed with the door open, for cripes' sake.

Reaching above me, I turned the doorknob, yanked it open, and scuttled out. Left the door hanging while I ran down the stairs and away from that balcony.

I'd return for that jug of Downy.

10

THE SHILL

MY FAVORITE PART of a long con, besides the rush of the con itself, was preparing a role. Penny had taught me how to hustle. How to survive and hide on the streets. Lex had taught me the dramatic art of the big bamboozle. There was no safety net in this kind of acting. That was part of the kick.

My small, symmetrical, almost nondescript features were easy to disguise. With makeup, Ellie Davis's face became fuller. Contour powder across my chin. Jawline. The tip of my forehead. Highlighter dotted my forehead and tops of my cheeks. My brows extended outward. Bangs fell to my eyes. My layered, blonde hair framed my face before hitting my shoulders.

The body was harder to disguise. I chose loose clothing for that reason. Nothing would show but my hands and face. Scarf around my neck. Padded bodysuit. Lifts in the boots. Trousers, blouse, and loose jacket in subdued colors. Something Ellie and her mother would have compromised over. All thanks to Neiman Marcus and Mrs. Davis's credit card.

On my way, I stopped at a print shop. Then parked three blocks away from the party. Trudged over in Ellie's schlepping gait.

The party was a front.

Platinum Partners played against the wall for this bit. A real bar. Low lighting. Shabby chic. Likely paid off for the night so they could control the venue. I'd checked it out earlier in the week. If the marks returned to the scene, they'd find this bar less glamorous. The staff less interesting. Looking dank and dingy instead of urban cool. But it'd still be there. Blacked-out ceiling, bad lighting, and all. With flat screens and beer-bellied occupants. The flat screens had been taken down for the evening. The beer bellies banished.

At the door, a bouncer had asked for my code. I handed him a piece of paper.

"What's this?" said the bouncer.

"Printed off my email," I said. "I'm an app developer. You know how many emails I get from black hats? I regularly scrub my files. When it comes to tickets, I kick it old school."

"How do I know it's you?"

"Call Tony Riggle. He interviewed me and sent the invitation. He's seen me."

The bouncer scanned my printout with his phone and waved me inside.

Inside my pocket, my phone was shut down. I didn't want to risk any probing, not knowing the capabilities of this crew. I scanned the room, moving toward the bar. One bartender. Tattooed chick. Shill but also a face, in case a pigeon decided to hang at the bar instead of mingling. Other women hung at the edges of the crowd, sipping longneck beers and glasses of wine. Appropriately dressed for this atmosphere. Tiny T-shirts and tight jeans. A few guys also acted as faces. Good looking without giving off the alpha male vibes that might intimidate someone. And then there were the fish. Small clusters of rich geeks, mostly huddled together. Still too nervous to mingle. A few older corporate types. Not hep to the sketchy vibe.

The venue was a bit of a letdown. I'd expected Platinum Partners to be more glamorous. Chandeliers and champagne. But the crew was smart, playing to a hipster theme. Keeping it casual. Chandeliers and champagne might have scared off these marks.

Ellie Davis had told the roper she hated formal. Tony Riggle had played into that, calling the happy hour a comfortable way of testing the waters. The bar looked like a step up from a Georgia Tech hangout. Where probably many of these engineers had graduated.

"Disappointed?" The accent was vague. Middle American. Soft-spoken.

I caught the words before I saw the man. Turned. He stuck out his hand.

"Oliver," he said and shook my hand. Smiled crookedly. But attractively. His blue eyes sparked behind thick, dark rims. He wore a gray cashmere hoodie with his jeans. Shoved his hands back into his hoodie pocket. Kept his shoulders slightly slumped. I could see it in his narrative. Habit from all those late nights of coding. "You look vaguely familiar."

"Ellie," I said. "You work here?"

Lex shook his head, but said, "A little. You?"

"I was invited."

"You must have had a busy week, Melanie Davis. Sorry, Ellie's a nickname?"

"Some weeks are busier than others. That's why I'm here."

"True." Lex blinked at me behind his glasses. "I heard you're from Silicon Valley."

"Not originally," I said. He was telling me they all knew my full name and background information. "Moved here from California. With my mom."

"We're seeing more startups in The ATL, now." Lex grinned. "Horse trading. Interesting choice for an app."

He got my joke. I hoped the rest of Platinum Partners didn't.

"And where do you work?" I cocked my head and gave him my own crooked smile.

His eyes warmed. "I joined a new firm. Recent venture. Thought I could help behind the scenes. I like to see how things work. They wanted me in front. So now I'm in sales."

"Profitable for you, I guess?"

"Sometimes it's not the salary. The job's more about a personal interest in the company."

"And what exactly does your company do?"

"It's so large that I don't know much beyond my division. My guess is we're connected. Possibly well-established. Maybe foreign ventures. But local at the same time. I'd say, heavy equipment."

Cripes. Heavy meant gangsters. A syndicate with foreign connections. Dot was just a handler who did penny-ante racketeering. I'd been correct thinking Platinum had felt bigger than Dot. But she'd been interested. Which might explain Lex's in.

"Are you looking to retire with your new company?" I said.

He laughed. "God, I hope not. I'm more of an entrepreneur. But they're well aware of my job hopping."

They had Lex's number, too. That made me nervous for him. Lex was strictly non-violent, skill-based grifting. He steered clear of anything covered under the RICO Act, the Federal law used to combat organized crime.

"Would I know your company?" I asked. "Maybe I have friends who work there."

"I doubt you've heard of the company, although you might know some of their associates. Maybe in their legal department? Pretty sure it's well fixed throughout metro Atlanta. Outside Atlanta, too, I bet. In the surrounding counties."

"I don't hang much with lawyers. Sorry."

Whoever ran Platinum Partners had the fix with metro-area law enforcement. No wonder Lex had said I should take the money and run. If Platinum figured out who I really was, Sheriff Goodhart would be on my tail. Plus a bunch of gangsters.

Lex's eyes shifted behind his glasses. He tapped his beer glass. Some kind of signal amongst the crew. "So it's your first meet-and-greet with Platinum?"

"My mom thought it'd be a good idea to get out and socialize. She felt like my earlier boyfriends weren't trustworthy. One stole from me." My voice hardened. "And I think he gave my stuff to another woman."

His smile didn't reach his eyes, but his gaze on mine didn't waver. "Your mum'd probably like you to play it safe." He spoke slowly, letting his accent slip. "Not keep anything that would get you in trouble."

"She'd trust me to know what I'm doing."

Our eyes didn't break contact. My pulse pounded. My skin felt prickly. I was suddenly aware of the layers of makeup. Like my skin couldn't breathe. Beneath my scarf, I began to sweat. I clutched my bottle of beer with both hands to keep from doing something stupid. Like reaching for him. Breaking character.

"I like my work. But I'm doing it for different reasons now," I said. "I want it to be less about me, you know? More to help others."

What was I proposing? Staying in the grift as a service? How did that help anyone? Lordy, I was losing my mind. The man made me mental. The perfect confidence man.

"A horse trading nonprofit?" His eyebrows quirked.

"In a sense. It's still fun. But without any buyer's remorse for the consumer. And I can take pride in my work. A guilt-free product."

"Guilt free. And unprofitable." He pursed his lips, then grinned. "As long as you're having fun. But be careful. Many sharks in the water these days. If they see you as competition, they won't care that you're a nonprofit. No remorse about what they eat. You know sharks. Swim or die."

I couldn't tell if that warning included himself. But I had a job to do. "It was nice to meet you, Oliver. I don't intend to be fish food. Don't worry."

"Ellie, you sound like the type of girl who knows how to take care of herself." He held out his hand. "Maybe see you later?"

"Maybe." As we shook hands, his thumb stroked my palm. My nerves prickled with pleasure. But I forced myself to focus on the letters he drew. An address. He wanted to meet me. "Depends."

"Right. Lots of people here tonight. I'm sure you want to meet others." He jerked his head toward the left of the bar. "I'll do the same."

He ambled to the bar. Joined a line of men and a few women. I stayed where I was. Sipped my beer. Watched the room. I didn't want to appear overeager to meet anyone. After all, Ellie Davis wouldn't know how to mingle confidently. Why else would she be here?

In my peripheral vision, I spotted someone walking toward me. Just as he approached, I turned and smiled at Tony Riggle.

"How's it going, Ellie? Having fun? Meet anybody yet?"

"It's good to see a familiar face, Tony," I said. "I met one guy. Oliver something. He's in sales. He was nice."

"But didn't hit it off?"

"Maybe?" I shrugged, toying with my hair. "I don't know. He was nice."

"I could see what he thought of you." Riggle smiled. "Just like in junior high, right?"

I worked up a blush. "Don't do that. I'd be so embarrassed. I'm glad you're here. It's hard meeting new people."

"You want to sit for a minute?" He pointed to a table and chairs. "What do you think of the bar?"

"It's cool." I sat and waited for him to scoot his chair closer to mine. Cozy. Working the angle. Just in case Oliver and I didn't hit it off, Tony Riggle could sweep me off my feet. But to what end? I wondered if Lex knew what Platinum's payoff was. If he were a shill, they wouldn't necessarily let him in on the actual bunk. "Looks like an old dive bar."

"It is."

"You come here often?" I leaned toward him. Played with my hair. Preening. But not excessively.

"Not really. Heard about it from a friend who lives nearby. When we were looking for venues for our next happy hour, it seemed like a fun place to come."

"You don't live nearby?" I stared. Awkwardly. Desperately.

"I live in Virginia Highlands. Not far." His smile rolled off his lips. "Quick Uber. But I've got to stick around for a while. I'm sort of working."

I forced another blush, darted my gaze away. Began twisting my rings. "Right. Of course."

Riggle laid a hand over my nervous fingers. "Ellie. Stick around." He smiled again and moved from the table.

I internally rolled my eyes and gazed at his retreat. Probably going in the back to complain about having to flirt with a cow. Maybe this was a simple badger game. Take me back to his place, where he'd have a hidden camera. Later use the video as extortion to fleece me.

But Penny had gotten engaged to Mark Davis. That was too long of a commitment for a badger game. Maybe she had really fallen in love with him. The setup was to find a match for wealthy singles. Were they planning on marrying off the crew and then siphoning funds from their rich spouses?

Would I have to get engaged to Tony Riggle to see how this played out?

Ugh.

My gaze cut from Riggle to the bar where a youngish man in a cashmere hoodie chatted with an older woman. She was at least twenty years older than him. Poor Lex.

I could get engaged to Oliver. Tell Tony Riggle that I had been interested in Lex. See what would happen.

Cripes, what was I thinking? Focus, Fin. You're not here for a date. What else can Platinum Partners do? Besides extortion, gangsters loved money laundering. Wouldn't they need a permanent address? Maybe trafficking? Couldn't see a bunch of rich tech geeks as mules. Financial fraud. Possibly. Gambling. Totally illegal in Georgia. But these fish didn't seem like the high stakes type.

But Penny had markers. Holding them for somebody. Or stolen. But why steal markers? They were IOUs between two parties. Might screw somebody's books, but she couldn't benefit unless she were getting a cut.

Of course, there was always blackmail. Who would Penny

blackmail? Somebody at Platinum? Penny wasn't stupid. You can't blackmail gangsters and live to tell the tale.

Of course, Penny didn't live.

I got up from the table and walked to the bar. Found a guy who looked like a pigeon. To see what would happen. Would they let me make my own match?

We were intercepted by another couple. Cute, nerdy girl and a techie.

"Hey, I'm Brian," said the techie. He wore a Peruvian poncho and jeans. Dark, curly hair with brown eyes. Glasses. Half-smile.

The girl inserted herself between us. Turned her back on me to shake hands with my pigeon. "I'm Moria. I teach preschool while I'm working on my modeling portfolio."

Maybe Platinum was just a pimp service for nerds. How depressing.

"Brian, what do you do?" I said, resigning myself to being ditched for a model. But that had been my plan, to meet more Platinum shills. Get some information. So why did getting dumped for somebody more attractive still hurt? Human nature was ridiculous.

"Cybersecurity."

I perked up. "Cool. Where?"

"Big corporation. Rather not say." He had an impish grin. "Security, you know."

I bored myself babbling to Brian about my horse app. While I explained coding horse DNA, I watched his body language. A bit stiff. I was boring him, too. But he made himself lean toward me. Occasionally touched my forearm, urging me to talk more. Kept his gaze on me.

"So this year's genetic pool should be amazing." I fished. Brian's bosses might be interested in calling horses. "Watch the tracks in another couple years."

"Awesome. You think you can call a derby winner?"

I smirked. "I wouldn't say that. But my app might."

She may be unlucky in love, but when it came to software, Ellie was cocky.

"I've been talking nonstop," I said. "Tell me about your job."

His gaze drifted over my shoulder, then back. "You know, mostly setting up biometric systems. Scanning software."

"Like facial recognition? Retinal scans?" Hopefully, they weren't using any of that tonight. Facial recognition would see through my makeup.

"And voice. Next, it'll be blood." He chuckled. "You know much about that?"

"Only what I've read online." I tried some new bait. "You do any hacking? I bet your firm's got all the toys."

He smiled. "Do you play around?"

"Sometimes." I hadn't prepared for this conversation. All my research had been for my fake app. I'd have to watch how deep I got. "Not trolling. Just seeing what code I can break."

He'd been edging me toward the bar. I let him slide in next to me, bump against my hip, turn his body toward mine. Brian ordered two more beers. After handing me mine, he lowered his arm to rest on the bar behind my back.

I kept my comments open but vague. Brian was testing to see what lines I might cross. Cyberly speaking. Then he switched subjects, asking about my family. They already had Melanie's name, address, and credit card number. She didn't know, but the Davises' mail had been diverted to a P.O. box. I had created dummy accounts online, rerouting search engines temporarily from sixty-something Melanie to thirty-something Ellie. The judge was a problem. But Davis was a common enough name. Mark had a different address. I hoped they wouldn't put the two together.

But I couldn't count on it.

Feeling tired, I spoke briefly about my fake mother and sister, then switched to music and movies. Netflix. Safer subjects.

Brian moved closer. Touched my shoulder occasionally. Then stroked my back. Coming on strong.

He turned to the bartender and tapped his bottle.

What did it mean? He had me hooked?

"Can I get your number?" he was saying.

I felt woozy. A little dizzy. I'd been careful about my beer. Never set it down. Sipped slowly. Bar betting 101: Watch for mickeys. But I didn't know the venue. The bartender could've put something in my bottle.

"Hang on. I'll be back." I pushed off the bar. Stumbled.

Brian grabbed my arm. "You okay? You want some help?"

"In a minute." Dammit. Probably a roofie. I sucked air through my nose and out my mouth. Focused hard on steering toward the toilets. Had Lex warned me? I could no longer remember.

"Let me help you." Brian took my arm. "Bathroom's this way."

"I don't want your help." I tried yanking my arm free.

He gripped it. "You're having trouble walking. Too much to drink. Happens to everyone."

"I only had two." We headed into a dark hall in the back.

"I'm sure you've had three or four since we've been talking. It's okay, Ellie. We're having a good time."

We stopped before a door. A wooden cutout of a bird silhouette hung on a nail. It jostled, tapping the wood. The other door had a rooster.

Brian leaned in close, raised my chin with his finger, and peered through my glasses to catch my eyes. He appeared fuzzy. Blurry.

Were my glasses dirty?

"I won't let anything happen to you. I'll wait here." He leaned forward and kissed me. Lightly. Not unpleasantly.

I had to hand it to Brian. He was good.

And I was in trouble.

11

THE COME-THROUGH

I'D HAD it all figured out and then been suckered punched by something as stupid as a roofie. Like I hadn't learned anything in ten years. But I still had a few wits. Knew I should remain in character, although my narrative had slipped sideways. I let Brian kiss me. Gave him a soggy smile and pushed into the bird's room. Locked the door. Looked around. And felt like throwing up.

A leaky sink. Two stalls. And a urinal. Why was there a urinal in the girl's restroom? And the room was disgusting. Smelled terrible and looked like it had been mopped with dirty water. A broken condom machine hung on the wall. I squinted at it. Came to a horrible realization. Squelched a scream as one of the stalls opened.

I spun around. My hands covering my mouth.

"Hello, love," said Lex. "You're looking somewhat—what is that wonderful expression you use—puny?"

"Roofie," I slurred. "Slow to kick in, I think."

"Not slow enough, daresay." Lex sighed. "What're you going to do?"

"I don't know," I said. "Maybe splash water on my face."

"And lose your makeup? They may be suspicious already."

"You don't know if they are?"

"I have no details about you beyond your basic background." He shook his head. "I'm supposed to make a match. Bonuses for the farther I go with my mark. A big settlement if I get engaged. I could marry if I want."

"What does that do? How's that a scam?"

"Passing information, I suppose. They're vague. Maybe hoping I'll get invested in my relationship and they can blackmail us both."

"Cripes." I shook my head. Made myself dizzy. Grabbed my face to stop it from spinning off. "What was Penny thinking?"

"Now you know. So now you need to leave."

I waved a finger slowly. "I don't know who murdered Penny. Or exactly why."

"Lord love you, Fin, but you're stubborn. Give it up already." Lex crossed his arms. "I told you this is a heavy racket. These matches must be insurance policies in a deep-pocket scheme."

"What are you going to do?" I rocked back on my heels and pitched. Grabbed a sink. Then slipped off.

Lex caught my arm, swung me into his body. "What do you mean?"

"Who you goin' to marry?" I circled my arms around his waist. Snuggled in. Just for a minute, I told myself. "The cougar?"

His teeth shone in the stark bathroom light. "Are you worried about me, love?"

"'Course I am." I rested my head on his shoulder. "I don't want you to marry the cougar. It sounds horrible."

"I'd be richer than Croesus, my darling. She owns her company. A life of ease and luxury." He kissed my hair, rubbed my neck. "I wouldn't have to work at all. Maybe play with stocks. Deliver insider trading news to some boiler room or other. Doesn't that sound nice?"

"No." I felt like crying. Maybe I was. "It sounds awful. You'd hate it."

"Would I?"

"You would. You'd be bored and resentful. Probably try something stupid and dangerous just for fun. Get yourself killed, or worse."

"What's worse than killed?" He tipped my chin up to look me in the eye. "Don't cry, love. Should I marry someone else instead?"

"I don't know." This time my blush was real. I tried to dip my chin, but he held it firm.

"Look at me, Fin."

I looked. His eyes were somber. His laugh lines had smoothed.

"I'm dead serious, Fin. This is not for you."

"It's not for you, either," I insisted. "Why are you doing it? For Dot?"

"Dot?" His eyebrows drew together. "I only do for Dot if I need something in return. That's how it works."

"She got you in this."

"I used one of her connections, yes, but that's it. You need to trust me more, Finley." He studied my face. "You're worse than a feral cat, love. I keep getting scratched. It hurts."

I jerked my chin away but eased my head back to his shoulder. "You're too involved. Too good at this."

He said nothing, rubbed circles on my back.

I closed my eyes. "Trust is for suckers. You taught me that, Lex."

"I did, didn't I?" He sighed. "Right, love. Time to get out before you pass out."

"Brian's waiting for me," I mumbled. "Outside the door. He kissed me."

"Bloody tosser. He's on the pull, that one."

"Looking for a bonus. Can you blame him?"

"Yes, I can blame him." Lex entangled me from his shoulder. "Right, love. Wakey-wakey. You've got to slide from the bar without Brian. Chuck him. Before they have you made. So quick, quick. I'll find you outside. You've been in tougher spots. I know you can do it."

I pouted. "What if I decide I like Oliver better?"

"Never break character, Fin. You know the rules." He smiled.

"But you give us hope, love. I'm worse than an addict that can't be knocked. I keep coming back to your game."

"I've never conned you, Lex. That's the difference between us."

He shook his head. "That's what you think."

BRIAN HUNG at the end of the hall where he could watch the party. When I stumbled from the bathroom, he hurried back to help me.

"You want another drink?" he said. "Or what if we went back to my place? We can talk. Get comfortable."

I needed to think, but all my processors were in extreme slo-mo. I leaned against him. "I'm not that easy, Brian."

"I can tell," he said. "A nice girl."

Not that nice. I'd picked his pockets. I had his phone. "You know what'd be great, Brian?"

"What's that, Ellie?" He smiled down at me.

"If you could get me a glass of water." I deliberately slurred my words and clung to him. Semi-deliberately. "That'd be super awesome. I feel like something really cold and refreshing. I'm kind of tired."

"Or another beer?"

"Super." Not drunk enough for you, Brian?

I detached myself from Brian. He hurried to the bar. Other couples had paired off. Oliver's date was looking at her watch. I tried not to take any satisfaction in that. Lex would get in trouble for screwing up his job.

Slide, Fin. I told myself. Take a bounce. Brian's at the bar. He'll be back in a minute.

I couldn't make my feet move. My eyes wandered the room. I caught a scent of something other than cologne and beer. Pipe tobacco. Did a slow turn. Spotted Mark Davis. In a deep conversation with the bartender. She stroked his hand while they talked.

He bounced back fast. Melanie would not approve, Mark.

But where was the goon?

Then I saw him. Sitting with a beer in the corner of the bar. By himself. Watching the room.

I reeled. Caught my footing. Did the one-foot-two-foot shuffle toward the bar. Parked next to the goon.

"Hey, I'm Ellie."

He peered down at me over the bottle he sipped. Sat his bottle on the bar. "Yeah? You're also drunker than a skunk."

I giggled. Sounded like he was from my hometown. Then I sucked in my breath. Maybe he was. Lordy. Working for the sheriff, maybe?

"You here looking for a date, too?" I asked.

He squinted at me and gave a firm shake of his head. Not interested in Ellie. Which was fine with me.

"Then what're you doing here?"

"Having a beer. It's a bar, ain't it?"

"Private party." I slurred. "How'd you get it in?"

"Tipped the bouncer." His eyes drew past me. "Someone's looking for you."

"Pro'ly Brian. I wish he'd get lost."

"Hassling you?"

"Gave me a roofie." I yawned. "I only had two beers. Figured it out when I couldn't walk. He's trying to get me drunker. For 'xtortion purposes, you know."

The guy's mouth drew tight. Then expanded. "Tell me about this party. Sounds like you have it figured out."

"Can't. Got to get out." I shoved off the bar. "I almost forgot. Supposed to slide."

His hand clamped onto my shoulder. "You know what's going on here?"

I stared up at him. He looked unfocused. Pixilated. The layers parted. Doubled. I blinked. They shifted again. Somewhere deep inside my body, the beer bubbled. A voice in my head rumbled about danger.

"Gotta go." I jerked, but the hand stayed fixed. A large hand. Strong. Had he always been this gigantic?

"You're coming with me." He hauled me off the bar, swinging me toward the door.

My feet dragged along the ground, the lifts inside my shoes making it difficult to gain purchase. He shoved me through the door. Cold air pricked my face like tiny daggers. I gulped and flailed my arms. His hand stayed clamped on my shoulder. We frogmarched down the sidewalk. Turned a corner. Then another. Slipped between buildings and into an alley.

Everything I had learned slid away. He was too large to fight. I could knee him, possibly. But I couldn't run. My limbs felt like overcooked noodles.

"Damn roofie," I cried. "Dammit."

He shoved me against a wall. My head fell back, smacking the concrete behind me.

"Wake up. Tell me what you know."

"Wait, wait." I shook my head. "Who do you work for?"

He slapped my face. Hard enough to make it sting. "Who are you?"

My eyes teared. "Don't. Please don't do this."

He held up his open palm, waved it before my face. "Wake up. Answer the damn question. Who are you?"

"I just want to know what happened to her."

"Happened to who?"

"Penny," I said. Then threw up on his shoes.

12

THE HURRAH

I WOKE UP IN A BED. Curled into a ball. Wearing a T-shirt and not much else. My legs kicked out. I sat up quickly. Too quickly. My brain sloshed inside my skull, bouncing off the sides. I squeezed my eyes shut. Clamped a hand over my mouth.

"No honking in bed. Bad form, love."

I opened one eye, then the other. Sunshine streamed through skylights. The low bed was in the corner of a large, open room. One wall had a kitchen with an island and stools. Another area had a couch, TV, and a long table covered in computer equipment. In the dancing dust motes, Lex stood with arms crossed over his bare chest. A pair of pajama pants hung off his lean hips.

"You acquired a loft," I rasped.

"I'd credit your powers of observation, but I'm too annoyed. What happened?"

"I should ask you the same. How'd I get here?"

"Found you literally crawling out of an alley. Like you'd been on a bender."

"Brian gave me a roofie."

"Why were you drinking at all? In a few months, she's forgotten the basics." He threw his hands in the air. Spun away.

Strode to the kitchen. "How could you have been so bleeding stupid? You could have been—" Picking up a pan, he slammed it on the stove.

I opened my mouth, then closed it. Lex didn't get annoyed. Or upset. I rested my head on my knees for a moment, then looked up. "Did you find a phone besides mine?"

"No phones at all."

"Cripes, the thug swiped them." I had stolen Brian's phone, but whatever. I flipped back the sheet. Slid to the end of the bed. "Where are my clothes?"

"Bathroom." He turned. His eyebrow arched. "Oh, are you going, then? Be a love, and leave a fiver for the maid. She'll have a job after you spent the night spewing your guts."

"You're mad because I threw up?"

"I'm angry because you almost got killed. Or raped. Or had your teeth kicked in." He crossed the room in long strides. Stood over me. Hands clenched at his sides. "You're on the level. Fine. You're a big girl. Know what you're doing. I may be gutted—lost my partner, lost my girl—but I understand. But for Penny, you'll jump back in and put yourself up as a vic? Like some bloody lop-eared sucker?"

"You don't get it. I owe it to Penny." I stared at the wall, avoiding the hurt burning in his eyes.

"She's dead, Fin. Not like she can collect."

I pressed my lips together. Spoke through gritted teeth. "It's not just about the score, Lex."

"You're the one who doesn't get it, Fin. They might have made you. I told you this was dangerous. I still don't know who *they* are."

"They figured out who I was?"

"They saw you leave with the private dick."

My head whipped back around, making my eyes bounce like ping pong balls. "Wait, he's a detective? Are you sure? He roughed me up in the alley."

"Roughed you up." Lex walked a tight circle, scrubbing his scalp. "Bloody hell, Fin. Bloody bleeding hell."

"We've been in situations before. Why are you so mad this time?"

He stopped before the bed. Towered over me, shaking. "Because *before* we were together. Why didn't you go outside and wait for me? Like I asked? I wrote the parking lot addy on your palm. You could have found my car, no one the wiser."

"I tried. Then I saw the goon and wanted to know his deal. I wasn't thinking straight because of the drug. The guy was in Penny's apartment earlier that day."

"Which meant you were at Penny's, too. What kind of idiot have you become? Return to the scene of the crime? Like a basic criminal?"

"I'm not a criminal." I reared back on my knees. Nose jutting in the air. "I'm doing this for Penny."

"That's rich. You're not a criminal. Let's see how many laws you've broken in this past week, shall we? Identity theft. Credit card fraud. Breaking and entering. Robbery. Penny might have been your best friend, but you still took her money, laptop, and I believe you're driving around in her car. That's grand theft auto, love."

"And you stole Penny's markers while you kissed me," I shouted.

"I would've kissed you whether you had the markers or not, you bloody fool." He quieted. Uncrossed his arms. Cocked his head. Put a knee on the bed. "That made it worse, did it? The snog?"

I scuttled backward. "I didn't say that."

"You just lost your character, Fin. That cold-hearted tough act. Poof. Gone." He placed a hand on the mattress. Then another. Crawling forward. "You were lying then, and you're lying now. You've got your tells. You do miss me."

My back hit the wall. "What are you doing, Lex?"

"Anger's a useless emotion, love. I'm chucking it for a different sentiment."

"Lex." I placed my hands on his shoulders, pushing him away. Then slipped them around and over his back. My hands remembering the slide of skin over skin. Caught myself. My fingers flew off his back.

But not quick enough. He noticed.

"Anyway." I crossed my arms. "I've been sick all night."

"A flirt you are. Come here, Fin." He pulled me down to lay my head on his chest. One arm wrapped around me. The other hand twined in my fingers. "What happened in the alley? How'd you scarper?"

"Puked all over him. He left me there."

"Such the charmer, you." Lex kissed my head. Smoothed my hair. "He was in Penny's apartment? Did he spot you?"

"No, he was in the bedroom when I entered. I hid in a kitchen cabinet until his back was turned."

Lex chuckled. "Learn anything useful?"

"He was waiting for someone to show. I don't know who he's working for. But I recognized the scent of his tobacco from my Platinum Partners interview."

"Odd, that."

"How did you know he was a detective?"

"Just a guess. Looks like one. Joe at the front door let him through, figuring it might cause more problems than not. So the dick could see it was just a party."

"Hookup party."

His chest rumbled with laughter. "It's a bar. Who isn't on the pull at a bar?"

"But you don't know who hired him?" I smoothed a hand over his chest, letting my fingers bump over the hard planes. He shivered. "Seems like something the sheriff would do."

"How would the sheriff know you would be at the party?" Lex caught my hand. Lifted it to kiss my fingers. "He'd be a step behind you, not in front. You smelled the tobacco at your interview. He was there first. Checking out Platinum. Didn't know you'd show at Penny's."

"Unless he was waiting for me to come back." I sighed. "But you're right. The detective was trying to get information from me. Wanted to know what I knew about the party. Who I was. If Daddy had hired him, he still would have slapped me around, but warned me off instead of questioning me."

"Did he..." The arm around me tightened. "He slapped you?"

I skipped the question. "How're we going to find out who he is?"

"I can ask if anyone recognized him."

"Maybe Tony Riggle knows him."

"Riggle." Lex ran his hand through my hair. Twisted a lock around his finger. "You got a little cozy with Riggle. How'd he seem to you? An inside man. Connected, that one. But not the brains."

"Who is the brains?"

"Dunno." He was quiet for a while. "No one seems to know much except there are several organizations working together. Big ones. I don't like it."

"They don't play well with others."

"Exactly." He kissed my hair. Nuzzled my cheek. "I miss this."

"Lex." I pushed up to look at him. "Are you going to help me find out who killed Penny? If I get her money back, I'm giving it to the greyhound rescue people."

He slid a hand beneath his head, staring up at me. "Penny's dogs, yeah? I guess that could be fun." His other hand ran up my arm. His hand spanned my neck. "Will you stick around this time?"

"If we're on the square? Both of us? Yes."

"We'll never be on the level, us." He grinned, pulling me back to him. "But that fine line may make an interesting place to walk. For a bit, anyway."

LATER, after a breakfast fry-up by Lex, we moved into his office area. I sat cross-legged on an office chair while he popped open laptops and printed off spreadsheets. Enjoying the lingering scent of sausage and coffee. But still too keyed up to relax.

"Here's what I could find on the Davis family. As well as some of the other Platinum clients." Lex dumped a ream of paper in my lap. "Not much on Mark."

"I hacked into his social media accounts. The guy's a loner. Masters in engineering plus an MBA. Immediately went to work and pushed his way up to the VP position. No social activities except through work. They think he's stodgy. Although he does Saturday night poker with the boys."

"Has a little gambling bug, does he?"

"I saw Mark at the mixer. Why would he go if he just lost his fiancée?"

"Because Platinum has him on the hook? We don't know exactly how they work yet."

"Or he murdered my best friend."

"And he's looking for another fiancée to murder? Is he a male black widow or a Jack the Ripper?"

"I don't know." I crossed my arms. "But he's suspicious."

"We know there's a criminal organization behind Platinum, love. Penny was working as a face. Let's look at these facts and set Mark as the serial fiancée killer aside for a minute." Lex dropped a kiss on the top of my head and paced to his desk. "Platinum gets their hooks in Mark through Penny. Once that's established, it's a matter of time before they start leaning on the judge."

"You think that's who they're after?"

"Mark's too boring. It has to be the judge."

"And this wouldn't be just a financial relationship. They'd want him for a court fix." I flipped through the stack of papers. "Similar deal on these other folks?"

"Different deals. Different industries. I think the organization liked having their fingers in a lot of pots, just using similar tools. Hook the marks, keep them in a relationship enough to set up long-term extortion, and then use them for whatever. The interview process is the perfect vehicle to screen the fish. How'd it look from your end? What was Brian after? Besides the usual."

I stuck my tongue out at the thought of Brian. "I thought it might be the horses, but he seemed more interested in my hacking abilities."

"Start you off with fun and games, see how far you'd go, then Bob's your uncle—raiding corporate files for fun and profit."

"That's what it sounded like. We were getting beyond my depth." I tapped the files. "Back to Penny. Where'd it go wrong? Who'd she tick off?"

Lex rocked back in his chair, watching me.

"Melanie Davis claimed Penny had a heart attack," I said. "Told me Mark found Penny. But a coroner called it before Penny even got to the hospital. No autopsy ordered, as far as anyone at the hospital knew. Crematorium picked up Penny soon after admittance DOA."

"This is all from Melanie Davis?"

I looked away. "No, I spoke to an old friend of Mom's. Nurse. She looked into it for me."

"Aha." The chair squeaked. "And how was that?"

"Bev didn't know much. But she did know Penny was an OD case. And we both know a corrupt coroner who'll call deaths for a payout. Hell, anyone on the seedier streets of Atlanta knows John Prince."

I glanced at Lex, saw the sympathy in his eyes, and busied myself. Flipped the paper. Stuck a finger into the ring on my necklace. Adjusted the chain.

"Someone's lying to the Davises or Melanie Davis is lying to you."

"That's what I figured." I placed the stack of papers on a side table. "But you're right. Icing Penny makes more sense as a hit. A heroin overdose is an embarrassment for a family like the Davises.

Melanie might be telling everyone heart attack as a cover. And those markers. That has organized crime written all over it."

"Didn't pull much off Penny's laptop," Lex said. "Maybe if I had the hard drive. We should retrieve it from your motel room with the rest of your stuff, yeah?"

"The rest of my stuff?" I arched a brow. "What? And move in here?"

"Safer." Lex held out his hands, palms up. "At least while we're working this job."

"Are we? Working together?"

"Of course." He grinned. "Why doubt it?"

"You know why. Where are Penny's markers?"

"In a safe place." He sighed at the look I gave him. "I'd rather not be explicit in case we run into some trouble. If they shake you down—"

"That's a load of bull. I'd rather have something to tell the thug who's shaking me down."

"And what if it's the police who're doing the shakedown, yeah? This is a complicated operation."

I studied him, wondering why the man who always knew so much knew so little. "You lost your date last night. Are you going to get in trouble? Do you need to report to the crew or anything?"

"I chatted her up but made sure nothing stuck. You know me, love."

"Right." Doubt began to seep in now that the rush of romance had faded. Lex still had Penny's markers, which made me wonder about their worth. Could they still be collected on? Fifty grand was a significant amount.

Lex had also spent a week accomplishing more research than I did. And didn't seem to have much to show for it. Except himself as a connection to Platinum Partners. Of which he seemed to know nothing. And he was avoiding discussing his part in it.

"I need to call the bar." I unfolded my legs and swiveled away from Lex. "That detective took my phone and Brian's. Maybe he left them there."

The only negative evidence on that phone was the photo I had taken of the obscure code from Tony Riggle's wallet. I'd uploaded it to a cloud and deleted the picture, but the photo could be accessed from the cloud if they had the phone. If someone knew how to find that image or knew how to pull wiped information, they'd have me made.

"I'll buy you another phone, love," said Lex.

So he could track me? Shouldn't he be worried about evidence on my phone?

"You'd have to show in character," Lex continued. "In case anyone's watching the bar. Like your friendly dick."

Made sense, but still. "Right. Don't worry yourself. I'll get a new phone today." I hopped from the chair and began to hunt for my shoes. "I should do that now. Before the church crowd is out and about. And I need to pick up Penny's car."

Lex watched me from his chair, his expression calm. "Finley."

"What?"

"Don't do this to us."

"I'm not doing anything."

"Fin. Your tells are obvious."

I felt close to tears, checked my voice. "You're a confidence man, Lex. You play it close to the vest, even with me. I knew this when I met you. It's my fault. After Mom, the only other person I trusted was Penny. And now I feel like I don't even know her."

"Right." He stood. Paced across the floor to me. Grabbed my hand. "Notice I wasn't on that list. But I understand about Penny."

"I need to go—"

"I have Penny's markers. I didn't give them to anyone. Or sell them to anyone." He looked at me steadily. "They are in a safety deposit box. I will give you a key."

My face felt hot. So did my eyes. I swallowed hard. "Okay."

"Better?" He raised my hand to his lips, looking at me over my knuckle. Lowered my hand, but kept it gripped in his. "Fin, I don't know how *not* to be who I am. I've been doing it too long."

I jerked a nod.

"Actions speak louder than words, yeah?" He pulled on my hand. "Let's run your errands. Like we're a real couple out for a Sunday. And while we're out, I'll make some calls."

Still too hard to trust him.

And too hard not to love him.

13

THE INSIDE MAN

THE LOFT WAS IN CABBAGETOWN, an area of old factories turned lofts. Arty and cool. Just east of downtown. Not far from the connector, which we took south until the I-85/I-75 split, then continued toward Griffin and my motel. I went along but made no plans. I'd get the laptop. Check on Penny's money. Over the years I'd learned—the hard way—to move money around, check on it constantly. Clean my own room as much as possible.

"One could never say Finley Goodhart likes to live large," said Lex, driving over the broken concrete in the motel's parking lot. "You'll be much more comfortable in my loft."

"You get noticed when you live large." I skipped the part about his loft. "Comfortable equals risk."

"Life is risky, Fin. Rabbits still make a den knowing the fox is nearby."

But the rabbit didn't live with the fox.

"Paranoia will drive yourself to an early grave."

Could he read my thoughts?

That's also called paranoia, Fin.

Lex parked, then turned to me. Laid a hand on my thigh. "Relax a bit, won't you? You're shaking my confidence and confidence is all I have."

"Sorry." I covered his hand with mine. "I won't rest easy until this is taken care of."

He gave me a quick smile, but I spotted the doubt in his eyes. Logically I knew I couldn't keep pushing him away and expecting him to rebound. But letting my guard down completely felt akin to that rabbit leaving her burrow, dodging the fox, and getting caught in a trap instead.

"Your dad ripped away everything you had. I can fathom it, Fin. Basic psychology. I once had—" He glanced away, clenched my hand in his, then turned back to fix me with a level gaze. "Well, no matter that. Past is past for me. But I get you. Just ease up, love. These past months without you were worse than anything I ever felt before."

"Why won't you talk about it? Your past."

"That yawn? I promise you this, Fin. Boring is something I'd never bring to our table." His smile became jaunty, eyes bright. Back to the mischievous boy next door. "Get your things out before they make you pay the full day. I'm going to check in with the Platinum crew. See what they made of your detective and Miss Ellie Davis's disappearance."

I didn't push. Something else I'd learned over the years. Lex never spoke about his life before the grift. But maybe he'd been born into it and knew nothing else.

I LEFT Lex to make his calls. He'd dart in and out of the conversation. Sneak away with information while keeping up a patter that would distract the speaker. I took my cautious approach to the room. Checked the stairwell and vending machine area. Quick scan of the parking lot from the second floor. Lex's ridiculously conspicuous Camaro had already blown my cover.

At my door, something felt wrong. I'd hung a "Do Not Disturb" sign. The cheap paper could have fallen off the doorknob. Only needed someone to brush up against it.

But, still.

Turned the key in the lock and waited. Listening. Then talked myself into entering.

The room had been tossed. Mattress pushed sideways. Drawers pulled out. My clothes dumped. My stomach ached like I'd been punched. I left the door hanging open. Moved out of the doorway to the wall next to the window. Surveyed the room, forcing myself not to rush about. Kept quiet.

The bathroom door was closed.

I felt behind the lined drapes for my cue case. It still rested upright on the window ledge. The perpetrator hadn't opened the curtains. Kept their burglary hidden from view. I pulled the case forward. Gripped it with both hands and held it in front of me. Tiptoed toward the bathroom door and swung the case up. Held it over my shoulder like a baseball bat. Waited another minute, listening. Kicked the door open and jumped aside.

Empty.

At the same moment, I heard a noise behind me. I pivoted.

"Bugger," said Lex from the doorway. "Someone's on to you."

THEY'D TAKEN Penny's laptop. And the money taped inside the toilet tank. They didn't find the stash taped to the bottom of the sink even though they'd pulled out everything from the sink cabinet. Tore open the toilet paper. And my overnight bag. My good cosmetics dumped. Cases broken. My makeup mirror had been smashed. And my suitcase ripped apart. All my hustling cash had been stolen from the false bottom.

"We'll put the stacks they didn't snatch in the safety deposit box with the markers, yeah?" said Lex after he'd helped me gather the few things that weren't ruined. We cleaned the room to avoid alerting the staff and carried everything out to his car. "It's just money, love."

"Penny's money." Her greyhounds were losing to this scum.

Bile burned in my chest. I slammed a grocery bag of clothes into Lex's trunk. "Who did this? Platinum's people?"

"The bloke I spoke to is playing it cool. Said he doesn't know anything about Ellie. But they're hot about the private dick." He circled an arm around me, pulled me into his side. "Stay at my place. Makes me anxious for you, this."

"What about you? If they figured out where I'm staying, they know who I am. And it won't take long to put me with you. Enough people know we were partners."

"*Are* partners. Let me worry about that one." He kissed the side of my head and closed his trunk.

"I don't get it. If my cover isn't blown, how would they find this place?" I set my cue case in the backseat. Climbed in the front and dropped back against the headrest. Lex slipped into the driver's seat and started the Camaro.

"Let's leave Penny's car for a while, then. You'll have a new phone. We'll buy you new clothes and whatever else you need."

I'd had to ditch stuff before. It didn't bother me that much anymore. Better not to attach myself to things anyway. But losing money always bugged me. I ran a finger over my necklace, playing with the ring and thinking. "What about Dot?"

"What about her?"

"She had you followed. They tossed Penny's apartment. It makes sense. Dot knows I keep outside of Atlanta. I've stayed in Griffin before, although not that particular motel."

Lex glanced at me, then returned his gaze to the road. Took the off-ramp toward the interstate. We were headed back toward Atlanta.

"Did Penny have something on Dot?" I turned in my seat to watch Lex. "Penny was working for Platinum, not Dot. Or is Dot part of this Platinum syndicate?"

"That is something you'd have to ask Dot yourself."

"Then I will. Let's do it now." My anger overrode my fear. I itched to confront the Amazon.

"It's possible this detective used your phone to find your

place," said Lex said. "I assume you used your phone at the motel. He could have tracked your pings. If he knows his stuff."

"If he's really a detective. Maybe he's just someone's muscle."

"True. Makes more sense if he's to blame for your room." Lex quieted. Eyes on the road. "There is another player. One whom I'm almost certain is not connected to either the Platinum syndicate or to Dot. At least not at the moment, anyway. They might have some insight."

"Who?"

"I don't have a name. Only heard a bit of this and that. Dot's mentioned the Mountain Posse, although that's her little joke. Trying to downplay their significance."

"Dixie Mafia?"

"Possibly at times. I don't know much. But they're heavy hitters outside Atlanta. Usual racket, but they lean more toward opiate trade, guns, contract stuff. Old school."

"They keep it up in the mountains?"

His eyes moved to mine. "As far as I know. I'm sure their network covers a broad area. But I hadn't heard of their connections to the south side, or middle Georgia for that matter. Politically speaking, anyway."

That meant no connection to the sheriff. That Lex knew of. I toyed with my necklace. "Why would we get in touch with another organization? It's dangerous enough as it is."

"Information. Hopefully, intelligence that's less biased than anything we'd learn from Dot." He pursed his lips. Nodded. "I'll make some calls while you shop. See if we can get a conference. Get yourself what you need, love. And not from Melanie Davis's card. I'm buying."

Lex didn't want me talking to Dot. Whether he was protecting himself or me, I wasn't sure. But I decided to follow and see where this new road led.

For now.

14

THE CONVINCER

THE CONTACT WAS in a small mountain town an hour's drive north of Atlanta. I felt relieved and concerned at the same time. Like any city, Atlanta had its crime lords. The usual gangs. Mostly involved in drugs. Some historic. Some new. Lots of interstate traffic. Atlanta's always been a roundhouse. Enough to attract internationally organized crime. Mexican. Russian. Chinese. La Cosa Nostra. Even plants from the Middle East. Besides drugs, the organizations had arms, fingers, and toes in a diverse criminal array: money laundering, gambling, financial fraud, and human trafficking. Scary stuff. But not unusual for a city its size.

Organized crime existed in the countryside, too. Ask any federal agent.

Or my father.

The Dixie Mafia liked rural areas where the policing was iffier and the law easier to buy off. They dealt in all the usual crimes covered in the RICO Act. But they were a less structured group of criminals. Not related by family or creed. I didn't even know if they'd refer to themselves as the Dixie Mafia. That was a term the Feds used. The one thing that held them together was money.

And when it came to money, there wasn't much they wouldn't do.

The problem with not having a familial or cultural allegiance, you didn't know if someone was an associate or not. And I liked to know where I stood. Like before this five-thousand-square-foot cabin in the North Georgia Mountains. Small town Georgia was my wheelhouse. But my feet did not feel like they stood on solid ground. Even though, physically, I was more than likely standing on granite.

"You found this person how?" I said to Lex.

"One of Dot's friends of a friend." He shrugged.

"I thought Dot had a prejudice against country people."

"There's country, and there's country." Lex placed a hand on the small of my back. Rubbed. Trying to soothe out my aggression. "You know Dot. The differentiation comes with the price tag."

Somewhere inside the cabin, a dog barked. A camera above the door swiveled to center us in its lens. Lex looked up and nodded. I adjusted my scarf so they could see my face, then folded my arms over my coat and cut my eyes toward the doorbell camera lens.

"Kind of overkill, ain't it?" I muttered.

The door opened. A colossal man stood in the doorway. He stepped back a few inches. His bulk made it difficult to squeeze past. Didn't move to make it any easier. No polite formalities. Not even a grunt.

Gigantor turned. We followed him down a cedar-lined hallway. Various antique armaments hung on the walls. The cabin smelled of woodsmoke and lemon furniture polish. At the end of the hall, the man knocked. Opened a door. Again stood halfway in the opening, forcing us to squeeze through awkwardly.

We entered a study or office. Spacious. More cedar walls, but with professional photographs of the Blue Ridge instead of old swords and flintlocks. A thick Oriental rug covered the floor. A low fire danced in a massive fireplace faced by leather chairs. Above the mantle was a large flat screen. The sound was turned off. Talking heads lit the screen. A stock ticker and news headlines ran beneath them.

"Stay a minute, Jeffrey," said the woman sitting at a desk in the back of the room. "The fire may need stoking."

Jeffrey nodded, then moved to kneel before the fireplace. Tossed in logs. Moved burnt pieces with a poker.

By Lex's deliberately relaxed stance, I could tell Jeffrey made him nervous. Particularly Jeffrey with a hot poker.

I turned my attention to Gigantor's boss. The kind of woman my father would call ridden hard and put away wet. No makeup to hide the lines in her face. Her graying ginger hair had been pulled back in a ponytail. She wore flannels and jeans. Could have been any woman from my hometown.

"You're working for Platinum," she said to Lex. When he nodded, she reached for a pack of Camel Lights on her desk and stood. "And who's this gal with you?"

"Finley Goodhart," I said. "I am not working for Platinum. My friend Penny Forbes was. I'm looking for her killer."

She took her time lighting the cigarette. As she inhaled, she studied us. Blew out the smoke. Studied her cigarette. "I own a lot of Vape stores. But I still prefer things the old-fashioned way."

Great, a hillbilly gangster who spoke in riddles.

"I'll talk to Finley alone," she said. "Jeffrey, take Mr. Leopold to the kitchen and make him a sandwich."

Lex slid me a look, but I nodded. His fingers brushed mine as he turned. We watched them exit. Lex shouldered past immobile Jeffrey. The door closed behind them.

"Who are you?" I said. "You should know right off, I'm not connected. I know Dot, but I don't work for her or any racket. I'm independent and plan to keep it that way. All I want to know is what happened to my friend."

Squinting through the smoke, the woman appraised me. Took one last, long drag.

"Sue Marshall," she said, exhaling the words with the smoke. Coughing, she extinguished the butt in the tray on her desk. "Y'all might want to rethink asking questions about that friend."

I kept my mouth shut. Head up. Spine straight.

"Look, I don't know the details about your friend. But judging that you came all the way up here from the city, I guess she got herself into some trouble." Sue tapped her pack on the desk, then laid it down. "Maybe pissed off the wrong people. But that'd be easy to do with those she was working for."

"You aren't associated with Platinum," I said.

"No, ma'am. I don't affiliate. Like you, I enjoy my independence. I'll enter into short-term deals, but those running Platinum wanted a big stake and a long-term commitment."

"How long did they plan to run the match service?"

She laughed, deep and croaky. "I don't know. It's just one of their functions. I liked that one."

"Penny became engaged to a guy whose father is a superior court judge."

"That so? I guess that could be handy. He'd know plenty about real estate deals. Liens and the like."

"And criminal court hearings."

"True." She picked up the pack again and tapped it on her palm, her eyes on me. "I hear you got a daddy who's associated with the law."

I took a step back. "I don't talk to him. I don't have anything to do with him."

"That so?" She shook out a cigarette. "He's affiliated."

"He's always been affiliated with someone or another. We had the nicest house in town, growing up. But that's not saying much if you saw my hometown."

She smiled. "What'd you hustle?"

"Pool, mainly. But I did work some scams with Penny. Some long and short cons with Lex." I folded my arms. "Started off as a way to tick off my father, but then it became a habit."

"You been doing it for a while." Placing the smoke in the corner of her mouth, she spoke around the cigarette. Reached for a lighter. "I checked. I always check. It wasn't no habit. You couldn't get a job if you tried."

"Yes, ma'am." I jerked a nod. "I succeeded in my quest to tick him off. Sheriff Goodhart ruined any chance I had at restitution."

"You could buy a new identity."

"I like my name. The first name in any case. It was my mother's family name. My last name reminds the sheriff that if I'm arrested, someone might connect the dots to him. And his job banks on reelection."

She laughed again, then lit her cigarette and blew out the smoke. "Oh, I like you."

I relaxed a little. But not much.

"Your partner's caught up in this new organization. Why's that?"

I was answering more questions than getting answers myself. Sue was feeling us out. I understood there was no Southern hospitality at play. These were her house rules.

"You'd have to ask him," I said. "My guess is he did it for me. To find out what he could about Penny."

"He didn't tell you?"

"Lex doesn't tell me much about himself, ma'am. But he agreed to help me figure out what happened to Penny." I hesitated. I wanted to ask Sue about the markers but wanted to word my question carefully.

Before I could ask the question, she spoke. "My ears heard he did it for Dot the Jamaican. For a nice sum, too. Lex Leopold had an agreement with Dot Campbell to spy on the Platinum organization for her. Same deal as your friend, Penny. One falls in the field, then that soldier's replaced by another."

I snapped shut my open mouth.

She gave me a long look and stubbed out the cigarette. "All right, that tells me everything. Don't ever try to hustle poker, hon."

Striding to the leather chairs near the fire, she sank into a deep chair. Pointed at the empty chair across from hers. "Sit. I'll tell you what I know."

I jerked my thoughts back into order. Followed her to the chair. Perched on the edge.

"If I was going to bite, you'd already be bit. Relax." She chuckled. "Never fall in love with a crook. But I guess your momma did, and now you, too."

Held my tongue. But slid back into the comfortable leather.

"Now, the organization that runs Platinum. Meant to be for high-end activities, high-dollar action. The principal parties connected under their umbrella are based out of four major organizations in Atlanta. Covers most of the metro area. Real international set. You ever see Russians, Chinese, Chicanos, and the mafia working together?"

This information ripped at the unraveling seams in my heart. Why would Lex sell himself out to work for these gangsters? Or Penny? I'd thought neither of them would deal with real mobsters. But maybe they'd do it for money? Some kind of loyalty to Dot?

Sue continued to talk, ignoring how the news had hit me. I didn't bother to hide it from her.

"I wasn't interested in their deal. Dot didn't get invited. Too low on the totem pole. That bugs her." She cackled. "I told her once, you get bigger, so does the target on your back. Competition is fierce between groups. And you risk the Big A."

Atlanta Federal Penitentiary.

I cleared my throat. "So who's the brain behind Platinum? How could they get any of these organizations to agree on who's running the show?"

"My first thought, too. Each group selected a chairman for the consortium's board. Four board members vote on everything. Then each board member elects their own representatives to work with the others in each part of the organization. After that, they hire from the outside. Like Lex and Penny. The contractors are not allowed to know anything about the structure or members. No chance to move up. No way for anyone to snitch this way."

"No wonder Lex couldn't learn anything."

Sue nodded. "He was telling the truth there."

I winced at her implication. "So you think whatever Penny did, she got herself iced by someone higher up."

"How was she killed?"

"Heroin overdose. A local coroner called it before she got to the hospital."

Sue studied the fire for a moment.

I felt relieved she didn't automatically assume Penny had overdosed on her own.

"I guess it could be a hit," she said. "It'd be easier to know who was lining the pocket of the coroner. Did she snitch, or what?"

"Doubt it." I took a deep breath. "Penny was holding markers for someone."

"A bookmaker?"

I shook my head. "They were all different. No names, obviously. But different chits. Different amounts. Large sums. Nothing penny-ante."

"Maybe they were hers."

"Penny wasn't a gambler. She grew up around the dog tracks because of her mom. Loved the dogs but didn't catch the bug."

"The consortium does have a casino. But maybe it was for a different kind of IOU." Sue stared into the fire. "Platinum is much more than a matchmaking service. That's just for roping the rich folks in, from what I understand. Then they get them hooked up to one of the other umbrella arms. Use their business for laundering. Get them into skimming. Land deals. What have you."

"I checked into their match service. I signed up, pretended to be an app developer. I think they were testing to see if I'd do any hacking."

Her nose wrinkled. "I like to keep things simple. I don't deal in blackmail like that because I wouldn't trust the canary not to sing. Or screw it up."

"I don't care about singing. I want to screw it up."

Sue Marshall's slow smile curled like a cat's tail. "That's what I hoped to hear. You and me are going to get along just fine."

That didn't make me feel any better. In fact, I felt a whole lot worse.

15

THE COME-ON

ON THE RIDE back to Atlanta, I explained the structure of Platinum Partners. Left off Sue Marshall's judgment of Lex. Sue didn't trust Lex. He was a con man. She shouldn't trust Lex. I didn't trust Lex. But I also didn't trust Sue.

Distrust was a well-learned habit. Nothing new there.

Why Sue thought so well of me, I didn't know. Other than we were both country. Maybe she felt she could understand me more than others. And I was too small-time to be a threat or enemy.

"You're in over your head with Platinum, Lex," I said.

"Not to worry, love. I didn't sign anything in blood. I am merely a shill in one small part of their hustle."

I glanced at him, wondering who controlled the strings. Dot or Platinum? "And how long does the hustle last?"

"As long as I need it to last." He patted my thigh, keeping his eyes on the road. "And Sue Marshall? Any worries there?"

"People like Sue Marshall always worry me. She wants something, but she's biding her time. I don't know how much this information was worth."

"Interesting bloke, that Jeffrey."

I noted he skipped any talk of payment to Sue. "How was the sandwich?"

"Rather good. Country ham. Jeffrey ate six." Lex's lips quirked. "Sue Marshall took over the racket from her brother—now deceased. Ambush, as Jeffrey put it. Like a scene from a Western. Quaint description for a hit. Sue's brother learned the business from their father, his father learned it from his own father, and so on. Genetic lines run straight into your prohibition back to the American Civil War. From Confederate counterfeiting to money laundering. Stills to narcotics. Gun running then, and now, too."

"Lovely." I heaved a sigh.

"I sense Sue Marshall is not satisfied with her Blue Ridge territory. She wants to edge south."

"Atlanta? She didn't want involvement in Platinum's dealings."

"No." Lex jerked his chin at the Sunday traffic returning to Atlanta. "Without realizing it, Jeffrey shared Sue's contempt for Atlanta. She's interested in circling around the Big Peach. More of a country campaign."

"Which explains her interest in my father."

"Aha." Lex cut his eyes toward me, then back to the clogged highway. "I was afraid of that."

"A little warning would have been nice."

"And have you on your guard? When it comes to the sheriff, you have a weakness in that armor you wear." He kept his eyes on the road. "No matter. She'll just want information about the sheriff. Cross that godforsaken bridge as it approaches."

"Lex—"

"No worries, love. I got enough out of Jeffrey to protect you."

"But I didn't learn enough about Platinum to protect you." I bit my lip, regretting my tone.

"So fierce, Fin." Lex smiled. "Quite heartening to hear his beloved's call to arms."

"Never mind that," I said. "As you said, we'll deal with Sue Marshall later. Right now we need to focus on Penny. Sue thought the markers might be a different kind of IOU."

"And Penny's debt was cashed in? Hard to wring blood from a stone."

I shuddered. "I guess you're right. There's still so much we don't know. Sue Marshall barely gave me a clue."

"I am sorry about that. I thought she'd know more. I'll see what I can learn from the inside."

"No!"

The vehemence in my voice startled Lex. The Camaro swerved into the next lane, triggering a long bout of honking.

"If Ellie hasn't been compromised, I'm still going to use her. As Ellie, I'm going to contact Tony Riggle. Threaten to call the police about Platinum. Tell him Brian gave me a roofie, then the detective took me outside and told me the whole thing was fake. I want to see what Tony Riggle will do."

"Seems risky, love."

"I think he'll try to buy me off."

"Here's what Riggle will do. Take your call but offer to meet somewhere. Between now and the meeting, they'll start digging. There was no reason to go beyond their basic search before. No red flags. Now they'll put you under the microscope. And when you meet, knowing who you really are..."

"Then I need an insurance policy. Like Mark Davis."

"They must want his father. We looked at Mark. There's nothing there."

"What if Mark didn't kill her but was set up for Penny's murder?"

"According to the law, she wasn't murdered."

"The case can always be reopened. In light of new evidence. And if someone has that evidence they may be waiting..."

"To use it for blackmail."

"Right."

"Except his father is a superior court judge, Fin."

Lex veered around a car and accelerated into the carpool lane. In the distance, Atlanta's skyline glowed in the dusky twilight.

Traffic began to thin as we merged onto the connector. The Camaro sped up. Joined the other commuters racing home.

"Judge Davis presides over felony criminal cases," he continued. "As in murder. He'd get the best attorney to prove Mark didn't do it. And the FBI to investigate Platinum."

"Before the press found out? A superior court judge, an elected official, has a son who's been arrested for first-degree murder by shooting his fiancée up with heroin to ensure she'd overdose? How long would it take the FBI to unravel Platinum? According to Sue Marshall, the four organizations send a few overseers, but everyone else is contracted with no knowledge of how Platinum works or why." I tapped his thigh. "Like you."

Before my fingers could escape, he rested his hand over mine. Curled his fingers into mine. "I see. You think the judge would rather protect his reputation than his son."

"I think the judge would rather pay off or work for the mob to protect both his reputation and his son."

Lex placed his hand back on the steering wheel. "Not many are as cynical as you, Fin."

"I've lived it."

He pressed his lips together, focused on the traffic.

"I want to know if Mark Davis believes Penny was murdered. If he killed Penny, he wouldn't encourage an investigation."

"If he believed she was murdered, someone like Mark Davis would have gone to the police. You know this. So what are you really saying?"

"If I can convince Mark that Platinum is behind Penny's murder, he might work with me. If he knows Platinum is after the judge, he may help us. And if Mark doesn't want to help, that might tell us something, too."

"You'd rather trust Mark Davis than the judge."

"I don't trust anyone." I folded my arms. "But I think it's a better angle. And we've got to find some way to work our way inside."

"At least you're saying 'we.'" Lex sighed then cut me a quick glance. "Mark's not a social chap, remember. We might have trouble drawing him out."

"Social enough to go to the mixer last night. One way or another, we'll learn if he's a good suspect for Penny's murder."

"That's interesting, there." Lex slipped into thinking mode. He accelerated up the off-ramp toward Turner Stadium. We were headed back to his loft. His newly acquired loft. But I kept my thoughts from straying to guessing at his past months' activities.

"Let's see what Mark knows first, yeah?" said Lex. "We don't know for sure why Penny was killed, let alone by whom. If Mark's already hooked into Platinum, he may rat us out rather than help. Methinks we need an insurance policy for our insurance policy."

"You said he looked clean."

"Most do on the surface. We don't know what he and Penny have been doing the past three months. She could work magic, that one. Mark could already be in deep."

"Fair point." I placed my hand back on his thigh. Tried to ignore the clamors of doubt in my head. Sue Marshall had set off more warning bells about Lex. But I needed him.

And for some reason, he needed me.

Was he helping me or using my situation to do Dot's dirty work? To work for Dot, spying on Platinum? I was probably a fool, thinking he'd risk Platinum to help me find out what happened to Penny. What had happened to Lex?

"Well, then, Elizabeth Ann." Lex squeezed my hand, but it was Carter who looked at me and grinned. "I'd say Mark's got some explaining to do. Y'all with me on this?"

I smiled. It felt like old times. Yet different.

More dangerous.

KNOWING Mark Davis was unlikely to meet us, we took a few days to study his habits. Found it easy to bump into him. Every

Wednesday, Mark and his sales directors took a business lunch at Noodle on Peachtree.

Or so said Mark's secretary after Lex charmed it from her.

Outside the doors of the trendy Asian restaurant, I applied mascara. My back to the party inside. Stomach growling at the scents wafting in the air. Like Dot's favorite, Bibimbap.

At Lex's signal, I pushed through the glass front door. Mark and his directors exited. I grabbed his elbow, said a surprised hello of recognition. Then threw myself into his arms and began sobbing into his suit coat. Embarrassed, he waved on his team.

A moment later, Carter rushed up to rescue Mark from an emotional Elizabeth Ann.

"She's been a mess." Carter handed me his handkerchief. "Ever since the celebration of life."

I dabbed at my eyes and wiped my nose. "A hot mess, that's what you mean, Carter. You must feel the same though, Mark. The loss grows day by day."

Mark nodded, then shook his head. "It's nice to see you again, but I should—"

Carter clasped a hand on Mark's back. "She makes a guy uncomfortable with all these tears, doesn't she? And look at your coat. Elizabeth Ann, you got makeup all over the man's coat."

"I am so sorry." I patted it with the handkerchief. "Oh Lord, now I've smeared it. Wait, let's go inside. I'll clean it up for you in a jiffy."

Yanking open Noodle's door, I waited until Carter had hustled Mark inside.

"Let me get that coat." I unbuttoned it. Slid it off Mark's shoulders. "Just hang out at the bar while I take your coat to the ladies. Carter, can't you buy him a Coke or something to make up for this? It won't take a minute. I think I've got a Tide pen or something in this purse."

While Mark gaped, I ran off with his coat. I hurried down the hall to the bathrooms. Glanced back. Carter spoke with his hands.

Distracting Mark from watching me disappear with his coat. I whipped around the corner and they disappeared from view.

In a bathroom stall, I pulled out a pack of makeup wipes. Cleaned up the mess, then went through Mark's pockets. Keys, chapstick, sunglasses. Wallet.

Never keep your wallet in your coat pocket, Mark.

Nothing interesting in his wallet. I slipped it back in the pocket. My fingers brushed against a slip of paper. Drew it out and unfolded it. More code. Similar run like I'd seen in Tony Riggle's wallet.

Bank numbers? Wasn't the right sequence. And too many letters.

Chewing my lip, I opened my purse and pulled out the new phone. Took a photo. Dropped the slip of paper into the coat pocket. Sauntered back to the bar.

"Mark, I am so sorry," I said, handing him his coat.

"It's okay." He slipped the coat back over his shoulders. Didn't even pat his pockets. Trusting soul. Maybe he would later. If I had been an ordinary thief, his politeness would have caused him a big headache. "I should get going."

"Did your momma tell you I got into Platinum Partners?" I cast the bait. "I met Melanie for coffee. We wanted to see if their screening was as exclusive as they said."

"You did what?" said Carter. "Elizabeth Ann. You didn't tell me anything about this."

"It's not like I was trying to get matched, Carter. We were doing it for Mark. Miss Melanie worried about you returning to that club."

Mark frowned. "You should leave it alone."

"Oh, I will. Although it was fun. We felt like spies," I said. "Miss Melanie's so worried about you. Did you know about the party last Saturday?"

"What kind of party?" asked Carter. "What sort of outfit is Platinum Partners, Mark? Should I be concerned?"

"If she doesn't go, I think—" Mark stopped. "Just get off their mailing list. It should be fine."

"You're not still going to their parties, are you Mark?" I said. "Your momma would be so upset."

"She worries too much." He shoved his hands in his pockets. "Anyway, it's not like I'm interested in finding anyone right now."

Really, Mark? Then why were you at the party?

I smiled. "We should stay in touch. If you ever do feel like getting back out there, I have a lot of single friends."

"Thanks." Mark didn't smile. "I need to get back to work."

"Me, too," said Carter. "I'll walk with you, Mark. Actually, I wanted to ask you something privately. See you later, hon."

I remained at the counter. Ordered a tea. Waited until they disappeared from view. Pulled out my phone and examined the picture I had taken. Had to be some kind of code. Fifteen random letters and numbers. I hadn't yet told Lex about finding the string of code in Tony Riggle's wallet. At the time, I had typed the combination in an online search, but nothing had come up. I didn't have the means, talent, or patience to jump that hurdle. And I'd been too focused on getting inside Platinum Partners.

Lex would dig for anything Mark knew or suspected about Platinum. Mark hadn't wanted me or his mother involved with the club. That could mean anything. He was a traditional sort of guy. I wasn't offended. Let Lex take the lead. Most men didn't want their mother poking into their business. Particularly when Melanie had made it clear she hadn't approved of Penny.

My thoughts rolled back to Penny. How would she perceive Mark's quiet stability? Even with her background, Penny hadn't revealed much. Took her jobs seriously. Hadn't been loud or brash. As a teen runaway, she'd skirted the system too long to try "normal." Or so I'd thought. Maybe Lex was right, and Mark had offered her an out. If she'd been born into a different family, I could see her choosing a career in business. She was good with numbers.

Which made the markers an even bigger question. Penny only

took calculated risks. Had she done such a good job as a roper for Platinum's matchmaking service that she'd been brought into another arm of the organization? The casino Sue had mentioned?

I was missing a big piece of the puzzle. The markers. Still no idea of their link.

After paying for the tea, I left the restaurant. Shivered and belted my Burberry, then walked several blocks until I reached the parking garage where we had left Lex's Camaro.

Before entering the garage, I stooped to pretend to wipe the toe of my boot. From my squat, I did a quick scan of the area. My eyes swiveled behind my sunglasses. Caught movement around the corner of the building on the next block.

Furtive movement.

I stood. Pointedly looked at the garage. Shook my head. Retraced my steps and darted around the corner.

No one. Just an office building. I pretended to admire my reflection. Tried different coat collar positions. Couldn't see into the window, but saw no moving shadows either.

To be sure, I continued up that block before circling back to the garage.

Once inside, I exited on the wrong floor and used the vantage point to watch the street for a few minutes.

Nothing.

Maybe I was getting paranoid like Lex had hinted.

Climbed the stairs. Found the Camaro. Leaned against the car and pulled out my phone. Studied the code. Decided to show it to Lex.

And looked up.

There he was. Looking young and handsome in a suit and wingtips. Grinning at me. All charm and insouciance. My heart lifted, but I refrained from giving him more than a smile.

Lord help me, but I was in love with a crook. Sue Marshall was right.

I hoped she wasn't right about everything.

16

THE TWIST

"HELLO, LOVE." Lex cocked his head, studying me. "Did I tell you Elizabeth Ann looks particularly fetching in boots and a mac?"

Ignoring my stuttering heart, I smiled. Careful not to let it get too wide or dimpled. "What did you learn from Mark?"

Lex paced forward and stopped before me, trapping me against the car between his hands. Leaning forward, he placed his forehead against mine. "Mark was gaga for our Penny."

"What?" I jerked my head back.

His eyes sparked. "And by his account, Penny felt the same."

"No. He just believed that. She played him."

"After a month into a deepening relationship, Penny confessed everything."

"What? No way."

"And when she tried to back out of Platinum, they held her over the fire for it."

I blinked. Felt grief bubble up my throat and bite my eyes. "So it was Platinum?"

"Mark thinks so." Lex caught my hand and squeezed it.

"And he wants to expose them?"

"Here's the tricky part. When they threatened Penny, Mark began paying them off. Said his family had money, but he refused to ask for it. They suggested he skim from the company funds. Set up a way for him to do this."

I took a deep breath. Why did the thought of Penny and Mark as an actual couple bother me?

"I know how they were doing it, too. Passing a code." I flashed the picture on my phone.

Lex enlarged it. Studied the string of numbers and letters.

"I found a similar code in Tony Riggle's wallet. He must pass them to the vics."

"SWIFT code for international banks mixed in with other numbers." Lex pursed his lips then tapped the screen. "Payment amount, likely."

"How did you do that so quickly?" I snatched the phone from his hand.

He tapped the side of his head and smiled. "Simple deduction. Safest place to make a deposit is an international bank. The letters are for a bank in Luxembourg even though they're separated by the numbers. All those L's and X's. Elementary, my dear Finley."

"Showoff."

He moved in closer. "I feel the need to impress you. Remind you of my skills." He ran a hand up my side.

I batted it away. "So Penny pretended to be in trouble so Mark could rescue her. It was part of the scam. Why didn't he go to the judge? Get the police in on it?"

"Probably to protect Penny. She'd told Mark not to do the skim. Said she'd find another way out. I'm not so sure she was scamming him, love." Lex arched a brow. "Mark went to the Platinum party because they'd contacted him. Wanted to know what had happened to Penny. He went to confront them."

"Tony Riggle didn't know Penny had been killed?"

"Apparently not."

"I'm so confused." I bit my lip to keep the tears from flowing.

Lex cupped my face. Caught a tear with his thumb, then kissed my cheek. "What if Penny felt the same about Mark? Would it comfort you to think Penny had some happiness before she died?"

"It should. But it actually makes me feel worse." My voice shook. "No. I don't believe it anyway. Not with Penny."

"I'm sorry." He held out an arm. No playful seduction. The sympathy in his voice sincere.

I stepped into him. Allowed myself the comfort he offered. Slid my arms around his waist. "You can't live like we do and expect to get out."

"Don't say that, darling." His arms tightened around me. "One can always hope for something better."

"Doesn't mean you'll get it." I rested my head on his chest. Against my neck, my necklace felt heavy and cold.

"And it doesn't mean you won't." He nestled his chin against my head. "Fin, is that what you truly want? To get out?"

"I can't. Unless I give up my identity and take a long hike. Then, maybe. But I don't want to leave." Leave you. I didn't want to leave Lex.

My mental dam cracked. Tears gushed. I felt too tired to stop them.

Silently, Lex held me. When I finally pushed away, I couldn't look at him. Afraid of what I'd see in his gaze.

He opened the passenger door. While I rooted for tissues, he climbed in beside me and started the Camaro.

"Tony Riggle's a hired gun." I forced myself to stop the pity party to focus back on Penny. The crying jag had at least given me some insight. "Someone higher up might have decided to get rid of Penny. Sue Marshall told me Platinum's hires don't know anything about the organization. And with four syndicates joined together, one could have decided to pop her without telling the others."

"True. Could get messy, that. They were earning off the skim and now that well is dried up. Someone's going to pay for that mistake." He glanced over at me. "We could let that situation play out. They'd deliver justice to the hot head who did in Penny, yeah?"

"I suppose. But it's not very satisfying," I said. "Plus we won't know what happened. What's Mark going to do now?"

"He went to the party to tell Riggle he wasn't going to pay any more. When you buggered off with the thug—"

"He forced me out the door."

"I left to look for you," Lex continued. "We missed the kerfuffle between Mark and Tony Riggle. Riggle said he didn't have any idea of what he was blathering on about. Had Mark escorted from the bar. The bouncer gave him a good crack."

"And then what?"

"The next day his contact called Mark. Make another payment or they'll expose him at his company. And implicate his family. Judge's son arrested for embezzlement and fraud. That sort of thing."

"Cripes."

Lex nodded.

"So no justice for Mark even if someone in Platinum gets axed over Penny."

Lex frowned. "You can't expect to take on the crime lords of Atlanta for poor Mark. You've gone from I want to know what happened to Penny to justice for Mark. He seems a decent chap and all, but that's quite a leap, Fin."

"But Lex." I folded a leg beneath me so I could sit facing him. "What if we could at least make the matchmaking con fold? That'd be something, right? Stop this kind of thing from happening to other people. We know what it takes to stop a con."

"Bugger it, Fin. This is dangerous. We don't get involved in rackets."

"You're already involved." I narrowed my eyes. "For Dot. Sue Marshall told me everything. First Penny, and then you. Because Dot wanted spies on the inside."

"And you'd believe her over me? Sue Marshall heads her own mob." Lex kept his gaze on the road, but I could see the pinch at the corner of his eyes.

"The point is, you're in. And that scares me. Really scares me, Lex."

He shook his head.

"Come on, help me shut down this matchmaking scam. It'll give you the excuse to get out. And it'll protect the fish who haven't already been hooked."

He darted a look at me. I could see the pain he couldn't completely hide.

I wanted to trust him. Even if it went against my better judgment. I touched his arm. "If we're partners, I want to protect you as much as you want to protect me."

He sighed. "Touché, Miss Goodhart."

I left my hand on his arm. Lex turned onto Peachtree Street. Heading back to his loft in Cabbagetown. Passed Noodle. Hipsters spilled out of The Vortex, full of burgers and tater tots. Watched a bus filled with senior citizens unloading in front of the Fox Theatre as we waited at a red light. Thought about various strategies to turn the tables on the matchmaking con. Hoped Lex was doing the same.

"Ellie and Oliver's covers haven't been blown yet," I said. "Mark must know Elizabeth Ann didn't go to Emory with Penny by now. I'm surprised he told you anything. Maybe he thinks Carter is a lot like himself. But he doesn't know Ellie and Oliver."

"I'm already working on the hustle, love." The charming man had returned. "Cheat the cons at their own game, yeah?"

17

THE SHADE

"WE'RE BEING FOLLOWED," said Lex. Instead of a right on DeKalb, he took a left on Decatur Street toward downtown Atlanta.

"I thought I saw someone when I was waiting for you." I adjusted my legs to sit half-turned in the seat. One hand on Lex's leg, for the appearance of a cozy chat—also because it felt right—my eyes on the back window. "Which car?"

"A pickup truck. Big one."

"The black F-150?"

"That's the one." Lex glanced at me. "There's a roundabout in the Pencil Factory Flats, but only one exit. Watch what happens."

He picked up speed on Decatur, passing the MARTA train on the aboveground track beside us. Made a quick left between the old Pencil Factory buildings, now converted to shops and apartments. Slowed to a crawl. The short road led nowhere, except to parking. Train tracks ran behind the buildings. At the back of the roundabout, Lex idled.

"He's not turning in," I said. "Must have gone past."

"We'll see."

We waited. Watched the road. Counted down the minutes. Lex

shifted to drive, eased around to the Decatur Street entrance, and stopped.

"Bugger all," said Lex. "They parked in front."

"I can't see inside the truck. The windows are tinted. Isn't that illegal?"

"You're asking me?" Lex chuckled. "All right then, care for a stroll?"

"You're going to park here?"

"Oakland Cemetery is on the other side of the tracks." He smirked. "We'll draw him out."

"In Oakland? What if they're with one of the syndicates?"

"And maybe they're not. Only one way to find out." Lex turned right, passing the truck. "Not only is Oakland a beautiful garden—"

"Full of dead people."

"If we need to, it's a great place to hide, as well," he winked. "Monuments and mausoleums galore. It is a lovely garden, Fin. You've never been?"

"I don't do cemeteries, Lex." I glanced out the back window. Saw the truck pull into traffic.

"You need more culture in your life than pool halls." He made a quick right on Grant Street. "Don't say I never take you places."

"Can't we just lose them on side streets?"

"We'll park at Tin Lizzy's. If all goes well, I'll buy you a beer."

"Stop having fun, Lex."

His brows quirked. "I can't help it, love. Something about the thrill of the chase. The old fox and hound."

"We're the fox, Lex. The fox does not have fun."

He pursed his lips. Hung a left on Memorial Drive. The south wall of the cemetery appeared. Lex accelerated. Made an abrupt right into an old strip mall, now retrofitted with bars and restaurants. Spun the wheel and slipped the Camaro between cars facing the restaurant.

"Too bad it's not the weekend," he said. "Easier to hide in a car park on the weekend."

"You can't hide an orange Camaro unless it's in a Camaro dealership."

He laughed. Popped his door. "Ready to run? We don't want to be caught here."

"Or in the street." Sliding out of the car, a gust of wind caught my hair and whipped it around my face. Flipping up my coat collar, I hurried to meet Lex.

He grabbed my hand, and we jogged across the parking lot. Down the street, vehicles idled at the red light. Traffic continued from the east.

"Come on, then. Before the light turns." Lex darted into the busy road, pulling me along behind him. Brakes squealed and a horn blew, loud and long.

"Sorry, mate." Lex waved. On the sidewalk, he pulled me against his body. Wrapped an arm around my back and kissed me. Hard.

Letting me go, he laughed. "Too fun."

"We could have been hit," I gasped.

"No worries, love." He reached for the cap of the cemetery's low brick wall. Placed a foot in an indentation in the bricks. Hoisted himself up, then over. On the other side, he grabbed for my hand. "Up and over."

"I'm in a dress. There's a gate just down the road."

"No time. Besides, the commuters will appreciate the show."

My clamber was not elegant. Nor smooth.

"We need to build your strength." Lex grasped me under my armpits and slid me over the wall. "There you go."

"Pool hustling doesn't usually require a weight regimen." I slipped my arms from his shoulders and tucked my hand in his. Before I began overthinking reasons not to hold hands.

He patted my bicep. "A pool hall never saw a lovelier form."

We stooped behind a sprawling magnolia and peered out. The F-150 had discovered our direction. It slowed, then made a sudden right. Pulled into a tattoo shop's parking lot. Parked facing the cemetery.

"I'm going to guess they have binoculars," said Lex. "Let's move deeper inside."

"Shouldn't we find a spot where we can watch them?" I glanced at the headstones behind us.

"We'll cut through the cemetery and ease behind the tattoo shop. Take a look from there." He grabbed my arm. "The bloke's getting out."

"It's the goon from the bar." My throat tightened. Another gust swept my hair across my face. I pushed it back. Caught the look of panic crossing Lex's face. He quickly disguised it.

But not quick enough.

I stepped forward. The hand on my arm tightened.

"His coat blew open. He's carrying." Lex pivoted, pulling me with him. We cut through the grass. Ran between the crumbling headstones.

"Do you still think he's a detective?"

"Legit PIs wouldn't give chase. We've done nothing to warrant more than surveillance."

We ran past rows of monuments. Tripped over ruts and divots in the compact ground where the graves had sunk. Jumped over a brick lane running between raised plots.

"This path," said Lex. The incline led us onto an open field of old stones. Behind us, something large crashed through a pile of leaves. "Bugger. Head toward the main road just up ahead. It's less exposed. More mausoleums and tight paths."

"What about less isolated?"

"The visitor's center is not too far ahead."

We jogged up the brick lane between raised family plots. The monuments and headstones grew larger. Massive memorial statues and Victorian-era mausoleums dotted the hillside. Brick paths and a few paved roads wound between them. Lex pulled me behind the gigantic Austell family mausoleum.

"Maybe we lost him." I leaned against the stone, winded.

"The exit out to Oakland Avenue is to our left. We could dart out and circle back, keeping low along the wall. Or we act as if we aren't hunted. Continue to the visitor's center like the usual tourist. You lead him onward. I'll duck back and corner him."

"Are you crazy?"

"As the proverbial fox, love. But I'm also quick like one."

"You don't know if he's after me or you."

"Nor if it's Carter or Elizabeth Ann. That's why we need to split up. He can't follow us both. I want to find out what he's after."

"You're going to try to talk to him?" I couldn't keep the panic from my voice.

"Darling, he won't shoot me in a cemetery. That's why I chose Oakland. Too many eyes about." He pointed to the cars parked along the road. "Keep to the middle, close to the visitor's center, yeah? There's a gift shop inside. Tour guides popping in and out. Restrooms to hide in."

Footsteps pattered on the brick path.

We ducked around to the back of the castle-like mausoleum. The footsteps paused, then hit the pavement. Lex eased toward the side the goon had rushed past. Motioned for me to follow. I peeked around the edge of the tomb. Saw the man cross the road and hurry up the path on the other side.

"Headed to Margaret Mitchell's grave, I suspect," Lex whispered.

"You know a lot about this place."

"Not too far from my new digs. These past months, I'd often take the air here. Good area to walk. Right peaceful."

"Makes you think about life and death, I suppose."

"Plenty of tourists here, too."

"You came here to work the pigeon drop?"

"Takes two, the pigeon drop. Missing my partner for that one. Didn't feel like turning a new partner out." He gave me a long look. "Didn't want another partner."

"That's why you started working with Dot?"

"A man's got to earn, Fin."

"You're going to get yourself killed working for someone like Dot."

He placed a hand on the stone above my head. Leaned in. "Working with Dot's not the only way to have me killed, Fin. Who is this bloke? You saw him at Penny's. Then at the bar. Tell me about him. Close your eyes. Give me the goods. Use that lovely memory of yours."

My heart sped up. "We don't have time. What if he comes back?"

"I've got eyes out. Take a breather. Big cemetery for him to cover."

I closed my eyes. Ignored the building fear pushing through my fingers and toes. Knocking at the walls of my heart. "He smokes a pipe. I told you that. Likes to talk with his hands. He's rough. And local."

"Local Atlanta or local Georgia?"

"Georgia. Maybe Atlanta. But his family isn't Atlanta. I could tell by the way he talked. Speaking to someone local, too. I'm pretty sure. He spoke easy. It's hard to explain."

"I got you."

"Likes to hear himself talk, too."

"Good. I can use that."

"Please don't." I opened my eyes. "He flung me up against a brick wall. He's strong, Lex."

"He's got more than a few stones on you, love. But yes, I understand your point. He could easily take me down. He could shoot me. But you know me." Lex winked. "Lucky Lex, as they say."

"No one calls you that."

"They should." Pulled me in for a quick kiss. "It's true."

"Luck runs out." I leaned back, my hands fisted on his chest. Feeling the anger bubbling out of my fear. "You think you can just hustle anyone. No matter who they're affiliated with or how dangerous they are. Maybe this guy murdered Penny. Why can't you take that more seriously? You're playing games with me while this roughneck is on our tail. This is what scares me."

"That's not what scares you, Fin. You know I can handle the heat." Lex drew an arm around my back. Tugged me against his lean body. Flipped us around to pin me against the Austell family tomb. "You're like me. You like the kick too much. That scares you."

His lips descended on mine, teasing and nipping. Plunging hard and deep. Backing me into the mausoleum. The stone bit my shoulders, fitting my body into his. My knee inched up the outside of his leg. He grasped my thigh. Hiked it higher. Pressed us closer.

Lex didn't care that tourists could eyeball us making out behind the dead Austells. Or that a goon was wandering the cemetery looking for us.

I almost didn't care, either. He made me want him despite where we were. And who we were.

My hands plunged inside his suit jacket. Slid over the hard planes of his chest. Around his waist. Up his back. I dug my fingers into his shoulders through his shirt. And held on.

Anything to keep him from leaving. To stop him from chasing after the thug.

"I know what you're doing," he murmured against my throat. "And I know something else."

His mouth slipped from my neck. Trailed kisses along my jaw. Lightly bit my earlobe. "You like this too much. Us. Together. And that's what really scares you."

I gasped.

He spun me around. Looped my arm in his. Walked me toward the edge of the Austell plot. My legs still wobbly. My nerves popping and buzzing. Thoughts flitting like butterflies among wildflowers. Not catching the shade he'd just pulled. Distracting me while I thought I was distracting him.

"Head toward the visitor's center. Keep an eye out. Let him find you, but don't let him overtake you."

"And how will I find you?" I glanced over my shoulder.

"I'll find you, love." He winked. "I always do."

18

THE BUTTON MAN

I STROLLED paths lined with Atlanta's famed dead. Somewhere behind me Lex did the same. Pretended to look at the familiar names that now marked our street signs and city buildings. Climbed the steps to tombs like I was interested in the hundred year-old-plus architecture, but using the vantage points to peer out. Searching for our thug. At a junction of roads, I found the visitor's center—a twenties-era-looking white stucco building with a bell tower. Spotted our John Doe to the right, standing before a tomb that looked like a tiny Greek temple. Hands on his hips, swiveling around. He stopped mid-swivel.

I'm not supposed to know him, I reminded myself. He only knew Ellie, not Elizabeth Ann. Forced my legs to keep to a stroll. I took a sharp left toward the visitor's center.

He was on me before I'd gone ten paces.

"Miss," he called. "Can you help me?"

Bugger. Polite Elizabeth Ann would help a tourist.

"I'm looking for the Confederate memorial," he said. Less than a foot behind me, I judged. Pool hall hustles taught me that art. Always be aware of your back. And whether they're in striking distance of your stick.

I slowly turned. Smiled. "You can't miss it. It's the tallest monument in the cemetery, I believe."

"What direction?" He pretended to look about. Frowned at the flap of my hand I used to indicate a vague direction.

I didn't know where it was, either. "They have a map in the visitor's center. That's where I'm headed."

"They want me to buy the map." He hooked a thumb toward the terraced plots behind us. "Would you mind just pointing it out? I'm sure we can see it from up there."

Would Elizabeth Ann be this stupid? Trusting a strange man much larger than her? Walk to that row of crypts with him? Probably. Politeness would overrule good judgment.

"I'm waiting on my boyfriend. I'm supposed to meet him inside the visitor's center."

"It'll only take a minute." He strode up the path to a row of monuments and mausoleums. Calling out questions over his shoulder. "Are you from Atlanta? What's your name?"

"I am. Elizabeth Ann. And yours?"

Where was Lex? I glanced around. He'd promised me this guy wouldn't shoot us in a cemetery full of tourists. I could get information as well as Lex.

I followed the lug up the brick rise. He'd already moved beyond the first plot, toward a tomb that looked like a stone beehive with inset stained glass.

Stained glass? Rich people wanting their death crib fancier than everyone else's. I'd had Mom cremated because it'd been cheaper. Even though Daddy had offered to pay for a fancy funeral. Like I'd let him play devoted husband. They weren't even married anymore. I shook off the thought, touched my necklace through my coat, then focused on the creep. Kept my distance. While the goon urged me closer with stupid questions.

"I'm Rick. I can't for the life of me see the monument." He had his hands on his hips again, turning about. Looking for Lex, likely. Maybe wanting Lex to know he had me up on this hill.

"Where are you from, Rick?" I said.

"Out of town." He stepped between the beehive tomb and the neighboring mausoleum. "Maybe the monument's in this direction?"

Forcing polite Elizabeth Ann to follow. I hung back. "I don't think it's over there."

"You sure?" He pointed. "Is that the monument?"

Cripes, he wanted me to walk in the alley between the tombs. I'd never do such a thing. How long should I play this game?

He thinks you're Elizabeth Ann. Don't let him think otherwise.

"Let me see." I moved forward. He sidestepped, placing himself opposite me. Easy to grab me. I stayed out of arm's length. But he had long arms.

"I sure appreciate this, Elizabeth Ann. Friend of Penny Forbes, right?"

Knowing I should be startled, I gasped.

This could be the way to get information from him. Stay in character, Fin.

"How—"

He smiled, moving closer. "I thought so. Hard to find information on Elizabeth Ann Lockhart. Just like Penny. Real strange. I figure you had one of those services clear your background from the internet. Like the college kids who graduate then learn companies can google all their drunk selfies."

My chuckle sounded weak. "I don't know you—"

"All you need to know is I know you."

I sidestepped.

Rick followed.

"What do you want?"

"Me? Not a thing. But the people I work for want you gone. And before you go, they want to know what you know about Penny Forbes."

How do I play this? I couldn't tell if he knew I was faking Elizabeth Ann or if he really thought Elizabeth Ann was faking her identity. "I don't know what you mean."

"I mean, I'm serious as hell." Like a gangster in some movie, he pulled back his coat. Showed me his holster. Unclipped it. Put his hand on the butt. Semi-automatic. It'd been a while since I'd been around guns, but he was right. It was a serious handgun.

"You want to leave your boyfriend here and come with me now? Or can I take your word that you'll meet me later? I *will* find you."

"What if I scream? Go to the police?"

"You and me both know you're not going to the police. I know where y'all are staying. Who you been seeing. Got a good idea what you've been doing. My employer doesn't like it."

"Who's your employer?"

Before I could jump back, he muscled me against the tomb wall. Forced an arm against my throat. "Not important."

I tried to swallow, but the weight forced my throat to catch. My heart fluttered. Couldn't snatch a breath. He shoved against my windpipe. I tried to cough. Pushed at his arm. Might as well have tried to move one of these tombs. Kicked at him. Like stubbing toes against a granite wall.

Rick leaned more weight into his arm. Smiled. Enjoying himself. "We know you don't matter one little bit. Who's gonna miss you if you're gone?"

Spots danced in my vision. I scratched at his sleeve. Began to panic. Thought about him tossing my body into one of these cold tombs.

"I'd miss her." The voice sounded like Carter, but the words were Lex's. "Quite a lot."

The weight eased off my throat. Rick turned to spot Lex, his arm still pressing me against the stone. I pulled in a shaky breath. My vision cleared and I sighted that semi-automatic. My hands flew from his arm and reached inside his coat. I grasped the butt of the handgun with both hands. He must have felt it slide from the holster. The arm flew off my neck to grasp my wrist. But I had the gun gripped tight. Blunt end shoved into his neck. Angled up because of my height.

I racked the slide.

"I'll do it," I said. "Self-defense with a witness. I know how to use it. Grew up around a cop."

"Some witness," he muttered. "Probably has a rap. Like you."

"Maybe you do, too," I said. "Get your hands off me. Squeeze me too tight, and I'll squeeze one off."

"You all right, Elizabeth Ann?" said Lex.

"I'm just fine." I planted my boots on the stone. "Rick, back up. Two steps. I'm going to follow."

We did our dance, giving me room to wiggle away.

"You're going to meet me," he hissed. "You'll get a call, and you'll go when and where I say."

Rick had a pair, I'd give him that. Not even sweating. Kept his focus on me. Hands out to his side. Palms out. But his eyes told me all kinds of things. How much he hated me. And how he'd have no problem doing me in. No regrets. The man did not like me using his piece on him.

I was keeping this gun. My back was to Lex now. "You tell your employer to go to hell."

Rick smiled. "I got your number. You better answer my call."

"Step carefully," said Lex. "The ground is uneven. I'm reaching for you."

Keeping my eye on Rick, I felt Lex's hand on my waist, guiding me back. He spun me. We leaped off the edge of the terrace and ran. A tiny truck—its bed filled with gardening equipment—had been parked on the road in front of the visitor's center. The motor was running. Tourists milled on the covered porch of the center.

"Get in," said Lex.

We dove into the seats. Lex accelerated past the visitor's center. The tourists waved us off, little green gift bags in hand. I checked the safety, laid the Glock on the seat, and turned toward the back window. Rick walked down the stone steps. No hurry. Watching us tear off in the gardening truck.

We were scared. He wasn't.

19

THE STEAM

"CAN'T GO TO YOUR PLACE." I had my fingers on my throat, massaging my windpipe. "Rick, that side of beef, knows where you live. Don't know if he knows who you are, though. He called me Elizabeth Ann Lockhart."

We'd left the truck at Tin Lizzy's. Sped off in the Camaro. Lex took the ramp to the connector and raced south. I was glad. Back to the country. I'd had enough of Atlanta.

Lex's mouth zipped tight. The fox wasn't enjoying the hunt anymore.

"Let it go, Lex. Now we know who he's after."

"Why didn't you go to the visitor's center? You were almost there. I left to grab wheels for a getaway."

"Because I was in character. I didn't want to throw off Elizabeth Ann if the goon thought that's who I was. He's working for someone. Kept talking about his employer. They want information about Penny. Then they want me—or at least, Elizabeth Ann—gone. Maybe permanently."

The Camaro's engine roared. Lex focused on the road. Getting us out of town. But also letting his anger drive the car.

"Slow down. Last thing we need is to get pulled over for speeding." I gripped his arm. "You're getting emotional. Love." I ground out the pet name. Making my point.

He let off the accelerator. Glanced at me. "You're not keeping your head, Fin. You want to keep up the con, but I can't make it work if I don't know exactly how you'll act."

"We never worked a con where my best friend was murdered, Lex."

"And I've never had someone want to murder my girl."

I took my hand off his arm. "Your girl?"

"Did you want me to say, my woman?"

"Ha."

"Playing it cool again, Finley?" He squinted at the lanes before him. Weaving in and out of traffic. "Ready to take me into that crypt and have your way, but the mention of any attachment gets me iced."

"Don't do this now. We've no business talking hearts and flowers with this kind of heat coming down on us." I folded my arms. "I'm going through with it. I've got no choice now. Someone wants Elizabeth Ann dead, and I've got to know who."

"Do I have a say? Or are you still making the rules for us?" He took one of the Morrow exits. Enough traffic to hide in. Less flashy, more blue collar. Warehouse stores and warehouses. Roads that twisted and turned. No straight lines. A layer of grime covered the street signs. Litter collected in the weeds along the road. Everyday people doing everyday things.

"You can do what you like, Lex."

"Bloody hell, Fin." He gritted his teeth.

"I knew what could happen, but I thought I could handle the goon."

"Oh, you handled him. You pissed him bloody well off."

I folded my arms. Unfolded them. Reached for my necklace. Let it drop against my chest. Thought about the gun now in his glove compartment. The memory of shoving it in the goon's throat. My stomach heaved. My temper overrode the sickness.

"You said he wouldn't try to kill us in Oakland, Lex. But he had a gun."

"That's why I bloody well needed to confront him. Not you."

"I couldn't take that risk." My eyes felt as hot as my throat. I sniffled. Pulled my knees up to my chest and wrapped my arms around them. Laid my head against my knees, hiding the tears I couldn't control. "I already lost Penny. I can't lose you, too. What do I have left if he kills you?"

"Finley."

"Don't." My words were muffled against my legs. "I'd rather it be me than you. I can't—I've got nothing as it is. Except you."

He reached across the center console. Cupped the back of my neck. "You're not going to lose me. I've been in tough spots. Even with the racket. Tougher than you faced. Tougher than you know. Please, Fin, trust me with that."

"This is a different kind of trust."

"I know you don't like the swagger. Just trying to distract you from worrying. You know this, Fin. You know I can sort myself. You know how I feel about you, as well." He rubbed my neck. "Fin, I—"

"Stop pressuring me with the relationship stuff." I jerked my head up. "There's too much at stake."

His hand flew off my neck. Returned to the steering wheel.

Why did this have to be so hard? I flopped back against the seat. Turned toward him. Wrapped my hand around his rigid bicep. Slid it over his shoulder.

"Sorry. I just—" I sighed. "Lex, why did you have to be a crook?"

His shoulders tensed, then relaxed.

"Why did you have to be an impertinent little pool hustler?" He chuckled. "Quite the distraction. Looking at me over your shoulder while you're bent over a pool table. Subtle, that."

"It worked."

"I'd spotted you weeks earlier. I knew your hustle."

"And let me do it anyway." I caught his eye. No twinkle.

Thoughtful. A bit mournful. "I need you, Lex. I want to stay part-ners. But I'm not ready for anything else. Yet."

"Right." He gently lifted my hand from his shoulder. Let it drop back into my lap. "Just remember, you're all I've got, as well."

He turned onto a local road. Drove into a small used car lot. Trailer for an office. An assortment of older vehicles with prices chalked in neon colors on the windshield. Nothing over five grand. An older guy sped out the trailer door. Heavy guy. Already panting.

I looked at Lex. "You're trading in the Camaro?"

"Orange is a bit passé, don't you think?" Lex winked. "I thought something more subtle would do. Perhaps a hatchback? In dirty gray? There's a mucky white sedan, as well. Whichever the lady prefers."

"You love this car."

"I loved winning the Camaro. Best bar bet I ever made." He sighed. "It's so American."

"Poor Lex," I said. "Back to my world. Cheap motels and dirty gray cars."

He shook his head. Gave me an imperceptible look. "I'm always focused on the long game, Fin. You should know that by now."

ALL LONG CONS require a certain set of steps to make them work, beginning with foundation work. Research and preparation. Hiring assistants, shills without an apparent connection but posi-tioned to encourage or distract the mark. Setting up a big store—the fake shop—if needed. It's a lot of work. Takes time and patience.

We didn't have time. And I lacked patience.

Something ate at me. Maybe Lex's setup seemed too smooth.

Maybe it was the crew involved. Mostly Dot's people. I didn't know them.

Maybe it was knowing someone wanted to kill me. That's a mood spoiler.

Lex thought so, too.

"You're driving me batty, Fin," said Lex. "I'm about to drop you at a pool hall. Let you hustle just to drive out that nervous energy."

"Why hasn't he called?" I waved my phone. "I'm ready for him."

"No, you're not. We're not." Lex folded his arms. He wore a soft T-shirt that clung to his biceps and chest. Sweats that barely hung on his lean hips. Lock of his sandy hair fallen over his temple.

That wasn't helping either. And he knew it.

Stuck in a tiny motel room with two singles. Determined to keep me hidden. At least until we knew the danger was past.

And this man was giving me space. Mental space, anyway. We didn't have any physical space.

But Lordy, with him prowling around me, looking like that, I didn't have much mental space either.

"We can still call this off," said Lex. "Get you out of town. It's safer."

"I'm not backing down."

He snorted. "That's the understatement of the year."

"I can't take much more of doing nothing." I dropped the phone on the bed. Paced the space between the beds. Climbed over the bed and flopped into the chair in the corner.

Lex watched me, then crossed to my side of the room. "I don't want you exposed any more than you need to be. There are a lot of working parts in this one. And we need our man Rick to wait until everyone is ready. Don't wish him on the stage sooner."

"I feel like I'm going crazy. Might need to score some Ritalin just to keep from climbing the walls."

"You're doing fine. Just hang tight. Tony Riggle's set." Lex leaned against the wall. "You worked him like a pro, Fin. And he did just as predicted. Offered Ellie her money back but gave you the option to try the Valentine party instead, dangling the bait of Brian and Oliver. Knowing Ellie would take the hook."

"Poor, insecure woman," I said.

"I blame her fake mother." Lex gave me a wry grin. "Oliver got the call from Riggle just after Ellie called him. And a reprimand for not doing more at the last party. I'm back to work, yeah?"

"Ellie's an idiot for chasing after men instead of getting her money back. Particularly when she'd been roofied by the thug. She could've sued them."

"That would have thrown a wrench in the works, yeah? Good to think she was just drunk. Tony Riggle played it smooth, saying the goon had been chucked from Platinum. Playing along like Rick was a member. You're meeting Riggle before the Valentine party?"

"It's not Tony Riggle who has me worried. He's acting exactly as we thought. Banking on Ellie's greed, like a typical con."

"Right." He ticked off points with his fingers. "Jello and your friend Bev agreed to help. Dot's handling the other shills."

I scowled.

"Can't be avoided. We need the extra players," he said smoothly. "And Mark Davis is willing to do his part."

"That feels weird," I said. "I don't like working with rubes."

"We'll have to be careful. But we need him."

"He still didn't mention the paper in his wallet. Or the markers. And him on the scene of Penny's death, it doesn't sit right. I don't trust him."

"He might not know about the markers. And we can't very well bring up the code, or he'll know you greased him. Elizabeth Ann doesn't pick pockets, Fin." He stretched, then interlocked his fingers on top of his head. His shirt rode higher, exposing the flesh pulled taut against his hip bones. "We'll find out more on Sunday."

"The insurance for our insurance?" I swallowed, my eyes flitting from his upraised biceps to his exposed waistline. Thoughts of

Mark's possible duplicity fled. My earlier frustration mounted. I grasped the chair arms, prepared to shove off, and run out the door.

"All going to plan." Lex pushed off the wall. "You know why we have to wait. I'm not letting you out there, vulnerable. I don't like what comes next."

"I've got to get out of this room, Lex. I'm climbing the walls."

"Soon enough. We'll cut loose after talking to Mark. But stay safe until then, yeah?"

"I still want to know who signed Penny's death certificate. We have time, Lex. Let's go up to Cherokee County Courthouse. It'll be fun. You could talk them into letting me see the death record."

Lex rolled his eyes, then cocked his head. A wrinkle formed between his eyes. "We've been over this. It's too risky. Not now. A coroner's easily bought and paid for. What's the point?"

"You know that signature won't be a Cherokee County coroner. We have a good idea of who it is. That could mean a lot to me."

"It'd mean a lot to me not having you murdered, Fin. You just want an excuse to leave."

"Don't you want to know who bought and paid for the coroner?"

"Not really." He paced across the room. Stopped before me. "Stay focused on the big picture, Fin. We aren't making an arrest. No need for chain of evidence. We're just folding the con. And getting Rick the heavy off your back."

"But—"

"Confidence men have no room for buts, Fin. We stick to the plan."

My head flopped back, and I moaned. "I want this over."

I felt him ease up to the chair. His foot nudged the chair leg. I closed my eyes, pulling in the scent of fresh shower and shave. My heart sped up. But I didn't move. Lex made his own rules now. He was done playing the chump.

"I can help you, Fin." He leaned over me. A hand on each chair arm. Trapping me inside. Not touching me. Just hovering. The right kind of heat pouring off his lean physique. He lowered his body. Inches from me. "Just say the word."

My head snapped back. I stared up at the blue eyes just inches from mine. Hooded. Dark. His mouth barely smiling. No smirk in sight. But lips curved with the promise of pleasure.

"But the word comes with strings," I said. "Doesn't it?'

His slow nod electrified every nerve in my body. "Tight strings. Words without escape clauses. I don't want it any other way this time."

"Come on, Lex."

He pushed off the chair and crossed the room. Quirked an eyebrow and picked up his phone. "Cold shower, love. Does wonders."

I was going to lose my bloody mind.

20

THE TEAR UP

"YOU ALWAYS FEEL this way before the action," said Lex. Reading my mind. Again. "Don't worry."

He winked. Sipped his coffee. Picked up his fork. Sticking to his narrative. Prepared to add the weight to assist Elizabeth Ann's push for Mark's in-and-in. We needed Mark to collaborate on the con, even if he didn't fully understand what we were doing.

We were in a Flying Biscuit, eating Sunday brunch like every other Atlantan. Hiding in the crowd—Sunday after-church mixed with Sunday slept-in—dressed as Elizabeth Ann and Carter. Bacon and fried green tomatoes. Biscuits and grits. Warm and sunny for winter. Air smelling like spring although it was February. Also typical for Atlanta. But we opted for a table in the back rather than the patio. Kept our voices low and eyes open.

Rick the goon had yet to call. Maybe he thought he'd driven us into hiding. Maybe he didn't have a directive from his employer. My daddy used to practice target shooting on the rats hiding in the woodpile. He was patient, too, just like Rick.

Now this rat was climbing out of the woodpile.

"We're missing something." I squirmed in my seat. Couldn't touch my food. My stomach felt like a trampoline.

Lex laid down his fork and covered my hand. "Stick with the

plan, Fin. If you go off script, I won't be there to catch you. Remember who we're dealing with."

"Elizabeth Ann and Ellie. Finley hangs back." I forced my hand to lay flat. Not to curl my fingers into his. "If something comes up, where can we meet?"

"Meeting may be tricky after today. Oliver is back to work for Platinum. They might be watching me." He lifted his hand. Leaving mine feeling cool. Lonely. "But I'll have eyes on you. Just keep your phone with you. I have faith in you, Fin. You'll do fine."

I wished I felt the same.

"We'd do this another way if we could."

"I know." I sighed. Spotted our rube. "Mark Davis is here. You ready?"

"Are you?"

"I hate this part."

"I do, too. But it'll work." He stood. Walked forward to greet Mark.

I hung back, arms crossed. Working up a few tears to make my eyes misty. They weren't hard to bring on. I'd miss Carter and Elizabeth Ann. Grifting was weird like that.

Listened to Carter and Mark say their "hey" and "how's it going." Carter a little uneasy. A little defensive. Mark picking up on the tension.

"You okay, Elizabeth Ann?" asked Mark.

I jerked a nod. "Sorry, we ordered without you. Carter was hungry."

Carter shot me a hard look. Leaned back in his seat. "There's been an incident. We were followed. Have you seen this big guy named Rick? He threatened Elizabeth Ann."

"Oh no," said Mark. "Like Penny was?"

"You know him?"

"No, but I don't know Penny's contact. I kind of figured Elizabeth Ann, knowing Penny, was...you know, like Penny. And you were...like me."

"I don't appreciate lies and deception," Carter leaned forward.

"No offense, Mark. It was more understanding in your case. Penny was hired to do what she did, then fell for you. She tried to make up for it."

"It's not like that." My voice sounded thick. I cleared my throat. "I didn't meet Carter like you met Penny, Mark. I haven't been involved in anything for a long time. Penny and I were young and did some stuff—"

"That you didn't tell me about. And now some guy is threatening you." Carter pushed away his coffee cup. "Sorry, Mark. This is not sitting well with me. At all."

"But what about the party? It's Saturday," said Mark. "We've been talking about taking this public."

"I've made the calls and will follow through. The reporter will still be there. But not me." Carter folded his arms. "Your dad can protect you, Mark. He's a judge. I don't have that kind of safety net. And if these felons are trying to get to me through Elizabeth Ann… Harsh as it sounds, I don't want to deal with it. It's not like we're married."

I winced. A tear leaked. Made me think about how I treated Lex. Did I make him feel like this?

Focus, Fin. Carter and Elizabeth Ann aren't real. Pull it together.

"But Carter, I don't even know them." My lip wobbled. "That guy, Rick, approached me. He's trying to blackmail us, but there's nothing there. Except I was friends with Penny. And did some stuff when we were young that I'm not proud of. But we were just kids."

"How do I know that it's in the past? That something else won't come up?" Carter scooted from the table. Legs spread wide. Chin tilted up. Around us, couples stared.

I averted my gaze. Felt my face heat up.

"Calm down, Carter," said Mark. "You're attracting attention."

"She set up an account with Platinum Partners without telling me. Using your mother's name, Mark. A nice girl wouldn't do that. It's deception. It could even be fraud, for all I know."

"But Melanie Davis was with me when I did it," I said. "We just wanted to see if they would accept me. To test their system. To show Mark that he shouldn't get involved with Platinum."

"And look what happened." Carter's voice dropped, but the venom remained. "You're in. And now some guy is threatening you, trying to get to me. If I'm not around, he can't threaten you, can he?"

"But Carter..." I flashed a quick look at Mark. His eyes had gone wide. Skin had paled. "We've got to help Mark."

"I'm sorry, Mark. But I'm out. I can't risk losing my job over this. Lord, I could be an accessory or something."

Mark swallowed hard. "I understand. We don't even know each other that well."

"Excuse me for airing our dirty laundry." Carter swiped his phone from the table. "I'll be at Mother's this weekend, Elizabeth Ann. Take what you want from the loft. We'll figure out the rest of the logistics another time."

I gave a curt nod, my face burning again. The tables around us had hushed. I watched him stride through the restaurant. Out the door. Silently said goodbye to Carter. Knowing I wouldn't see him again. My throat felt clotted. My eyes stung. Carter and Elizabeth Ann were really done.

Lordy, Fin. Once again, Carter's not real, remember? Get your head in the game and use the boo-hoo on Mark.

I turned to Mark, grabbed his sleeve. Knowing it would make him uncomfortable, but also knowing Mark was a sucker for the damsel in distress.

Poor Mark.

"I'm sorry you had to see that. I really want to help you." I cleared my throat. Dabbed at my eyes with a napkin. "Penny had a chance for a real life with you, Mark. Just like I did with—" Cripes, I'd almost said *Lex*. "Carter. And now that's ruined. I should have told him the truth like Penny did for you."

Mark looked stricken. He patted my arm. Retracted his hand. I clutched it before he could pull away.

"Penny and I were young and foolish. We both grew up rough —well, that's why I couldn't get into Platinum Partners without your mother's help." I released his hand. Touched my heart. Dropped my voice to a sad whisper. "But I'd rather Melanie not know about this. It's so humiliating."

"Lord, no. I don't want to involve Mother."

I decided to press my advantage. Lex wasn't around to stop my questions. He wouldn't like me going off script, but I had to know more about Penny's death.

"Your momma said you found Penny. I don't want to bring up hurtful memories, but..." I took a long breath, letting my chest rise and fall slowly. "You said Penny was murdered. But weren't the police there? Wouldn't they...I don't know, have some insight? Couldn't they do something?"

"It looked like she'd... There was a needle in her arm. A neighbor had called the police because my dog was going nuts. The policeman had already arrived. I let him in the house. He called the coroner and reported it. The coroner arrived, and they took her away. Case closed, I guess."

His voice roughened, grew harsher. "But I didn't believe it. I couldn't believe it. She'd told me about her mother. Penny didn't even like to drink. Took herbal stuff instead of over-the-counter medicine. I would have noticed something earlier if she'd had a problem."

I rubbed his shoulder. "I thought the same thing. Her mother had been in prison most of the time I'd known Penny."

"Plus, we were happy. Really happy. Except for this thing with Platinum—and she thought she'd figured it out. Penny did not overdose on her own."

"Maybe that was the problem. We need to get you off the hook, Mark." My voice had hardened. I'd almost forgotten myself. Switched back to Elizabeth Ann. "With Platinum Partners, I mean. What can I do?"

"You don't need to help me. You should worry about yourself."

I clutched my throat. "They'll leave me alone now, won't they?"

"I honestly don't know. The whole thing is surreal."

"What am I going to do?" I thought about Penny dying. Lex leaving. Forcing the tears to start again. Wasn't hard.

This time he took my hand. "I'll help you, Elizabeth Ann. I can't believe Carter would abandon you like this."

"We've had a rocky relationship. It's not his fault. I'm not the right kind of woman—" I shook my head, my eyes brimming again.

Okay. Enough with the waterworks. Talk about overkill.

"Don't say that. You and Penny were caught up in circumstances that weren't your fault." He squeezed my hand.

Poor, soft-hearted Mark. But I was helping him, wasn't I? Folding the con for him? But it wouldn't bring Penny back. Lex was wrong about letting that go. I wanted to know exactly what happened.

Mark's eyes grew steely. "I'm not paying them off anymore. Carter and I had a plan."

"Oh, my." Getting back into character, I slipped my hand from his. Touched my hair. Placed my hand back on my chest. Fingered my necklace. Let my hand fall to his arm. "What are you going to do?"

"Expose these blackmailers, so they're arrested. I'm going through with our plan with or without Carter."

"Let me help you," I said. "Really, Mark. I can handle it."

"And I'm going to bankrupt them. I know how to reverse the funds, get the money back. My last payout is at the Valentine's Day party. I'll get the new code then. In a few days, I'm pulling everything. I already tried smaller amounts, and it works."

I pulled my hand back. My heart sped up. "You what?"

"My senior project at Tech was software security and design testing for E-commerce, M-commerce, and banks. I can reverse engineer anything with that software because I wrote it."

"Aren't you worried they'll catch what you're doing?"

"They're only looking to see if I made the deposit." His eyes glinted. "I had a theory based on their banking setup that my withdrawals would be lost in their other transactions. I can't be the only one. So I'm going to pull all the money and flag it. Our government can't do anything, but the Central Bank of Luxembourg will see it."

Mark's skimming from the skim. Cripes.

"These are serious gangsters." I couldn't cut the panic from my voice. "Mark, this scares me."

"They won't see the flag. By the time they figure it out, I'm confident we'll be out of the mess. I can get the money back to my company. The extra money will be siphoned to another account. The police can figure out where it's supposed to go."

Lordy, he was blind. Mark might have brought down the house on Penny. He might have killed his fiancée trying to out-con the gangsters.

His gentle face hardened. "I'm not letting them get away with this, Elizabeth Ann."

We'd totally missed the mark on Mark. And I'd been cut off from Lex. I'd have to rewrite the script and hope for the best.

21

THE SIDE

MARK TOOK me to Lex's loft. I packed a few things, making a
show of it. In front of the building, I hugged him, then kissed his
cheek. Hoping someone saw. Like Rick the goon. Felt certain other
people were watching, too. Lex had arranged a spotter. I felt safe
enough. We'd contacted Dot to help put together the crew. No
choice there. She could be watching me, overseeing the setup.
Making sure we were playing it right. Maybe Sue Marshall had
eyes on us, too. I still didn't know what she wanted from me.

I waved Mark off, insisting I could Uber home. He'd be in
touch. Soon. Poor Mark. Not hard to understand how quickly he
fell for Penny. She probably read him faster than I did. Major white
knight complex. Mark was so sincere. So upright. Platinum had
really picked the wrong dupe. I just couldn't understand how
someone as tough as Penny had fallen for him.

Maybe sincere and upright were too alien for me.

My part was done for the day. Time to lose the eyeballs.

I Ubered to Lenox Mall in Buckhead. Spent time in Macy's. In
and out of dressing rooms. Shopping but making quick turns
between aisles. Bobbing in and out of sight for anyone who
watched. Typical Sunday crowds. Easy to hide in.

Ducked into the movie theater. Into a bathroom. Out the back door. Snuck through the parking lot with my new clothes on. Ball cap. Sunglasses. Hopped on MARTA. Switched trains downtown. Got off at Inman Park. Caught another Uber to Penny's car.

Thank the stars. The Honda had been in the lot for a week. Ticket, but no boot. I knew people who could un-boot a car, but I didn't want to involve anyone else nor take the time.

Tossed the ticket. Checked the car. Headed out of Atlanta. I had a funny feeling about a cop and coroner who arrived on scene like that. Likely story about the neighbor, too.

I still wanted that death certificate. If there were no investigation into Penny's demise, that certificate would be filed away without notice. I could anonymously send the copy to an interested party, thereby bringing attention to Penny's murder. If all Mark said was true, it would bring him justice. Throw more shade at these gangsters. And possibly at a shady sheriff and corrupt coroner.

Poor, gullible Mark.

But gullible Mark was stealing from Platinum. That's how they'd see it, anyway. Was that naïveté or something else? His father was a judge who oversaw criminal trials. At the dinner table, Judge Davis must have shared organized crime stories. Like I grew up hearing about arrests. At least, the arrests who hadn't paid or traded information to escape their bust.

Mark must know the consequences for ripping off a mobster. I reflected on that for a minute. Maybe the judge told the stories differently. Maybe Mark was innocent. He wasn't stupid, but could he be that naïve?

One way to find out. Someone needed to keep an eye on Mark.

Lex wouldn't be happy with my change in plans, but I couldn't sit around waiting for this to come crashing down on our heads.

MARK'S HOME wasn't in Atlanta, which had surprised me. His parents lived in Atlanta. Posh home in Buckhead. They also had a place out by that country club where the celebration of life had been held, and another condo in Florida. Mark chose to live outside the metro area. A pain-in-the-butt commute. If he had lived inside the perimeter, he wouldn't have these issues with fake coroner pronouncements. But who can predict that sort of thing?

Although someone might have concluded that point, which was why the fake coroner was sent.

I drove with those thoughts toward Mark's suburban house in Woodstock. The man had chosen a brick two-story with a half-acre wooded lot. Something a family of four would have loved. Kind of odd for an unmarried man.

I could see Penny's dogs loving this yard, though. Mark had a dog. Some kind of lab or retriever mix. It jogged the fence line in the backyard, following my car as I traveled his street.

Maybe Penny fell in love with Mark's home. Or the idea of his home.

Why did I have such a hard time believing Penny had loved Mark?

His road ended in a cul-de-sac. I spotted the pickup truck in time. Whipped onto an intersecting street that also ended in a cul-de-sac. Then parked on the curve to hyperventilate.

Why was Rick in Mark's neighborhood? Was he watching Mark's house? Or did he think I'd show up?

I craned my neck, checking the houses around me. Sunday night television lit most of the homes. A few were dark. I took Rick's Glock from the glove compartment. I wasn't sure how to carry it. I'd been lugging it in Elizabeth Ann's purse, making my shoulder ache. My father had taught me how to use firearms, but I'd never carried. Neither did Lex. We'd had weapons flashed at us, but usually by some thug kid trying to act tough.

The Glock was too big for my back pocket. I shoved it in my waistline and pulled my T-shirt over it. After I'd checked the safety six times. A little worried I'd shoot myself.

This street where I parked ran perpendicular to Mark's. But Mark's road curved, like so many suburban subdivision streets.

Very few straight lines in Georgia. I couldn't hike up the road without Rick spotting me.

A tree line ran between the lots. I cut through the yard of one of the unoccupied homes. Tried to draw closer to Mark's. Fences stopped me. With the winding street and similar-looking homes, I wasn't even sure which one was Mark's.

I could watch Rick. Make sure he didn't make a move on Mark. Maybe Platinum had figured out his double-cross.

Which didn't seem altogether smart, but not altogether stupid either. If I could get close enough without him noticing. I had the Glock, after all.

On the other side of the street, I cut through two neighboring yards. Felt confident Rick was focused on Mark's house and not his own back.

I slipped alongside a dark home. Cut close to their garage. Most of the homes on this street had vehicles parked in their drives. A Tahoe in this one. But looked like no one was home. I hunkered behind a tree next to the driveway, intent on watching the F-150. His truck was dark, but something glinted occasionally. Flashes of infrared light. Night vision binoculars, I'd bet anything.

Did he know Mark had stolen from the skim? I chewed my lip, fearing for Mark. Not that I completely trusted Mark, I told myself. He seemed like a nice guy. I just couldn't figure him. Or Penny's relationship with him.

The metallic pop of a vehicle door broke my concentration. Not Rick's door. He was still watching the street. I turned to look behind me.

They were on me before I registered the sound had come from the Tahoe. Hand over my mouth. Bag over my head. Wrists zip-tied. My kicking feet gathered. Ankles zip-tied. At least two people. The zip-tier patted me down. Took the Glock. Under the bag, the other thug kept his thick, garlic-scented hand fixed firmly over my mouth.

"Keep your mouth shut, or he'll hear you. He starts shooting, and I'm using your body as a shield," whispered Garlic Hand.

I bucked. Got my head clocked with the Glock. Felt like the Glock, anyway. For a minute, they sat on me. Pinned me to the ground. Laying low. Thirty seconds later, I was lifted, Garlic's hand still slapped tight against my mouth. We fitted awkwardly in the back seat of the Tahoe. Garlic must have slid in first. Kept his hand over my mouth, then pulled me against him.

Another door opened and shut. They waited, Garlic speaking quiet threats about girls who screamed, bit, or jabbed their elbows. The motor started.

And we sailed down the drive.

22

THE BUILD-UP

GARLIC HAND SHOVED me to the other side of the vehicle. My rapid panting quickly heated the bag, making my face sweat. Felt my body quaking. Forced myself to slow down my breathing.

Think, Fin. Who are these two? Where are we going?

Both impossible to answer inside a bag.

"Is he following us?" I asked. "Rick. The guy in the pickup."

Nothing.

Sue Marshall had said there were at least four crime syndicates involved with Platinum Partners. I hoped I wasn't a casualty in some gang war over Mark's embezzlement. I wasn't even sure who I was supposed to be: Elizabeth, Ellie, or Finley.

"Do y'all even know who I am?"

The driver turned on music. Loud. Hip-Hop. The speaker next to my leg buzzed, vibrating from the heavy bass.

Beneath my bag, I gritted my teeth. This was what I got for losing Lex's spotter and going off script. Tried to get some perspective. The threats had stopped. No gun shoved into my side. Lex had said a little fear was good. It would keep me vigilant.

Vigilant enough to want to pee my pants.

What felt like an hour later, the Tahoe slowed. Centrifugal force knocked me into the door. Probably an off ramp. With my hands and ankles bound, I had to wriggle my shoulders and thighs to push upright.

My stomach began to jump, then cramp. Thinking about what might come next. The Tahoe slowed further. Stops and starts. Must be traffic and red lights. Car lights shone through the dark bag while we were on the highways and interstates. More light poured in. Streetlights, maybe. Must be in the city. But where?

More slowing. More turns. The Tahoe crawled. We stopped. A door opened. Then another. Fresh air blew inside the car. Beneath the bag, I gulped to taste it. Someone grabbed my elbow and yanked me out. I stumbled. Before I could catch my balance, I was lifted and bent over a shoulder. Fireman carry.

"You kick me," said a low voice, "and I'll shoot you in the knee."

I was more worried about hurling down his back than kicking him. We mounted stairs. Banged my forehead against his back. Crick in my neck. A door opened. We took a few more steps. I was tossed on the floor. My forehead smacked wood. I scrambled to sit up. Someone shoved me down. The bag was ripped from my head.

My cheek was pressed against the floor. I blinked and tried to focus. Bright light blinding me. Someone knelt behind me, cutting the zip-ties. A pair of Adidas stopped before me. I recognized the crazy chuckle coming from the owner of the Adidas.

"Dot," I said weakly.

"You are one crazy girl, Finley Goodhart. What you doing in Mark Davis's neighborhood?"

"What were you doing kidnapping me from Mark Davis's neighborhood?"

She laughed, then yanked me up by the back of my hoodie. I jerked to sitting. My knees bent and splayed. I craned my neck to see the Amazon.

"This was no kidnap," said Dot. "It's a rescue mission."

"Hard to tell with the hood and the cuffs," I said. "I don't have a lot of experience in kidnapping, but you make a pretty good case for it."

"Get up." She kicked my leg. Not hard, but enough to take notice. "Don't barf on my floor, neither."

"You're my spotter?"

"These two was watching Mark Davis. Saw you acting the fool. Told them to pick you up."

She pointed at the two men who had wandered to the zoo wall. Watching a snake swallow a mouse. Throat bulging. Tail and feet still hanging out its mouth.

"Don't tap the glass, Lewis. You'll upset her digestion. Takes a while for that one to eat."

A shudder ran over me. I looked away.

"Lewis. Bruce. You boys get out of here now." Dot wandered to her chair. Plopped into it. Waited for the door to shut behind them. "Finley, you come talk to me." She held up the Glock. "What're you doing with this?"

"It's the detective's. Rick. He's no detective, though."

"I know what he is. Rick Grave's a contract dude. Whatever you want, he'll do."

"A contract killer?"

"I don't know that, exactly. Maybe. He's a cleaner. Cleans up situations. But someone hired him for something."

"Who does he work for?"

"Not for me."

"Was he watching Mark, or me?"

"Tonight, Mark. Sometimes you. Earlier, you and Mark. You getting sweet on Mark? I told Leopold you were kissing him."

"On the cheek." I rolled my eyes. "Lex knows my role."

She laughed. "I don't care about you and Lex. But you are not following the plan. And that's a problem, Finley Goodhart. I have an interest in this project. And now you owe me for time and inconvenience."

I gritted my teeth. Stared at the ceiling and counted to ten. Why did we have to involve Dot? She was worse than a cheap airline, nickel-and-diming us for every little thing.

"Why do you have an interest in this?" I said. "Folding Platinum Partner's cupid division hurts you because you'll no longer have someone on the inside. I know what Penny and Lex were doing for you."

"Cupid division." She snorted. "Platinum Partners *is* the name of their cupid division. That partnership doesn't have a name. And folding that arm—any arm—helps me. They're like an octopus. Cut off enough arms, and they got nothing to feed themselves with. Atlanta doesn't need a hungry octopus eating up all their rich folks."

"Like you care about Atlanta. You don't want that kind of competition."

"Whatever." She shrugged. "I'm not getting into some kind of semantic-type argument with you, Finley."

"Where's Lex? I need to talk to him."

"You see Lex Leopold in this room? He's probably doing what he's supposed to be doing. Unlike you. Which is why you always be a two-bit hustler. You can't focus on the long con unless Lex is holding your hand."

I sucked in my breath, feeling the anger roll from my toes to my teeth. "I'm doing what's necessary."

"Too many cooks, and the soup spoils when the players are deciding for themselves what's necessary." She folded her arms. "You ready to talk to me?"

"What do you want?"

"That's exactly what I want to hear. I'm glad you are amenable to alleviating this disruption." Her voice hardened. "I want to hear what you discussed with Sue Marshall."

I blinked. "That's it?"

"If I think of something else, I'll let you know. Also, I'm keeping this Glock." She popped the chair lever and leaned back, hands behind her head. "Start talking."

"Sue told me about the groups that made up Platinum Partners. Basically explained how the organization worked. That's about it."

"What'd she say about me?"

"That you weren't a part of the consortium, but you sent your soldiers to spy on the organization. Like I said, I know what Penny and Lex were doing for you." I folded my arms, studying Dot. I left out Sue Marshall's disparagement of Dot, knowing that'd do no good. "And Sue wanted to know about my father."

Dot jerked the lever on her chair and flew forward, finger pointing at me. "See? This is why you want to keep with Dot. Sue's after the sheriff through you."

I shrugged. "I've got no play with the sheriff. You know that."

"Don't trust that Mountain Posse, Finley. Stick with who you know." She thumped her chest. "You've known me a long time now."

I doubted Dot felt any kinship towards me. This display of emotion must have more to do with keeping Sue Marshall in the mountains and out of central Georgia. I shrugged. "I got no allegiance to Sue Marshall. You know me, Dot. I've got no allegiance to anybody."

"'cept yourself."

"That's known as survival. Now, how can I contact Lex? I really need to talk to him."

"Let me tell you something. I hear about you and Sue Marshall... What you doing looking around? Look at me when I'm talking to you, Finley."

"I'm looking for the dead horse you keep flogging."

She barked a laugh. "Think you're so smart. I don't think you appreciate me enough."

"Probably not." I edged toward the door. "Nice chat, Dot. But I've got to find a way to get to the north side and pick up my car."

"You ain't going nowhere, Finley. Lex was worried about you having too much time on your hands. He thinks you're going to get yourself killed. Now Lex appreciates what I bring to the table, so I like to appease him. I'm gonna keep you right here until we need you."

Bugger.

"I've got a job to do, too," I said.

"And when you need to clock in, we'll bring you where you need to go."

"What do you have on Lex?"

"That's between me and Lex."

"What if he went on the level?" It was out of my mouth before I could stop it. "What if, after this, Lex didn't work for you anymore? If he decided I was more important than running cons for you?"

Dot shook her head slowly, chuckling. "You fooling yourself, Finley. Neither you nor Lex Leopold is ever going straight. First off, you owe me too much. Second, it's in your blood. No way you can wring that out."

"Maybe we'll join an AA for ex-cons. Kick the habit."

"Maybe you'll do what I tell you to do." She was out of her chair, towering over me. Head cocked, whites of her eyes glinting. "I lost a good earner when Penny died. I don't know what happened, but I have an idea you know more than you're telling. You're lucky Lex is covering your ass. Now I can have Lewis and Bruce dump you in front of Rick Graves's truck. And you can interrogate the cleaner with all these useless questions and see how long it takes him to shoot you."

"Or," she continued. "You can sleep off all this anger in my guest room. Which is much nicer than the skanky motels you usually stay in."

DOT'S GUEST room was indeed much nicer than my skanky motel rooms. But I wasn't going to admit it. The next morning, I rolled out of bed. Found a duffel bag containing my clothes and personal items, Elizabeth Ann's purse, and a new burner phone.

I dialed Lex's last number, but he'd killed the account. Listening to the automated voice telling me the number was no longer in service brought on a few tears. I told myself it was frustration, nothing else. He had to dump Carter for the con, and that meant dumping everything associated with Elizabeth Ann.

Not Finley, I told myself. Just Elizabeth Ann.

Fanning my disappointment, I stoked that low, burning rage I had for Dot. Staying at her place meant being on my toes. I left the guest room and found Dot eating cereal in the kitchen space. For some reason, it stopped me short.

"What?" she said. "You never see anyone eat Fruity Pebbles before? You a Cocoa Krispies-type? Don't tell me you only eat that granola crap."

"I've just never seen you eat. Anything."

"I told you I like that Korean BBQ." She squinted at me, then glanced at the neon-colored rice in her bowl. "You want some?"

"Sure." I felt uneasy. Glanced at the wall. The pets weren't dining. The mouse was gone.

"Most of them are nocturnal." She nodded at the zoo. Put down her spoon and reached into the cupboard to grab a bowl. "They creep you out, don't they?"

I nodded.

"Good." She shoved the cereal box at me. "Eat up."

"What am I going to owe you for the cereal?"

"Who you think I am? Hades? And you're Persephone?" She rolled her eyes. "You are a guest in my home. For a minute, anyway. This ain't a restaurant, though. As my momma once said, you get what you get. Or I'll give you something to cry about."

"Where did my stuff come from?" My voice rose before I could stop it. "Did Lex come by? I really need to talk to him."

"Lewis and Bruce picked it up. Brought your Honda back, too." Her eyebrow rose. "Penny's car. That's something else I want to know. Where's Penny's money?"

"What are you talking about? You took it from her apartment."

"Then why am I asking?"

We eyeballed each other over spoonfuls of Fruity Pebbles. This was weird. Having an almost normal conversation with Dot the

Jamaican. She didn't look like she wanted to kill me. Dot almost looked...amused.

"The day of Penny's celebration of life, Lewis and Bruce tailed Lex and followed us to Penny's," I said. "They tore apart her apartment. I checked later. The money was gone."

"They were tailing you, Finley, not Lex. And found nothing. So where's the money?"

"Lex said they were tailing—" I stopped. Filed that away. He probably knew they were tailing me and didn't want me to go after Dot. "I only found Penny's walking-around money. Around five G's. Is that what you mean? Because that's mostly gone, too."

"What do I care about a few thousand?" She cocked her head. "But what happened to the walking-around money? You spend it?"

"No, of course not. I was planning on giving it to Penny's dogs." I sighed. "I was spotted. Cleaned me out. Tore up my motel room. I thought it was you. Probably Rick Graves."

"Always thinking the worst about good old Dot."

"Your reputation proceeds you. And you did beat the hell out of me once."

"And don't you forget it. You were cleaned out because you live in motels. Put your money in a bank like a grown-up, Finley, and you won't lose it." She snorted. "Wait. You can't, can you? Your daddy fixed that for you, didn't he? No credit history. No real job."

"Thanks for bringing that up."

"I'm just cutting up." She chuckled. "Finley, you're like a porcupine. No one can get near you, 'cause you always got those stickers out. Lex Leopold's got holes all over his body, I bet. Stupid man."

"Quills." I took a bite of cereal, chewed, and considered. "Why didn't you tell me about Penny when I first came to you?"

"You know my rules. I only trade when it comes to information." Her lip curled. "And you're uppity, Finley. Prickly and uppity. I don't like that."

"This coming from a gangster."

"I ain't no gangbanger. I'm a fixer and a handler. And do a little of this and that on the side. Mostly merchandising."

Obtaining and selling hot items. She also ran a small protection racket, Lewis and Bruce's regular job. But why split hairs with someone like Dot? "You're interested in organizing, though. You're smart, and you'd like to dip into more than you do."

Dot shrugged. Seemed pleased I called her smart. "There are certain avenues I'd consider."

"I don't want to consider crime anymore." I waved my spoon. "I'm done."

She snorted.

"I'm serious. After this, I'm getting out."

"And you want to take Lex Leopold with you." She shook her head. "Ain't going to happen. You got too much hanging over your head to make it out there. And he's too involved."

"Involved in what?"

"I'm not getting into this with you. I don't talk about other folks' business. You want to know, you ask Leopold."

"What about Penny? She's gone. Did she owe you? Hold markers for you? Is that why you want her money?"

"Penny paid her debts by working. But there are other people's debts. The money that disappeared would have cleared those debts."

"Whose debts?"

"Her momma's." Dot tossed her bowl in the sink. The spoon clattered after it. "Penny's momma is back in prison. And left a big ol' mess for Penny to clean up."

"Again? Who did her mom owe?"

"The usual. Dealers. Loan sharks. I tell you what. Penny did not learn her work ethic from her momma."

"You think that's who killed Penny?"

"It's a possibility, but doesn't make much sense. And I don't think they stole Penny's money, either. Otherwise, this Rick Graves dude wouldn't be stalking you and Mark Davis."

"Lex said you can't make a dead person pay up."

"Smart boy."

"Lex isn't interested in solving Penny's murder," I spoke slowly. Considering these new factors. "He's just helping to fold the con."

"Not much of a payout for him in solving Penny's murder. In this particular case, Lex's only interest is in saving your butt." She folded her arms. Leaned against the counter. "Though I don't know why he cares so much for that skinny, little butt of yours. With you so prickly. You need to treat him better, Finley."

"I know." I sighed. "I have trust issues."

The phone on the counter buzzed. We stared at it.

"That's my old phone," I said. "Elizabeth Ann's phone. Why do you have it?"

"I'm keeping tabs on your con." Dot picked up the cell phone. Checked the caller ID: Name unknown. She handed me the phone. "This could be it. You ready?"

23

THE PICKUP GUY

"WE'RE gonna talk about Penny Forbes today," growled the voice. Rick Graves.

"On the phone?" I stalled. Looked at Dot. She listened on the speaker.

Dot nodded.

"Meet me at Penny's apartment. Today. One o'clock. Bring her keys. All of them."

"I want to speak directly with your employer."

"Good one," Dot mouthed.

"Penny's. One o'clock." He hung up.

"Do you think he knows who I am?" I said to Dot. "Or does he think I'm Elizabeth Ann?"

"What does that matter? Either one of you can get killed. You're dead either way."

"That doesn't help." I chewed my lip. "I've got to take off. He'll ping me to the nearest cell phone tower. You don't want this guy finding your place."

"Take Penny's car. Lewis and Bruce are still watching Mark Davis. Drive somewhere and call Rick Graves back. Make him ping you in a different spot. Then do it again. Keep bouncing around."

"Should I show up at one o'clock?"

"You crazy, girl? Of course you don't show."

"What if Graves goes after Mark?"

"Why would he go after Mark? You're the one who pissed him off."

But Mark was stealing from Platinum Partners. I couldn't tell Dot about Mark. She'd want the money he skimmed. And would want Mark to continue embezzling. I needed to protect Mark. At least for now.

"Please have Lex contact me," I said. "It's important."

"You'll see Lex when you're supposed to see him, Finley. You know how this works. Don't blow this for us. Stick with the plan. Otherwise, you're the one who gets tossed in the grave with Penny. And nobody wants that." She laughed. "Most of us don't, anyway."

I ZIPPED AROUND THE INTERSTATES, pinging Rick Graves. Atlanta made it easy. From Dot's place near the airport, I headed south. Toward Columbus. Then sped west. Stopped across the border, near Auburn, Alabama. Shot back up I-85. Hit I-270 circling Atlanta and sped east to Stone Mountain. Made hang-up calls from all those stops. Kept circling until I reached I-75. Then headed northwest toward Chattanooga.

I felt like those ducks in that shooting game. A moving target.

At one o'clock, I stopped for gas in Cartersville, an hour northwest of Atlanta. Called Graves again.

"You're not where you're supposed to be. I warned you," he said. "It's going to get ugly."

"Tell your employer that thanks to them, I've got no home. No man. No money. And my best friend is dead. I've got nothing but ugly."

"But you're still alive. For now."

"What do y'all want with Mark Davis? Why are you watching him?"

"Stay away from Mark Davis. Don't play games with him."

Interesting.

"You mean games like Penny played?" I fished.

"What do you know about Penny Forbes?"

"I've a pretty good idea how she died and who did it." I dangled more bait. "And who covered it up."

Silence.

I thought about Rick Graves's investigative techniques. Lex and the Platinum crew had thought he was a detective. I'd bet he learned investigation in a law enforcement class. "Tell the sheriff I have evidence."

"The sheriff..." he spoke slowly.

"I think you know who I mean." I felt fairly certain. Not one hundred percent. But I needed some kind of coverage. Hoped the death certificate details would be enough. "Don't get me wrong. I think you're scum, Rick Graves, but I don't care about you. My concern is for your boss. That's who ordered the hit on Penny, right?"

"I see what you're getting at."

"I thought so. Think about it some more before we talk again."

I hung up.

Walked into the gas station. Found the bathroom. And threw up.

I STAYED in Cartersville until nightfall. Sat in Penny's car watching the sun set on Lake Allatoona. Thinking. Wishing Lex was with me. The more I dug around into Penny's murder, the more confused I became.

Even if we folded Platinum Partners, Mark was in danger. If Graves worked with the sheriff, they were caught up in at least one of the crime rings that owned Platinum Partners. I needed to convince Mark to stop stealing back his money. And to leave the rest of the money in the account. Let the crime lords deal with whoever iced Penny.

But if I stayed on this hunt to discover who killed Penny, I could learn something else. Maybe John Prince, the coroner who worked for Sheriff Goodhart, signed that death certificate. I'd have real evidence to put Prince away. Possibly take the sheriff down with him.

I let my brain play with that idea. I could give the death certificate to the Feds. Let them work it out. To cop a plea, John Prince would point his finger at Sheriff Goodhart. I could read about it in the news. No confrontation. He wouldn't know who turned him in.

But I also could keep the death certificate until I found a better piece of evidence. Something bigger. And that little document might protect me. In case the sheriff and I did tangle again. Blackmail for protection.

Can't do anything until you have the death certificate, Fin. No point in making future plans if some gangster wants you dead right now. Plus, Mark still needs your help.

CARTERSVILLE WAS NOT FAR from Woodstock. At least for an Atlanta driver. Took me an hour to find a payphone, though. Couldn't trust the burner phone for this.

I called Mark. "Drive to your local McDonald's," I said. "Use the drive-through and keep your doors unlocked."

"What should I order?"

For someone embezzling from the mob, Mark was one chill dude.

"Very funny," I said. "I'm going to sneak into your vehicle when you pull through. Make sure to park in your garage when you get home, so no one sees me."

"Do you like Big Macs, Elizabeth Ann?"

I thought for a minute. "Quarter pounder with cheese, small fries, and a large Coke."

"Large fry and we'll split it."

"Mark, aren't you wondering why I'm smuggling myself into your car?"

"I stopped wondering about a lot of things after I met Penny." He hung up.

I parked two lots down from the McDonald's. Keeping low, I wormed my way through cars and into the building. Sipped a sweet tea until I saw Mark's SUV pull into the lot. Exited the McDonald's. Skirted the side of the building. Slipped beside the dumpster in the back. Mark's BMW X1 pulled around. He stopped to pay. Hunkering below his windows, I slipped alongside the car. Opened the back door. Crawled inside and squatted on the floor behind his seat.

"Evenin', Elizabeth Ann. Ready for dinner?"

My mother would like Mark, I thought. But my mother had liked my father at one time.

Don't trust him completely, Fin. Keep with the Elizabeth Ann narrative.

The golden retriever mix climbed over the center console and hopped to the floor beside me. Gave my armpit a good sniff, then licked my face. I rubbed his ears. "Hey, buddy."

"That's Elmore," said Mark. "You want your fries now or later?"

"If I take the fries now, do I have a fighting chance with Elmore?"

Elmore flipped onto his back, exposing his belly. I scratched. His leg thumped against the seat.

"Not really." Mark reached behind him. My Coke dangled from his hand. "This will have to hold you until we get home."

AT MARK'S HOUSE, I waited for his garage door to close before I climbed out of the car. Elmore followed me. Tail wagging. Nudging me along. We followed Mark into the kitchen. He flipped on the lights. I skirted the windows. Inched to the sink. Turned on the water.

"Elmore's a terrible guard dog," I said to Mark. "Does he always greet people who sneak into your car like that? He almost licked me to death."

"He's a people pleaser." Mark handed me the fries. "And I think he misses Penny."

"I miss Penny." I took a fry, offered the box to Mark. He held out a fry to Elmore, then took one himself.

"Me, too." He stared at the sink. "Why are we running the water?"

"Mark, your house could be bugged."

Mark handed me my burger. Paper rattling in his shaky hands. Not as cool as he played it.

"Why do you think that?" he said.

"Because Graves—the guy who threatened me—he's been watching your house. Mark, I'm really worried about you."

He smiled weakly. "That's nice."

Elmore lunged. I scooped the dangling fry box from Mark's hands. Gave Elmore a fry. Nibbled one while I studied Mark. "I don't think you get it. You need to stop pulling money from the accounts."

"It'll be over soon, Elizabeth Ann. On Saturday."

"Have you heard from Carter?"

"Carter's out. He said that when he left you."

"I thought maybe he—" I stopped myself. Lex wouldn't change narratives. "Right. I'm worried about Saturday, too."

"Come sit with me," said Mark. "I'm really tired. Extortion and embezzlement are lonely work."

I did not understand this guy. Did he have no self-preservation instincts? "Mark, do you understand the type of people who would bug your house?"

"Yes, I do. It's not bugged, Elizabeth Ann. I had it swept."

I shut off the water. Placed my hands on my hips. "Mark, you're confusing me."

"I confuse a lot of people." He grabbed the fries and strolled toward the hall, waving a hand. "Come on."

24

THE BAGMAN

I FOLLOWED Mark into his living room. Big flat screen, cushy chairs and couch, a wall of books. On a table next to the couch rested a framed picture of Mark and Penny. I walked to the photo and picked it up. They were on a beach. Laughing. Arms around each other.

"Where was this?" I swallowed a surging knot of grief.

"Aruba. At Christmas."

"Penny went to Aruba for Christmas?" In the past, that holiday had been our best time for running charity scams. A necessary earning time because January was slow. And cold. I'd spent this Christmas at Jello's, practicing pool shots. The college boys had gone home. Just Jello, the barflies, and me. Fighting the desire to call Lex and apologize for leaving him. Fighting the temptation to get caught up in the grift again. Thought it better to wallow in self-pity, alone.

And Penny was in Aruba soaking up the rays with Mark Davis. Never would have guessed that in a million years.

"That's where we were engaged." Mark collapsed on the couch.

Elmore trotted through the room. Shoved his face between Mark's knees and stole a mouthful of fries.

"We talked about staying," said Mark. "Buying a house to rent to vacationers. It was a joke, but now I wish we'd done it."

It was like I hadn't known Penny at all. In the photo, she wore a bikini and sarong. Her tight brown curls were salt-sprayed. Wide smile. Arms wrapped around Mark's waist. Looking up at him. Adoration in her brown eyes.

"She looks…happy," I murmured. But she looked more than happy. She looked at peace. I'd never seen Penny like that.

I set the photo on the table and faced Mark. "I don't get it. Why were you with someone like Penny?"

"You doubt Penny loved me."

"I doubt a lot of things, Mark. Don't take it personally. But I knew Penny from the streets. She was the Artful Dodger to my Oliver Twist."

His eyebrows shot to his hairline.

"Before I ran away, I went to a good high school. Private, actually. I read books. I wasn't raised an orphan."

"That came later?"

"In a way." I was inching away from Elizabeth Ann's narrative, toward Finley Goodhart's. Mark made it easy.

Don't let down your guard, Fin.

"Anyway, the *Pretty Woman* thing you had going on with Penny. Kind of hard to believe."

"I believe in second chances. And she explained everything about a month into our relationship. I told you that."

He rubbed Elmore's ears. "I wasn't completely gullible, though. When we met, I kept things…slow. Old fashioned dates. I was a little wary of Platinum Partners. And I don't have a lot of experience with women. Haven't been able to—" Distress pinched his face.

I sank onto the couch next to Mark and reached for a fry. Elmore rested his head on my lap. I gave him the fry. He climbed on my lap, and I hugged his furry neck. Giving Mark time to continue. Work through those painful memories.

"I asked around," he said. "No one knew Penny. She was on her company's records, even in the company phone directory. But if I'd call random departments and ask for her, no one knew who she was."

Penny had a good setup, but Mark wasn't stupid.

"Those were some serious red flags. But you continued to date her?"

"I confronted her about it. She apologized, told me the truth. I told her I forgave her. But I had fallen in love with her anyway. There's just something about Penny."

"Penny was special. One in a million. I wish I had some of what she had."

But Mark was looking at the photo, not at me. Absently, he reached toward Elmore and scratched his back. Elmore slid between us, rolling over. Mark laid a hand on Elmore's belly, but his focus was somewhere else.

"When I told Penny I forgave her, she broke down. I don't think anyone had ever said that to her before."

"Yeah, probably not." I reached for my necklace, twisting it around my fingers.

"She wanted a church wedding. Penny had made a lot of changes in her life. But that was before Platinum found out she wasn't putting the pressure on me to embezzle."

I rubbed Elmore, digging my fingers into his fur. It was like listening to a story of someone I hadn't known. But, I could see it. I wanted to change my ways, too, didn't I? And after her childhood, Penny deserved that kind of peace.

Yet Penny still had her apartment with hidden money. Penny was complicated. But Mark was, too. There was more to this story he wasn't sharing. Something behind his eyes. I'd wait. He needed to spill. Listening was the least I could do.

"I hate to bring this up," I said. "But a mutual friend said Penny's momma owed a lot of money. Do you know if Penny paid it off?"

"I paid it off."

"Wow." This guy was serious about staying on that white steed.

"I have a trust. It seemed a good thing to do with the money. It wasn't Penny's fault that her mom's a junkie."

"Penny kept markers. Maybe they were her mom's?"

His brow creased. "I don't know about that. Was her mom an artist?"

I shook my head. He didn't know about the markers.

Elmore raised his head and rolled over. Jumping on my lap, he pushed off my stomach and leapt to the floor. I toppled forward in the deep cushions.

Mark caught my arm. "Sorry, Elmore thinks he's smaller and lighter—"

"Elizabeth Ann?" Melanie stood in the doorway. "What are you... I'm sorry, Mark. I didn't know you had company. I just stopped by to say hello."

I grabbed the couch arm and pulled myself upright, away from Mark. "Hey, Miss Melanie. We're just talking about Penny."

"This is unexpected," said Mark. "Do you want a glass of wine? Fries?"

"No, thank you." Melanie's nose wrinkled. She hesitated in the doorway before striding forward. "I don't want to interrupt. I was just surprised to see Elizabeth Ann here."

I smiled. "I was unexpected, too."

"Actually, we've been consoling each other," said Mark. "Carter left her."

"I see." She looked from Mark to me. "I'm sorry to hear that, Elizabeth Ann."

The look that crossed Melanie's face said it all. The "my son's taken up with another Penny-type" look. She was probably happy for Carter.

"It's been good to see you, Mark," I said. "I'll catch an Uber. We'll talk later."

Nothing more could be said with Melanie here. And her presence made me less worried about his safety. Plus, I'd already slipped from my original Elizabeth Ann backstory. No need for

Melanie to learn any more than she already had. She hadn't walked down Mark's road with me.

"You don't have to go, Elizabeth Ann," said Mark. "It's late."

"It's fine." I rose from the couch. "Miss Melanie, I can tell you're uncomfortable. But Mark knows about our little Platinum Partners charade. Carter didn't like it, but Mark was glad for my honesty."

Behind his mother, Mark shook his head. I got it. Melanie didn't know the full story about Platinum. Which meant she didn't know about the real Penny.

"I'm glad Mark'll have nothing more to do with them," said Melanie. "Goodness knows I have plenty of friends with daughters. No need to use a *service*."

Service sounded synonymous with *prostitute*. Mark's face made it obvious he caught the same meaning.

"Mother—"

She held up a hand. "I know you young people feel differently. I'll find the wine myself."

As Melanie strode to the kitchen, I pulled out my phone and pressed the Uber app.

"Let me take you to your car," said Mark.

"Your mom?"

He shrugged. "She'll be here when I get back."

"I don't think she's happy with finding me here."

He cut a hard look toward the kitchen. "I'm too tired to care."

I DUCKED as Mark drove his SUV out of the garage. "Do you see a truck at the end of the cul-de-sac?" At Mark's nod, I waited until he'd turned out of his subdivision, then peeked through the back window.

"He's following us." I slid my head below the seat. "Keep driving. Find a busier road. We'll see if we can lose him in the red lights."

"How long have you been doing this sort of thing?" asked Mark.

"Hiding in BMWs?" I said. "Today's my first."

"I noticed you said BMW. Sounds like a partial truth."

"And you had your house swept for bugs. You do that often?"

"It was a first." He glanced at me. "Pardon me if this offends you, but you sound a little less sorority, a little more country the more I get to know you."

Cripes, Fin. You lost your character. Lex would be disappointed. But Mark was different. I felt like I had to go off script. "I didn't grow up in the city. I'm from south of Atlanta. I think it's safe to call my hometown country."

"Where did you meet Penny?"

"In Atlanta. I was a high school runaway. I met Penny at a shelter." I was giving away a lot. Chill, Fin. "Remember, your mom sent Penny's stuff there. They can use it."

"But not all of Penny's stuff."

I looked up at Mark. "What are you saying?"

"I know about her apartment. I know who you are. You're Finley."

I banged my head against the seat back. He'd made me. I was losing my touch. Because Mark was such a nice guy? Or did he know from the beginning because Penny had told him about me?

Maybe he knows for another reason. Don't forget, this guy is embezzling from the mob. Keep your head in the game, Fin. You don't know everything.

"Why didn't you go to your dad, the judge, about any of this?" I pointed at an intersection. "Take a right here, then another right. Cut down that side street and back onto the main road."

Mark focused on the road, eyes skittering to his rear view mirror. "I'd rather not involve my parents. They didn't like Penny. You could probably tell. "

"I'm sure they wouldn't want their son involved in organized crime, either. Penny's dead. But now you're in danger. The judge probably knows some great prosecutors who could help you. FBI, too."

"I need to concentrate," he said, whipping his wheel to the right. "I can't seem to lose him."

"Traffic is too light. Monday night." I glanced out the rear, then peered out the front window. "Do you know where the closest police station is?"

"I think so."

"Here's what you do. Drive to the station. Run inside. Tell them you need to report a drunk driver. They'll have to take it."

"Isn't that fraud?"

"It's a misdemeanor in Georgia. You're worried about a misdemeanor, Mark? You're already a felon." I shook my head. "Anyway, report the truck. You don't have to prove he's drunk, but he's acting like it. They might pick him up."

"And if they interrogate him?"

"You think this guy wants the police to know he's a cleaner?"

"A cleaner?" Mark's forehead wrinkled. "What is that? And how do you know the law in Georgia?"

"You're not talking about your dad, Mark. And I'm not talking about mine." I pulled out my phone. "Take the main strip. I think you'll be safe enough. Rick Graves won't follow you into the police station. He's a contract hire. Probably working for someone at Platinum Partners."

"He won't follow me? Where will you be?"

"I can't appear in a police station, Mark."

"Why? Are you on a wanted poster?"

"I'm texting a friend. She's got eyes on Graves. We'll coordinate this. I'll grab a ride with her surveillance crew. We'll make sure you get home safe." Lewis and Bruce were going to love this. They'd probably zip-tie me again. I'd raise holy hell if they bagged me.

"Listen, Elizabeth Ann. Finley. Whoever you are." Mark glanced at me, his eyes hard. "I appreciate that you want to protect me. You may be a hoodlum, but I'm not putting you in danger."

"Hoodlum?" I snorted. Spotted the McDonald's down the road. Tucked my phone inside the purse and flipped the strap over my shoulder. "Rick Graves is three cars back right now. We don't know if he's going to keep following you or try something. Besides, he doesn't know I'm in your car. How could he? He thinks you're alone."

"If you won't go to the police station with me, I'm taking you home. You'll stay at my house."

I didn't have time for white knight syndrome. And I wasn't being kept prisoner for my own safety again. As the BMW slowed for the next light, I opened the door and dove for the curb.

25

THE SEND

I KICKED THE DOOR SHUT. Hopped the curb, the sidewalk, and the green space alongside it. Ran into the parking lot and ducked behind a car. The stoplight turned. Mark rolled the passenger window down, looking for me, but didn't call out. Behind him, a horn honked, and he was forced to drive on.

Two cars back, the pickup rolled, then drove forward, toward me. I squatted in the shadow of the parked car, holding my breath. Didn't look like Graves saw me. He had his window down, knocking tobacco from his pipe. Head angled to his shoulder. Talking on his phone.

Where were Lewis and Bruce in the Tahoe? I squinted down the street. Between the dark and the headlights, I couldn't determine the make of the vehicles beyond Rick Graves's F-150.

I looked behind me. An AutoZone shop. Closed. I didn't want to get stuck in an empty lot. The McDonald's was a block away, my car beyond that. I took off, running bent over. Through the AutoZone parking lot. Hopped the divider between businesses. Mini strip mall. Flung myself against the sidewall and checked for the pickup. Couldn't see it.

Graves hadn't seen me. I felt bad for Mark, but if he stuck with my plan, he'd be safe. I jogged behind the strip mall, stopping at the edge to peer around. A drive connected the McDonald's to this parking lot. I'd be exposed, but there were more cars and more people at the McDonald's. I glanced at my phone and found a text from Dot.

"When u didn't show at P's apt, yr dude went back to new BF's house."

Nice. Dot calling Mark my new boyfriend. But at least I knew Graves hadn't been tailing me. Hadn't seen me climb into Mark's car. I was safe.

"BF's on the move," I typed. "Tell your boys to watch his back. Black BMW X1. Get him home safe."

"You need a lift?"

"Wheels r nearby. If BF takes trip to locals, it's to lose tail. My advice. Tell boys to wait. Don't get uptight if he takes some time in the donut shop."

"U r 1 CB."

Crazy Bitch. Thanks for that, Dot. I shoved the phone in my pocket. Fast-walked across the connecting drive and entered the McDonald's. Took a quick right to the bathroom. Called Mark.

"No need to talk, just listen," I said. "I checked with my friend. Rick Graves has been watching you most of the afternoon and evening. He doesn't know I was there. But don't worry. There are two big guys in a Tahoe watching Graves. If you get in trouble, they'll help."

"Finley, I lost the F-150. He's nowhere in sight."

"Are you at the police station?"

"I didn't need to go there. A couple blocks after you got out, he took a right. I went left at the next intersection. Haven't seen him since."

"Do you see the Tahoe?"

"Wait. Let me pull into this lot."

I danced in the stall, waiting. Why didn't Graves stay on him? Maybe he still was, and Mark wasn't good at clocking tails.

"Okay, I see the Tahoe. They're pulling in." I could hear Mark swallow. "Are they— What are they?"

"They're just going to follow you, not shake you down." Although that was probably Lewis and Bruce's specialty. "Friends of a friend."

Great. Now I sounded like Dot.

"Finley, I'm worried about you."

"You're sweet, Mark. But I've been taking care of myself for a long time." Not like this, but whatever. "I'm near my car. Call me if you're in trouble."

Cripes. *I* was in trouble. I didn't know where Graves went. I felt sure he hadn't seen me, then decided that was stupid. Sure was for horseshoes.

I cracked the bathroom door. The hall was clear. I shut the door. Wished I could call Lex. But I was off script. He was back to work with Platinum. To make our con work, I couldn't jeopardize his role. We didn't know who Graves worked for. If we had contact, they could possibly connect Lex to Mark. The last thing I wanted was to shorten the lines between Lex and these gangsters.

All right. I'm on my own. Lewis and Bruce were watching Mark. That's good. He's safe. I just needed to hotfoot it to my car. Take off.

Back to Dot's? I shook my head. Couldn't have Graves connect us. That would also blow the con.

A shelter? That had worked for me in the past. But I didn't want to endanger any of the women there.

I'd figure it out. Georgia's a big state. And there's always Alabama, Tennessee, and North Carolina nearby. Head to the mountains, maybe.

Lordy. That's a lot of driving in one day.

I peeked again. Slipped out of the bathroom. At the end of the hall, scanned the mostly empty restaurant. Didn't see Graves. Flipped up my hoodie and slid into a booth, searching the side parking lot. Didn't see the truck. Exited the booth and the door. Studied the parking lot. No F-150.

Two lots over, I told myself. You only have two parking lots to cross. You can see the Krystal's from here.

Stepped off the sidewalk and halfway across the drive-through lane, I glanced left. The F-150 idled in front of the McDonald's, hiding around the corner. Parked against the Playland fence. I bolted. Hopped the low cement wall between lots. Glanced behind me. The truck had left McDonald's.

Cripes.

Didn't want to take a longer route. My car was so close. But I ran for the dry cleaner's drive-through entrance next door. Circled the building. Panting. Lungs aching. Inhaling the scent of burger grease and french fry oil. Peered around the building. Couldn't see anything.

Next door, Penny's Honda was parked behind another fast food restaurant. The lot was separated by a thick chain stretched between cement barriers, to keep the fast food traffic from cutting through the dry cleaning lot. The chain was knee high; no problem there. But I'd have to run diagonally to hop the chain.

Couldn't wait here. Either run back to McDonald's and possibly get stuck. Or make a run for Penny's car. And possibly get caught.

I ran.

Graves waited for me again, the F-150 in front of the dry cleaner's parking lot. He'd already jumped out of the idling truck. Dashed toward me, his long legs easily overtaking my sprint. Tackled me to the ground. I hit the pavement with the palms of my hands and knees. Felt my jeans tear. He grabbed me by my hoodie, yanked me to standing.

"Enough with the games," he said. Shoved me forward. "Get in the truck."

I glanced right and left where folks drifted near the restaurants. Getting in and out of their cars. Not paying attention. Yet.

I screamed rape.

Graves dropped the hold on my hoodie and backed up a step.

It was all I needed.

Still belting out one long, continuous shriek, I ran for the Krystal's next door. Didn't look back. Hopped the chain. My voice petered out. Passed a group of teenagers. They'd pulled out phones, filming the crazy girl running through the parking lot. I fished for my keys. Pulled them out of Elizabeth Ann's crossbody purse. Bleeped the lock on the Honda. Dove inside and started the car. My body shook. My chest ached. Cold sweat soaked my neck.

I started the engine. Tore out of the parking lot, bumped into the road. Checked my mirror. The F-150 gunned its motor behind the minivan at my rear.

Graves was infuriated with me now.

I wouldn't cry. Hoodlums don't cry. Mark's safe. Lex is probably safe. Penny's in a better place. I'll get out of this.

26

THE WEIGHT

I DIDN'T KNOW my way around Woodstock. Didn't want to get stuck. I drove the main road. Ran lights when I could. Turned south on Bells Ferry. Traffic was light. But Graves stayed on my bumper. Turned on his brights, trying to blind me. I mumbled the prayers my mother had once taught me and took the right onto the highway exit at the last minute. I shot ahead of the few cars heading west. The truck was gaining.

My phone rang, but I couldn't pick up.

Where was I going? I couldn't stay on the highway. I'd hit I-75 soon. I was too far north of my roots. I didn't know any back roads up here.

Could I risk the interstate? What choice did I have?

I took the exit onto the interstate too fast. Clutched the steering wheel. Kept the turn tight. Feeling like I might flip. Telling myself not to get sick. Flattened the accelerator and cut in front of the slow traffic sitting in the right lane.

Graves stayed on me, gunning his motor. Lights blinding me. Close enough to bump me. Tapped me once and I flew ahead. The Honda veered right. Clamped my hands at ten and two, trying to cut back into my lane without oversteering. My heart beat in my temples. Fearing a bump that would send me into the sidewall, I cut across lanes to the far left. Hit my brakes to slow down.

The truck shot past me, then slowed. I stomped my brakes again. Hoped to stay behind him.

My phone rang again.

The F-150's brake lights flashed. I slowed further.

I wanted to scream, but my throat was still raw.

Another pickup, a massive work truck with an extended cab, sitting high on jacked-up tires, roared past me. Graves's truck continued to slow, trying to reach me. I pumped my brakes and fell further behind. Cars behind me honked and sped around me. The bigger truck gained speed. Switched lanes. Pulled alongside the F-150. And cut into his lane.

For three long seconds, the monster truck drove Graves's truck across the remaining two lanes of traffic. Heading for the dividing wall.

My jaw unhinged. I jerked the wheel to the right. Aimed for the shoulder. Around me, other vehicles had slowed and were doing the same.

The F-150 accelerated, shaking the bigger truck loose. Scraped the sidewall and shot ahead. The monster truck followed, this time cutting to the right lane. Aiming for Graves's left side.

I stopped on the shoulder. Slipped the car into park. Hit my emergency flashers. Watched the scene before me, but not wanting to watch. My phone rang again, but I couldn't take my eyes off the trucks.

The monster truck herded Graves toward the next exit. Nudging and bumping the F-150 across lanes until it was close to the shoulder. Keeping pace with Graves. Not letting the F-150 over.

Graves had no choice but to take the ramp. But his truck swerved left and the massive pickup plowed into it. Even at this distance, I could hear that terrible screech of metal on metal. Both trucks careened sideways. Blocking the exit ramp. Lights shone on the embankment wall.

I froze in my seat. Afraid to move forward. Couldn't go back-ward. I gasped and realized my fingers had twisted my necklace into a noose. I released the chain. My phone rang. This time I picked it up. My hello was barely audible.

"Fin." Lex's bark sounded pained. "Tell me you're all right."

"I'm okay." My voice shook. "There's been an accident."

"Are you hurt?"

"Not my accident."

"Don't cry, love." His voice broke. "My darling girl, please don't cry. You're going to make it."

"Where are you, Lex? I need you." I wiped my eyes, cleared my thoughts. "Really need to talk to you."

"Not where I bloody want to be. My spotter said the bleeding bugger's on you. What were you doing at Mark Davis's? Fin, I set this up to protect you. You keep going off script."

"How did you—" Lex had eyes on me. Whose eyes? Why wouldn't he tell me? "Rick Graves tried to nab me. I got away. He followed and tried to run me off the road. But then, this truck... Where are you?"

"I'm sorry. I'm not anywhere close. Working a job, so I have to be quick. But I... You're okay, Fin."

"Lex..." My voice trembled. "I don't know where to go. This is spinning out of control. I've never been this scared."

"Fin, we have a plan. Go to Dot's. She's waiting for you."

"But—"

"It'll work. Please trust me, Fin." He took a deep breath. "You have to trust someone. Even if he's a crook."

"But there's more to this. I need to talk to you about Mark."

A woman's voice interrupted our conversation. He hung up.

I squinted at the exit down the road. There was movement near the wreck. Police sirens wailed in the distance. I had to slide.

The sirens' wail intensified. I jammed the Honda into drive, accelerated, and moved across two lanes to the middle. I fixed my eyes on the upcoming exit. The F-150 still rested sideways in the lane. Sidewall crumpled. But the big truck was reversing. Turning around in the exit lane. The engine roared. It shot forward, down the ramp, bumping over the grassy shoulder, pulling under the underpass. The bumper hung loose.

I squinted at Rick Graves's truck. Didn't want to look, but forced my eyes to search for him. Couldn't see the driver. His passenger door hung open. The overpass street light spotlighted a figure scrambling up the shoulder toward the road above.

Behind me, the police sirens howled. My heart hammering, I sped forward and passed the big truck. It pulled out behind me. Took a deep breath and looked over my shoulder. A giant man sat behind the wheel. In the glow of the dashboard, it looked like Jeffrey.

Lex's eyes were Sue Marshall's. He'd made a deal with her. Or she'd made a deal with him.

WITHOUT A PLAN, I returned to Dot's, hoping she wouldn't barricade me in the apartment. The devil I knew seemed preferable to all the unknowns hiding in the dark.

"You okay?" When I'd arrived, Dot paced toward the door to meet me, robe billowing out behind her. Adidas squeaking on her wood floor. "What happened?"

First time I'd heard Dot sound concerned. I explained the truck pile-up and my escape. "Did Mark get home safely?"

"Lewis and Bruce are there now. Said it's quiet. The mother left before Mark returned." She chuckled. "They're ticked they missed that scene on the interstate. They don't like surveillance duty. They're bored. Call it babysitting."

"So kidnapping me was a break from boredom? They get a kick from zip-tying people?"

"I told them to keep you quiet. That's what they came up with." Dot opened a cupboard and pulled down another box of cereal. Cinnamon Toast Crunch. "The cleaner hasn't shown at Mark's yet."

"Rick Graves will need a new vehicle first." My knees felt like jello. I grabbed a kitchen stool and sank onto it, not wanting Dot to see how the truck chase had affected me. "If he's after me, why does he keep watching Mark's house? Just hoping I'll show? I think I'm missing something."

"Why'd the cleaner want to meet you at Penny's?"

"I don't know. He wants information on Penny. And wants her keys. But he got in her apartment before, looking for something. So what keys does he need? To her car?"

Dot set two bowls on the counter. Grabbed milk from her under-counter fridge. "Maybe he didn't take Penny's cache. That's why he's stalking you and Mark. He thinks one of you has it or knows where to find it."

"But why would a mobster know about Penny's greyhound money? Mark paid off her momma's debts."

"Mark did what, now?" Dot laid down her spoon and cocked her head. "Speak up, girl."

"Earlier tonight I learned a lot about Mark and Penny. The relationship was legit."

"No." Dot folded her arms. "She was working a job."

"And she fell for him. Dot, she told him everything. He forgave her. And he used his trust to pay off what Penny's momma owed. But he didn't know about the markers."

Dot shook her head. Her brow furrowed.

"He doesn't know about you. Don't worry."

"That's not what bugs me."

"You mean, how could someone like Mark love someone like Penny? Especially knowing she was trapping him into embezzling." Dot opened her mouth, but I cut her off. "Mark said Penny changed. She was working for you. You must have noticed something."

Dot focused on her cereal like she wanted to keep her mouth and hands busy. The thought of Penny and Mark shook her, maybe more than it did me. She set her spoon on the counter and looked up. "How much were those markers?"

"About fifty grand."

"That's about what her momma owed." Dot sighed.

"Penny kept her mother's markers? She wasn't sentimental." I held up a spoon. "Maybe she wrote them to herself. To pay back Mark."

"Could be. Penny always paid her debts by working. She didn't like owing."

"Did she tell you she wanted out? Before she was killed?"

Dot shrugged and turned away from me. Rinsed her bowl and put it in the little dishwasher that pulled out from under her counter.

"Dot, I'm just trying to figure out what really happened to Penny. That's all I've been doing this whole time. And now I've got this goon trying to kill me. Maybe going after Mark. There's more to it than folding this con."

"Penny was worried about someone." Dot leaned back on the counter. Her chin lifted, looking down at me. "Wouldn't tell me who. And she did want out."

"Did you know Platinum Partners was blackmailing Mark into skimming from his company?"

"I didn't know the details, but I had a pretty good idea they weren't running no charity."

I'd found Dot's sore spot. She might actually have remorse over Penny's death. Which might explain why she was helping me. "This would have been a lot easier if you'd told me in the beginning."

"Wasn't your business back then." She crossed her arms. "Still ain't, except now there's a cleaner after you."

"Did Lex know in the beginning?"

"Wasn't his business, either. Not until Leopold offered to take Penny's place. And that was after you showed up here acting all high and mighty about Penny. Then went AWOL on him again."

"Lex offered to take Penny's place? I thought you hired him."

She spoke quietly. "You assume a lot, Finley."

My heart sped up. "Why did he offer to do Penny's job?"

"I think you know why."

"And now he's in deep with Platinum. Had to go back to work to help me shut it down."

She pursed her lips. "You're so stupid, Finley."

I really was stupid. And now Lex also owed Sue Marshall for my protection. "I've got to make sure this double-cross with Platinum works. We've got to shut it down to get Lex out."

"Maybe you should've thought of that before you went running off to get yourself killed by that cleaner. You're paying back Lex real well. Only so much that man can take. He hates it when you go off script."

Lex said I had to trust someone. I should have trusted him. Now I had to trust Dot. It almost physically hurt, but I needed to face reality. All this time, I'd thought hating on Dot was street smarts. But a lot of it was pride. I'd run hustles with Lex, but I didn't want him doing jobs for Dot.

I was the one with the flawed ethics, using wrongs to make things right. And going with gut instincts instead of carefully laid plans.

"Dot, there's more to the story with Mark. But before I tell you, I need some kind of promise swearing you won't get involved with Mark."

"You afraid I'm going to hook up with Penny's dude or somethin'?" She squinted. "Or is this to do with the skim?"

"I'm willing to owe you for this."

Dot's teeth gleamed. "Must be worth a lot."

"It means changing our setup. Lex needs to know. I think the party will still work. And the press conference bit, but we're going to need to tweak the plan."

"I'm listening."

When I finished telling her about Mark's embezzling efforts, she whistled. "Penny's little man has a dark side."

"I think it's a light side," I said. "He's trying to do the right thing."

"I don't know about that, Finley. Robbing people is still robbing people."

27

THE IN-AND-IN

DOT and I stayed up most of the night, brainstorming and strategizing. Said she'd try to update Lex. I would do the same with Mark. Dot didn't trust Mark. I worried she couldn't contact Lex.

We both feared the cleaner ending the charade altogether.

I dressed as Elizabeth Ann, headed to Midtown, and parked a few blocks from Mark's building. Took my time scoping the area. Looking for Graves. And Jeffrey. Waited for Mark in the lobby when it seemed clear.

"Elizabeth Ann." Mark shook my hand, glanced around the lobby. "A nice surprise. What can I do for you?"

"We need to make some adjustments to our party." I tapped the crossbody bag slung over my shoulder. Spoke loud enough for the receptionist to hear. "I brought some samples for you to check. You know. Paper goods, centerpieces, that sort of thing. I also have a large floor plan I'd like you to look at. Do you have an empty conference room? I think it'd be better to discuss this somewhere besides your office. There's a lot to spread out."

He nodded, motioned for me to follow. Spoke a few words to the receptionist about using a conference room.

In the elevator, I apologized for showing up at his office. "I thought it might be safer than your house. Security would spot Graves hanging around. And I figured you wouldn't want me in your actual office."

"And Mother won't bother us here. Sorry about last night."

"What would she do if she thought we were involved?" I said. "I thought Miss Melanie would stroke, seeing me at your house. She doesn't like you slumming, Mark."

His cheeks heated. Kept his eyes on the blinking floor numbers. "Slumming is a harsh word."

"I'm serious, Mark. Would the judge take a lot of heat if you got engaged to someone like Penny again? I don't know how your society works. Where I'm from, it'd rain down all sorts of hellfire on my parents. People talk. And they'd keep talking, even if things didn't work out."

"Just what are you saying, Elizabeth Ann?" Mark turned to me. Took my hand. Winked. "Are you proposing?"

I winked, squeezed his hand, and smiled.

AFTER WE WENT over the plans, Mark and I had lunch at Noodle. Dot was right. The Bibimbap was tasty. And Mark understanding.

He drove me to his county courthouse. Helped me obtain Penny's death certificate. Neither of us was family, but someone recognized him as the fiancé. The son of a judge can pull a few strings.

"The pronouncer's the EMT," said Mark, studying the form.

We strode through the courthouse. His eyes on the certificate. My hand on his sleeve. I guided us to the front doors.

He handed me the paper. "I recognize the name from the ambulance crew. But that name on the bottom, he's not the county coroner. A medical examiner?"

"No." I halted on the front steps, slipped the paper into my satchel, and scanned the parking lot. "You met him the night

Penny died. John Prince is a coroner, but in a different county. And now I finally have some real evidence against him."

"That night was a blur," said Mark. "The shock of finding Penny, I guess. My parents arrived to help me."

"Your parents were there?"

"I called them, and they came immediately."

"So they knew how Penny died." I cocked my head. "Your mom told me Penny had a heart attack."

"Technically, Penny's heart arrested. Mother was embarrassed." Mark shoved his hands in his pocket. Kept his eyes on his shoes. "You're right. This is going to be hard on them."

"I thought Penny's death had something to do with your father. Platinum trying to get their hands on a judge."

"Nope, my dad's clean as they get. He'd never allow any of this to happen. Would have shaken Penny off, if it had been him. He takes his job very seriously."

"He would have let Penny take the heat?"

"Judge Davis has met a lot of criminals. He's not known for his compassion."

"Did your parents know who Penny really was?"

Mark's head snapped up. His eyes hardened. "I'd never betray Penny like that. They were cold enough to her. I'd rather deal with Platinum Partners than my parents. That's why I took money from my company, rather than our family bank."

"That's one thing we have in common. I chose criminals over family, too." I patted my satchel. "But now I have something that will help me deal with mine if it ever comes to it. Thanks, Mark."

He drew me into a long hug. "I should thank you, Elizabeth Ann. Finley. Whoever you are. No one I know would have done what you have for someone like Penny."

I looked up at Mark and winked. "You forget, I'm like Penny, too. And we ain't done yet."

WHILE MARK RETURNED to work that week, I returned to Dot's. I'd promised to keep to our new plan. She'd let me out to do the job. I played hoops behind the garage to keep from crawling the walls. Also to avoid her zoo. The Gila monster looked at me funny.

Ellie had a meeting with Tony Riggle on the Friday before Valentine's Day. Lex planned to have Ellie appear at the Platinum Partners Valentine party to assist with the sting. As reassurance after my previous party fail, Riggle required my in-and-in. We also needed Riggle as insurance for the sting. I needed to collect more than a party invite today.

Ellie had asked to meet Tony Riggle at the office where they'd had the interview. He persuaded her to meet him at Octane Coffee Bar instead.

Ellie didn't know that office had been a temporary front. But I did.

Coffee, tea, or me, I thought, walking through the High Museum courtyard. The Octane he chose was connected to the Woodruff Arts Center complex next door. Hip, sleek, and modern. Smelling delicious. I grabbed a house blend in a ceramic mug and waited. Octane closed at seven. Easy for Riggle to wriggle away without commitment.

Riggle entered, bought his coffee, and slid into a chair across from me. Inched it closer. "Ellie, it's good to see you. I heard you haven't talked to Brian or anyone else since the last party. Are you still coming?"

"Frankly, dude, I'm still not comfortable with what happened. How can you assure me that guy is not going to be at the party again? I found out his name. Rick Graves." I slipped my hands beneath the table. Felt for my phone in my pocket. Slipped it onto my lap. Leaned forward. "I joined this club to get away from jack-asses like him."

Riggle leaned forward. Began to nod. "I apologize for what happened. It was completely inappropriate. He won't be there. As I told you earlier, he was kicked out."

About one nod per second. Riggle was good. Trying to make

me mirror him. Feel more positive. He adjusted his tie. Preening. Wanting to win me over.

I gave him an encouraging nod. "Yes, but I think I just want my money back," I said, showing him I wasn't completely certain. Wanting him to convince me. Make him think it was his idea to convince me to go to this party.

"I'm sorry you feel this way." He placed his forearms on the table, palms up. "I swear to you Ellie, if that guy shows up, I'll personally get rid of him."

I clasped the coffee cup he had just touched. Like I was considering his request. Movement near the window caught my eye. My concentration slipped. I glanced over. Jeffrey peered through the window.

Did that mean Graves was near? My heart sped up. I felt sweat break out on my neck.

I quickly swung my attention back to Riggle. Looked at him over my glasses. Touched my hair. Hoped my makeup wouldn't sweat off. Did Riggle hire Graves? But Graves had questions about Platinum. Still didn't make sense. Maybe Graves went to the party to check on Riggle.

My thoughts spun away from our original narrative, picking out a new storyline. If Graves was nearby, I needed to work fast. A quick blow-off to get rid of Riggle. But not before I got what I needed.

"Dude, he could have attacked me. Seriously. Rick Graves pulled me into an alley. Luckily, I puked on him. And…" I lowered my voice. Widened my eyes behind the glasses. "The more I think about it, I believe he roofied me. I'm good at holding my liquor. That's the only explanation I can think of. What if he starts stalking me? I mean, shouldn't I report him to the police?"

Riggle took my hand. "I appreciate what you've been through, Ellie. So much." He squeezed my hand and let it go. "The man should be in jail. You're right. Let me look into it for you. We have lawyers. They can file the necessary paperwork."

"Won't the police want me to make a statement or something?"

He patted my hand. "Of course. Email it to me and I'll give it to our lawyers."

"Are you sure? Sounds like a CYA."

His face reddened. Didn't like the mention of company protocol to protect themselves. I had to play it cool. He might try to shake Ellie off as too much trouble. But I couldn't pass Ellie off as completely naïve. She was smart.

"I just want to make it easier for you," said Riggle. "But you have to do what's right."

"All right. I was really hoping to meet a nice guy. I'm so disappointed, to be honest. With the horse app taking off, it seemed like good timing." I dangled my bait, knowing they were interested in my hacking abilities. "I'm being courted by a new opportunity. App development for cybersecurity. If I take it, I'll be too busy to do the dating stuff."

"That's exciting." He touched my coffee cup, then clasped his hands together. "What do you say, just one more party before you decide to quit? I'd hate for you to miss an opportunity to meet your soulmate while you still have free time. This party will have a different mix. Plus it's Valentine's Day. Everyone's in the mood for love. I'm confident you'll meet someone."

I winked. "There's always you, Tony."

He laughed and pushed his chair back. "I'd really get in trouble with the members if I started scooping up all the hot prospects."

Nice save, Riggle. I watched him rise, giving the impression he was taking his time, even though I knew he was dying to leave. I wondered if he hated the job. Was Riggle just a contract worker or sent from one of the organizations to head Platinum Partners?

"Before you go." My finger twisted a lock of hair. "Can I have the name of your boss or the president of Platinum Partners? I want to write them about how you handled this Rick Graves situation."

"You don't need to do that. It's my job."

"I'm happy to do it. It might mean a promotion or pay raise for you. And if it goes to your boss directly, they'll know it's legitimate."

"Why don't you give me the letter in a sealed envelope at the party? I can deliver it to my boss for you."

Excellent, I thought. Just what I hoped he'd say.

28

THE BOTCH JOB

I WAITED until Riggle had left. Stood near the window in front of a newspaper rack to track his movement off the property and to the street. Took Riggle's coffee cup to the bathroom. Pulled out a roll of tape and eyeshadow from Ellie's backpack. I dusted his coffee cup with the shadow, then applied the tape. Stuck it on a piece of paper, filed it in Ellie's bag. Pulled out my phone, uploaded the picture I took of Riggle while he bought his coffee. Then uploaded our recorded conversation to the cloud.

That done, I needed to escape the coffee shop before Graves found me. I slipped from the bathroom. Stood to the side of the wall of windows and peered out.

No Rick Graves.

This was getting old. And scary. I'd parked in the garage behind the complex. MARTA was nearby. I could cut through the courtyard to the street that ran behind the arts complex. Bypass the parking garage. If I crossed that street and cut through the bus loop, I could enter the subway. But if Graves hid nearby, there was a serious chance he could nab me anyway. Better to hit Peachtree Street. More people around. Catch a ride.

I was spending a lot on Uber these days.

Wait, I had a bodyguard. And I was in disguise. Rick Graves looked for Elizabeth Ann. Although Ellie had driven her car.

I found Jeffrey skulking around the sculptures in the High's courtyard facing the Woodruff. Looking decidedly unimpressed. And bored. I dropped Ellie's frames in my bag and donned a large pair of sunglasses. Shoved my hands in my puffy, down-filled coat that emphasized Ellie's size and strolled around the three-dimensional house that looked like a two-dimensional drawing.

"Anyone else around?" I said as I passed Jeffrey.

He covered for his double-take by sneezing. Jeffrey hadn't known Ellie either. Probably why he was peering in the coffee shop window.

I stopped ten feet away to admire the piece. I could see Jeffrey around the corner from the brightly colored installation.

His shoulders lifted slightly.

I turned my back on the house. Jeffrey would follow me to the parking garage. Must have parked there too. I cut across the lawn to the pavement, scanning the various entrances to the buildings. Jeffrey lumbered somewhere behind me.

In the parking garage, I chose the stairs. Penny's car was parked on the third floor. The stairway smelled musty and slightly putrid, like old garbage. But I didn't like the way an elevator opened. A surprise each time. My boots clattered on the metal runners. I hurried, not wanting to find myself trapped in the narrow stairwell.

At the bottom, I heard Jeffrey's long-winded sigh. Not a fan of stairs, I gathered.

On the third floor, the thick stairwell door had a small window. I shoved my sunglasses to the top of Ellie's wig and stood on my toes to peer through the wire-hatched glass. The door faced the elevator. I couldn't see the parking area beyond. I glanced behind me, listening for Jeffrey's labored breath or heavy steps. Heard neither. The behemoth took his time, hating those stairs.

I turned back to the window. Saw a man gliding around the corner of the elevator bank.

Graves.

Wearing that trench coat he favored. He reached inside the coat. Facing the elevator, back to me. I shrank from the window, flattened against the door. My body didn't want to seem to move.

Slide, Fin. Slide.

I shot toward the staircase, hissing a whispered warning to Jeffrey. Began retracing my steps. Treading on my toes for silence. Gripping the handrail, so I didn't do something stupid, like fall.

A loud pop broke the silence. I turned to look up. Then hung over the banister to look down.

No Jeffrey. Had he run out at the sound? Waited for me at the bottom?

My heart leaped into my throat. Another crack, no mistaking the noise this time. Sounded like a firecracker in a metal can. I pulled in the rotting stench and held it a second, willing myself to stay calm. Let it out slowly. Adrenaline rushed in. Pushed my feet down the stairs. I ticked off escape routes in my head, letting my feet do the work. Taking a break from thinking about what I'd just heard.

On the bottom stair, my thoughts snapped back. I lurched out the open entrance to the stairwell. Glanced at the elevator. Heading to the first floor.

Jeffrey had taken the elevator. And he or Graves were on their way down.

In the stairwell, a metallic boom reverberated. The stair door. Someone was coming down the stairs.

I couldn't be caught in the garage. Or the open courtyard.

Heavy footsteps clattered on the metal stairs. The elevator had passed the second floor. I darted around the side of the vestibule wall. Rows of cars filled the first-floor parking.

Hide along the wall? What if he finds me? I couldn't make a quick escape trapped between cars.

The elevator pinged. I peered around the corner of the wall. The doors slid open. My breath caught in my throat. A rushing roar filled my head.

Jeffrey lay in a heap on the floor. Head against chest. Back against the wall. Legs sprawled. One blossoming spot of red growing on his coat. One long line of red on the wall behind him. His hand held a gun. Some kind of pistol.

I bit my lip hard. Spots danced in my eyes. I squeezed them shut.

I could do this. No choice. Just go.

I opened my eyes. Dropped the sunglasses back to my nose. Forced my body to cross the small vestibule in two leaps. Jumped into the elevator, nearly stepping on Jeffrey's knee. Shuddering, I hit the close door button. Pushed the number three. And smacked the close door eight more times. No emergency stop. My finger wavered over the alarm. I pulled it back.

"Jeffrey." The words sounded like a long gasp. "Hang on. I'm going to get you out of here."

Whipping away from the open door, I slunk into the corner opposite Jeffrey. Stood on my toes, holding the stupid puffy coat close to my body. Trying to shrink against the wall. Fixed my eyes on a point that wasn't Jeffrey or that splash of color on the wall.

Listen for Graves. Just keep cool and listen.

The doors began to slide shut. I heard him now. Feet slowing on the stairs.

Please close faster, I prayed. Let this elevator take me away before Graves notices the elevator moving at all.

The doors shut. Jeffrey and I crept back to the third floor. Heard my breath shooting in and out of my nose before I registered the dizziness. My face felt hot and my body felt cold. My head reeled. I looked down and my stomach bubbled up my throat. Burned hot in my chest.

This man's shot because of you, Fin. He may still be alive.

Holding my breath, I knelt next to him. Kept my eyes on the elevator door and used my peripheral vision to check for a pulse. Hyper-blinked, closed my eyes, and opened them. My fingers felt far away from my body.

When I was twelve, my mother, expecting me to become the

neighborhood babysitter, had brought me to the hospital to learn CPR. I had done so well, they thought I could follow the rounds. Dressed me in scrubs. A future nurse in the making. The first room needed a simple suture. A child with a long cut on his arm. The doctor sat before the child. He turned on his stool to motion me over. Pulled the cotton gauze away and a drop of blood hit the floor.

I'd passed out before they'd threaded the needle.

Jeffrey's breath came out in a rattling hiss. Eyes wouldn't open.

You can't pass out on him. Don't vomit, either. That man just saved your life.

The voice in my head sounded like Mom's. But it'd been so long since I'd heard her voice, I wasn't sure.

"Jeffrey? Are you still with me?"

He clutched the pistol in one hand. Was his hand shaking? Maybe he wanted to lift the piece. I covered his hand.

"It's okay, Jeffrey."

A tremor wracked his body. Beneath my hand, his muscles strained.

The elevator shuddered to a halt. The swing and teeter all the more apparent while kneeling on the floor. My stomach moved with it. I shrank against Jeffrey, my breath shooting out in short gasps.

The doors slid open. I saw his feet and the bottom of the coat. Without hesitation, Jeffrey's gun lifted, angled up toward Graves. And fired.

The feet—dirty brown boots—slid backward. The coat swung open. I turned my head, hunching my shoulders. Heard the gun fire again. Deafening in the small space.

But not enough to silence the awful thud of a body hitting concrete.

The doors banged. The elevator teetered. And the grinding creep began again.

My head jerked up. The number three button glowed through

Ellie's tinted shades. Graves had tried to catch us on the second floor.

I forced my eyes to Jeffrey. And realized my hand still covered his. I had lifted his gun arm. Jeffrey's fingers were clamped around the butt. My fingers covered his.

Except for the one still inside the trigger guard.

I dropped his hand. It thudded against his thigh. I raised my eyes to the ceiling. Searching for I didn't know what.

Could I still save Jeffrey?

I pressed my fingers against his thick neck. They came away sticky. I blew out my breath slowly. Propped up the sunglasses with my free hand. Forced my eyes to look at his face. Then his beard. Finally his neck. Saw the blood oozing from the back of his head. Jerked my hand away. Then held my hand over his mouth. I needed to be sure.

Had I been holding a dead man's hand? Shot another man with a dead man's gun?

Gagging, I wiped the area I'd touched on his neck and backed away. Pushed myself to standing. Careful not to touch the walls. Wiped the buttons with my sleeve. Couldn't believe I thought to do it even as I was doing it. But my body had disconnected from my brain. Which suited me fine. The top of my head felt like it would spin off.

The doors opened. I half expected to see Graves, grinning and holding his piece. My final words I'd hear on earth would be some smart-ass comment about my shooting skills.

I stuck my head out of the elevator, searching the empty vestibule. No Graves. Some idea tried to push its way forward. The memory of that thump. A body hitting the floor. I shoved the thought away and turned back to stare at Jeffrey. My breath slowing. The dancing dots receding.

Jeffrey was gone. Except for his body. And I couldn't report it. Couldn't give testimony. I couldn't move him. This was a crime scene. Besides, Jeffrey was too heavy to move.

I knelt again. Forced slow breaths in and out of my mouth.

Kept my eyes off the splashes of red. I searched his pockets, like some kind of graveyard thief. Left his handgun. He didn't have ID on him. But I took his phone and wallet anyway. And a ring he wore on his pinky.

A class ring. He'd played football. And wrestled. A few years younger than me.

Poor Jeffrey. He'd become another crime statistic, marring this beautiful area of town. Frightening the tourists from the High and the Atlanta Symphony Orchestra. I liked the art museum and the ASO. And now some out-of-towners would be too scared to try them.

I hit the emergency alarm with my elbow, hoping security would show before a tourist found him. My anger snapped me out of my funk, tearing off some screen that had fogged my brain.

Graves. My heart shifted, began to thrum like a bird's.

I might have killed someone. And I was too afraid to look.

29

THE BOOSTER

I HAD THREE CHOICES.

Stay and let the police take me in.

Descend the stairs to the second floor and look for Graves. A sheriff's daughter should know enough to check to see if he was truly dead. Try to save him if he wasn't.

But I was the kind of sheriff's daughter who took choice number three. Heeled it to my car and got out before security showed. Representing the kind of sheriff whose daughter would take the coward's way out.

But this was on me, not him. Making me no better than the sheriff or these gangsters who killed to suit their narratives.

After I escaped Peachtree Street traffic, I tried to call Lex. He answered as Oliver. My voice wouldn't work. I gasped and gulped, but the words wouldn't form.

I hung up, pulled to the side of the Connector, and threw up.

Sobbing, I navigated out of Atlanta. Outside Buford, I pulled over. Cleaned myself up. I used a number Sue Marshall had given me and left a message that I was coming with bad news. Made it to the mountains by memory. Finding her house on a dark road was tricky. Spent the entire trip searching for the right words.

In the end, I just handed her Jeffrey's wallet, ring, and phone.

Sue stared at the items, then motioned me inside the cabin. I followed her down the hall of old weapons and into the cozy den. Once again, a fire blazed and the TV flickered silent news reports. I felt like I was inside someone else's story.

"What happened?" she said, moving toward her desk.

I stopped on the rug before the fire. Rubbed my hands on the puffy coat. I'd torn Ellie's wig off in the car, but my hair still felt sticky with sweat. My face greasy from the heavy makeup. Tried to clean my hand with wet wipes and couldn't quite get the grime off. Like that woman in the Shakespeare play we were reading when I quit high school.

Damn spot.

Needed to get it together. Not the place to have a meltdown.

Sue turned from her desk, lit cigarette in her hand. "Was it the cleaner?"

I jerked a nod.

"Don't stand there shaking," she said. "Sit down."

"I'm sorry, ma'am." I sank onto the edge of a leather chair. "He caught us in a parking garage. At the Woodruff Arts Center. It'll be big news. I didn't know what to do, other than take his personal effects and leave him."

"How was it done?"

"Two shots. One in the chest. One hit the back of his neck. He was in an elevator. I don't know if he spun around or maybe the bullet ricocheted..." My voice trailed off. That was something my father would have speculated. It didn't matter. Jeffrey was dead either way.

"And you were?"

"In the stairwell."

Her eyebrows followed the pluming smoke. "Why wasn't Jeffrey in the stairwell with you?"

I shrugged. "I don't trust elevators."

"Damn fool." She sucked hard on the cigarette and wandered to the window on the far wall.

"Rick Graves was waiting in front of the elevator on the third floor. Probably hit Jeffrey as soon as the doors opened. Then I got in the elevator with Jeffrey on the first floor. He must have punched the button before falling. Graves caught us again between floors. And I..."

My brain stuttered. Should I make a confession to someone like Sue Marshall?

That person inside me, the one who kept me alive when I was seventeen, screamed, "No!"

"Jeffrey," I continued, feeling the shame burn up my spine and heat my neck. "Had his piece out and ready. We got off two shots before the elevator closed."

Exasperation rather than sorrow punctuated my sigh. I was no longer seventeen. And even if I had killed Graves, I wasn't cold-blooded. "I mean, I fired the two shots. Jeffrey was dead by the time we reached the third floor. I got out without checking on Graves. Grabbed Jeffrey's personal stuff but left the weapon. Thought it best for discovery. In case there were questions..."

Because I was gutless. Because I wanted the police to think Jeffrey had killed Graves. I was never getting out of this hole I had just dug. Unless I gave myself up.

In the window's reflection, I could see Sue examining the growing ash on her cigarette. Mouth pulled tight. Lines deepening like trenches.

"I'm sorry, ma'am. Really sorry." Felt the dam ready to burst again and had to swallow to keep that misery from bubbling over. It wouldn't be appreciated here. "Jeffrey kept me alive on the inter-state. I didn't even know he was there. For such a big guy, I couldn't sight him. And he had my back today. I owe Jeffrey my life."

"You'll need someone new."

My heart lurched. This woman was all brass tacks. Jeffrey wasn't even cold. "I don't know..."

She cocked her head. "If there's a contract on you, they'll send someone else. You plan on bailing?"

"No, I've got to see this through. Too many people depend on this working." Felt another shudder working through me. "And I need to make right what just happened."

"I'll take care of his family. They know what Jeffrey does."

Jeffrey's family. His parents? Or was he married? Kids? My stomach squeezed.

"Tomorrow's the Valentine party," I said. "If it works like we planned, I was thinking afterward… It might not be too late to go to the police. Even anonymously—"

"Girl, you listen to me." She strode to the desk and stubbed out the cigarette. "You want to help Jeffrey, you're going to keep your mouth shut."

"It's bad enough I left a murder. I was a witness. I could be—"

"The cleaner shot first. What you did was self-defense."

I swallowed back whatever words wanted to escape.

"Was there a camera?"

"I don't think so."

"Did you leave prints?"

I shook my head.

"At least you had the brains to take care of that. I'll make some calls. Find out what's happened and what I can fix."

"But—"

"I'd advise you to not say another word on this subject."

I stared at the fire. Wondering how I always managed to make wrong out of trying to do what I thought was right.

"Let me think about who should cover you now. According to Jeffrey, you can occasionally shake a tail, but you ain't so good at hiding out. He burned a lot of gas following your GPS movements."

My head jerked up. "Lex has you tracking me with my phone."

Sue gave me a look like she couldn't quite judge how big of an idiot I was. "Yes. Anyway, I'll discuss it with Leopold. It's better if you don't know who I assign. I should've pulled Jeffrey off after the truck incident, put in someone new."

I took a long breath. Turned back to the fire.

She strode from the desk to sit across from me. "You're chafing at that, ain't you? Me taking this up with Leopold. Because you want to run the show instead?"

"Because I don't want there to be a show. Because I don't know what Lex owes you for this. I feel like something y'all are bartering over. And I'm in the dark about his part of the trade-off."

"Ask him."

"Lex won't tell me. He doesn't tell me anything." I relaxed my fists and flattened my palms. "That's not the point. He's paying a price for me that he shouldn't have to pay."

"That's his problem, not yours."

"It is my problem." I wanted him to follow a different path and he couldn't if he owed people like Sue and Dot. But I couldn't explain my screwy moral philosophy to someone like Sue Marshall.

"We can make a transfer." Sue leaned forward. "I don't care who pays me, as long as I get paid."

"I don't have that kind of money."

"Neither did he. You can work for me instead. I'd prefer it anyway. I'd rather deal with my own kind."

That's what I feared. Lex working for Sue Marshall. This wasn't grifting. Her clan played hard and dangerous. Real gangsters. Not even meeting Dot's wannabe aspirations. I'd be expelling one measly demon for seven newer and bigger ones.

"You don't want to work for me." Sue smiled slowly. "I'll make it easy on you. An introduction. That's all I need from you. I think Jeffrey's life is worth at least that, don't you?"

Dread sent icy shivers trickling down my back. She didn't care about Jeffrey. Lex and I saw this coming. She'd known who I was from the beginning. Wouldn't have dealt with Lex otherwise. She didn't trust him. Had tried to play me against Lex, hinting I'd end up like my mother.

Lex and Dot had seen through her. Lex was willing to offer himself instead of me. For my protection. Why hadn't he just used Dot?

Because I'd hated Dot. He didn't want me fighting with her

and getting in trouble. On account of this demented notion of good and bad I'd created.

"You want me to introduce you to Sheriff Goodhart." I kept my voice calm. "You know I've avoided him as much as possible the last ten years. He ruined my life."

"You've wanted freedom more than revenge. You fear him." She paused, letting that fact sink in. "But he hasn't bothered you in a long while. If you were to pop up on his radar, I think he'd take notice."

She knew a lot. But Sue Marshall didn't know, because of Penny, I now had my revenge. Or at least some ammunition, in the form of a bogus death certificate, that would help me get my revenge.

"I'm dead to the sheriff."

"But your *father* doesn't want you dead." She paused. "Unlike other people."

I cut my gaze toward the fire, not wanting her to see the fear and anger I felt fizzing in my veins. I gripped the chair arms to keep myself seated.

The last time I tried to get my father's attention was by getting arrested. He'd dismissed the charges. Wouldn't even let the arresting officer question me. But did have a female cop beat the snot out of me to teach me a lesson. She'd apologized after. Said some kids had to learn the hard way.

The sheriff knew I skated along the edges of the underworld. But to make this kind of introduction meant I'd moved into serious crime. That could draw more than a beating. He wouldn't want the association. And he'd resent my interference.

Sue was wrong. Sheriff Goodhart might actually want me dead. He banked on keeping his name clean in the right circles. And keeping it dirty in the wrong ones.

This wasn't the revenge I wanted. But if I did this for Sue, Lex would be safe from her. If I didn't, she'd use Lex like she did Jeffrey. Replacing one fallen soldier with another. But not as a bodyguard. Lex wasn't physically intimidating. She'd use him for running guns, drugs, or something even worse.

Lex would hate me for trading my life for his. Not out of pride but out of fear for what would happen to me. After the way I'd treated him... Dot was right. There were limits to what a man could take. This could end us for good.

"This introduction would wipe Lex's debt to you?" I said.

"We'd shake on it."

"I don't want anyone new for Jeffrey. I'll dig in. Not much time left until the party anyway." After the party, I didn't care much what happened. I'd have to attend to certain consequences.

"Suit yourself." She tapped the chair arm. "Do we have a deal?"

"I'll make a deal. But I need to clarify the terms."

I'd do this for Lex. And hoped he'd forgive me.

30

THE BILL IN

DESPITE THE EARLY morning hour and my exhaustion, I drove out of the mountains. Didn't want to be anywhere near Sue Marshall. I was closest to Mark Davis's house, but I chose to shoot south of Atlanta to Penny's apartment in Newnan. I collapsed on Penny's torn-up bed and cried myself to sleep.

Didn't waste too many tears, though. I was that tired.

Sometime before dawn, a noise woke me. Shivering, I crawled into the closet and rolled myself into a ball. Heard the bedroom door open.

"Fin?"

I pushed open the closet door. Could barely make out Lex in the dark. He stood for a moment, a dark shadow searching the room, then turned on the light. His haggard features pulled together. He dropped to the floor. Crawled into the closet and gathered me into his arms. I didn't realize I was shaking until I sank against his chest.

"It's all right, love. Whatever happened, it's all right."

"Do you know what I've done?"

He tipped my face back. "I only know you're here and alive. And that's all I care about."

Pulling me to my feet, he led me back to the bed. Laid down

next to me.

"On my phone, I saw you leave Atlanta and drive to the mountains. And that was after you tried to call me." He kissed my hair. Tightened his arms around me. "I can see where you are, but I can't see you. Thought it'd gone all pear-shaped."

"In a way, it did."

"What happened? Why go to Sue Marshall's?"

I squeezed my eyes shut. Curled into him. "I can't tell you. But after we're done tomorrow, I may have to cut out. For good."

"No." He placed his lips near my ear. "Don't let her use you. I've got us covered."

I couldn't tell Lex what had happened in the garage. But I rolled over to face him and placed my hand on his face. Stroked his cheek. "Lex, I think I know where Penny's money is. It might help. If things do go...pear-shaped."

"Keep it safe." He rubbed his cheek against my hand. "Tomorrow is tricky. We've not done anything like this before. Did you confirm with Bev? And Jelly? They'll motor you out of town. My people are ready to go. The reporter, too."

"They know what to do."

"Fin." Lex's hands cupped my face. "I had hoped that one day we'd... Like Mark and Penny. I've never wanted that—never thought about it—with anyone else."

I opened my mouth, but he shook his head. Kissed me quiet.

"Don't say anything yet. I've been thinking about what you said. About getting out of the grift. Or at least using it to help people. This, what we're doing for Penny, has been the hardest thing I've ever done. Especially watching what you're going through. Not being with you. But I can see how much it means to you. To fix what happened for Penny."

"Lex..." I longed to tell him that I wanted it, too. After seeing Penny's engagement picture, I'd almost envisioned a life with Lex. But now it was too late. I'd killed a man. A bad man. But still, I'd taken a life. I couldn't have Lex caught up in that any more than I could have him working for Sue

Marshall, or even Dot. Especially since he was doing it for me.

"I've done enough to screw up your life." I ducked my head into the crook of his neck.

"Guilt doesn't do you any good, remember, love? It's all about restitution." He drew his arm around me.

"I'm trying, Lex. But it's not my past that haunts me now, it's my future. And it might be better—"

"Don't say anything more, Fin. Let's just sleep."

In the morning, he was gone.

I did a final search of Penny's, then hauled butt back to Dot's. Gave her the print of the greyhound chasing the rabbit.

She admired the painting. Said it wasn't her style. But I heard her humming as she ducked down the hall to put it in her bedroom.

"Why'd you go to Penny's last night?" said Dot when she returned. "Still looking for her money? You know, they're still looking for her money, too. Last place you want to be is Penny's. That's where they'd want to take you."

I shrugged.

"You up to something?" Dot squinted at me. "What's the matter?"

My face felt hot. "Besides Penny and Lex, I haven't had a lot of friends in the last ten years."

"So?"

"I'm sorry for how I've been acting toward you."

Dot cocked her head. Looked down her nose. Then slapped me on the shoulder. "'S'all right."

"I still think you're a bad influence on Lex."

"I still think you're a two-bit hustler. But you ain't a bad roommate."

"Dot, you might hear something about me. Later. In the wind. Don't get any ideas. Just know what I'm doing now, it's for Penny. And what I might do later, that'd be for Lex."

"I swear I've met some stupid people in my life, but none as stupid as you." She flung her hands in the air. Strode to the wall zoo and peered into a large tank. She spoke to a turtle. "I don't want to know her business. Why she have to make everything so complicated?"

"I know you're doing this for Penny, too," I said. "No matter what you tell yourself."

The turtle lunged. Snapped at Dot. Slid into the muddy pool. Dot looked over her shoulder. "Get ready. Big job today. You don't have time for all this preaching."

———

THE PLATINUM PARTNERS' invitation had announced their Valentine party would be held at a small venue in Buckhead. After triple-checking our preparations, I drove to Mark's house so we could be seen arriving together. Lewis and Bruce had already parked in front of Mark's. That was Dot, not taking any chances. She was keeping her eyes on the prize—Mark. Dot still assumed Jeffrey would watch me at the party. As part of my deal with Sue Marshall, I'd agreed to keep my mouth shut about his death. And Graves's.

I cleared my head of other thoughts on the drive up to Woodstock. I needed it firmly back in the game. Put yesterday's tragedy behind me to fix everything for Penny, Mark, and Lex. And all the people Lex had gotten to help us. Focused on a trick I used when I was younger, when my situation got me down. I imagined a room inside my head. A closet inside the room. A box inside the closet. Placed the thoughts and feelings about my parents and former life inside the box. Closed the lid. Locked the closet. And shut the door on the room.

Today I shut the door on Lex. And Penny. Jeffrey, Rick Graves, Sue Marshall. Dot. Even the sheriff.

I only opened myself to the characters we'd play. Today I'd stick to my narrative.

For the most part.

At Mark's house, I saw his dog Elmore grinning at me through the window. And felt a little better. Mark's garage was open, a space waiting for Penny's car. After I parked, he opened my door and took my hand. Helped me exit gracefully.

"Elizabeth Ann. You look beautiful."

I felt my neck grow hot. I'd worn a little black dress featuring a flashy collar-to-hem zipper and knockoff Manolos. Both had figuratively fallen off of one of Dot's trucks. "Not too bad yourself, Davis. Nice suit. How's Elmore?"

"I think he misses you."

"Probably misses the fries. I should have brought him a bone or something."

"Your carriage." He opened the BMW door for me.

"For not dating much, you seem to know what you're doing."

"I had several years of cotillion."

"Me, too." I shrugged at Mark's raised eyebrows. "Life before the streets."

I put a package in his trunk, then slipped inside the car holding my purse and a large satchel. Felt like Cinderella. With a bag full of glass slippers.

However, my illusion might not make it until midnight.

The drive to Atlanta wasn't awkward. Almost like we were on a date, speaking only of the evening's plans. Two blocks before we reached the party, he pulled over. I hopped out with the satchel. On the sidewalk, I leaned into his open window.

"I won't be long." Touched his cheek. Felt his smile in the palm of my hand.

"Be careful."

I sauntered toward the front door of Sixes. Paid my admission to the club and wove between clumps of partiers. Found the bathroom. Changed in a stall, balancing in my heels to climb into Ellie's padded body suit. Elizabeth Ann wore a chignon, which made it easier to slip on Ellie's wig. The makeup was trickier in the bad lighting, but I'd brought inserts to stuff inside my cheeks to round them out.

Dressed as Ellie, I found an empty table. A DJ set up on the stage. The club starting to fill. I set my satchel on the ground near my chair. Slipped my phone from my purse and studied it. Held it to my ear.

"I liked that dress," said the man at the table next to me. "Pity you had to change."

I didn't glance over. Didn't trust what I'd do at the sight of him. "Dot found it." I spoke into my phone, but Lex could hear me. "It's also practical to wear under these clothes."

"A zipper is practical for many things." I could feel his snigger but knew it disappeared quickly. "I don't see your eyes. Where's Sue's man?"

"I'm okay, Lex. Just have to get through tonight."

"What about Mark Davis?"

"He's fine for now. We'll see how it goes." I pretended to dip into my purse, looking for a pen. Glanced over at Lex. He was also on a phone, texting. Looked up. Our eyes held for a long moment before we broke away. I scribbled on a napkin. "I trust Mark now. I like him, Lex."

"I can tell."

"You were right about a lot of things."

"Only one thing that's really important, love."

"I'll miss you."

He sighed. "Better late than never, yeah?"

I left the napkin and the satchel, and moved through the crowds and out the door. Mark had left to park. I hurried to the restaurant, Ellie's platforms already making my feet ache. The day had been warm—typical Atlanta February—but the temperature dropped with the sun. No puffy coat today. Didn't want the hassle of ditching something that big. But the cold didn't affect me. My nerves were juiced. The thrill of the game had grasped me. My excitement tasted as sharp as the air. My pulse hammered with each step.

Same feeling I used to get, running cons with Lex or Penny.

I reached the restaurant without incident. Mark waited in front.

He carried a computer case slung around his shoulders. As I reached him, he cocked his head. Searching my face. Elizabeth Ann was gone. I had bigger everything, including the blonde hair that feathered around my face. My platforms, tinted lenses, and scarf disguised the rest.

"It's me," I said, reaching him.

"Wow." He scanned my body. "The car is with the valet."

"Good. You'll get it back later." I smiled. "Are you ready?"

He offered his arm. I tucked my elbow through his. Inside the restaurant's entryway, the same bouncer from the previous party sat on a stool.

I held out my phone. Licked my lips. Wondered if the bouncer recognized Ellie.

"Are you together?" asked the bouncer. "This is a singles party."

"We met at your last one." I held up my phone. "Here's my invite." Didn't print it this time in case I needed it for Elizabeth Ann.

He studied me, then Mark. Crossed his arms. Taking his time to think through Platinum's dating structure and this anomaly.

"Isn't that the point of your parties?" I said, using Ellie's snark. "To find dates?"

Beside me, Mark shuffled his feet. "I need to talk to Riggle."

Keep cool, Mark.

The bouncer scanned my phone. "You're in." He eyeballed Mark. "Invitation?"

Mark fumbled for his phone. Held it up for the bartender to scan.

We pushed through the door and separated. Mark headed to the bar to speak to Tony Riggle. I hung back. Giving him time for the setup. We were only to be seen together by the bouncer. Cover if anyone later asked questions about how Elizabeth Ann got into the party. Throw shade at the bouncer.

The venue was more traditional, more elegant, than the last. A small stage had been set up in the front window. A three-piece jazz band played. Ice buckets filled with champagne decorated the tables. Hearts hung on wires. Roses bloomed from vases. Most of the patrons stood near the marble-topped bar. They looked simultaneously hopeful and uncomfortable. A mix of dress casual and business wear.

A server approached us. "Are you Ellie?"

"Tony Riggle's expecting this." I handed her Ellie's envelope.

She winked. "Right."

I scanned the room for Lex. My stomach lurched. Found him at the bar. Sitting with the older woman from the previous party. She talked. He smiled. Filled her glass with champagne. He'd swapped the hoodie for a button down. Blonde hair, still rumpled. Glasses. Hunched shoulders. Oliver looked more like the professorial assistant from Jello's bar than the tech nerd from the Platinum Partners mixer.

I turned my back on Oliver. Glanced at my watch. Took in the rest of the scene. Mark had his laptop open on the bar. Typing. Around him, couples drank and talked.

Tony Riggle pushed through a swinging door. And spotted Mark at the bar.

Showtime.

I took on Ellie's heavy, clumsy stride. "Hey, Tony," I said, intercepting him. "I'm here."

"Nice to see you, Ellie. Let me catch you in a minute. I've got to greet someone." His glance strayed toward Mark. Gave me a dismissive pat on the arm and began to walk away.

"Yeah, I kept going back and forth about everything." I stayed behind him. Within earshot. "Thinking about how everything works here. I'm still a little confused. But I thought I'd check it out one more time."

"Why don't you grab a table?" Riggle spoke over his shoulder. "We can talk more in a minute."

"And came to some conclusions," I continued. "After doing some research. Like major research. Which, admittedly, I should have done before starting this process."

At the bar, Mark had set up his laptop between couples. Riggle shouldered his way next to him. I followed. The couples, looking irritated, moved down the bar.

"What are you doing?" Riggle whispered to Mark. "Not here."

"This is the last time I'm doing this," said Mark. "It's now or never."

"You know that's not necessary," said Riggle. "Put away your computer."

"Don't you want to hear my conclusions, Tony?" I raised my voice. "I even ran some of my hypotheses in my testing software."

"Riggle, can I talk to you for a minute?" Lex pushed his way into our huddle. "A bit of an emergency is brewing."

The back of Riggle's neck had turned a deep crimson. He spun to face Lex. "Not now, Oliver. I'm busy."

"I don't think this can wait."

"Did you get my envelope, Tony?" I blinked at him behind Ellie's glasses.

Sweat beaded on Tony Riggle's temples. His eyes locked on something behind me. I turned to look. In the entry hall, a camera team argued with the bouncer.

"That's what I'm trying to tell you, mate," said Lex. "A news crew is trying to barge in."

"Yeah, that's kind of my fault," I said.

"Ellie?" Riggle glanced over his shoulder.

"Riggle, I'm leaving in a minute." Mark stuck his hand between us. "Give it to me now. We agreed this is the last time."

Riggle pivoted, slapped a piece of paper in Mark's hand, and headed for the front door.

"You got this?" I murmured to Mark.

He turned back to the laptop. "I need ten minutes."

"You're on," whispered Lex. "I've got Mark."

I hurried across the room, Ellie's vivid floral pantsuit billowing around me. Pushed past Riggle and yanked the door open.

"They're with me," I said.

The bouncer pivoted on the stool. The reporter and cameraman scooted around the bouncer and rushed through the door.

"What's going on?" said Riggle. "This is a private party, Ellie. If you have an issue, we need to talk privately."

"I tried doing that yesterday, Tony. You're just not listening." My voice rose. Couples at the closest tables stopped chatting to watch us. I moved around Riggle, leading the crew into the restaurant. Stopped at a central point between the tables and bar. "Maybe you'll talk to them. Explain what's going on here."

The reporter shoved her microphone toward Riggle. "Hi, I'm Stephanie Nix with the Consumer Fraud Investigation Team. We had a call about this organization perpetrating to be a singles matching club, but our sources tell us you're actually backed by a criminal organization."

"What?" Riggle stepped back. Halted. Widened his stance. "I'm sorry, but you were told wrong. We're a private club acting as a matchmaking service. If this woman told you we're doing something illegal, she's seriously deluded. In fact, she's been stalking me."

"Stalking?" I pursed my lips. "I don't think so. I've talked to you twice since the last party, but only because I was roofied and attacked in an alley."

Stephanie adjusted the microphone. "Tell us more. Who roofied you? Were they connected to Platinum Partners?"

"No more." Riggle thrust his hand in front of the camera lens. "This is a private event. Get out."

"Sorry, but we're live," said Stephanie. "Everyone watching the seven o'clock news can see you. You might want to handle this differently."

"What?"

She pointed. On the flat screen above the bar, a hand slipped from view, revealing Tony Riggle. The server placed a remote on the bar and walked away.

I smiled and waved at the camera. "Hey, Atlanta. Happy Valentine's Day!"

"And that's exactly why we're here," said Stephanie. "No time like Valentine's Day to reveal deceptive scams bilking poor, trusting souls looking for love. Like Ellie Davis."

Around us, a crowd grew. Riggle was trapped between me and the reporter. Nothing draws people more quickly than a professional video camera. Some stood behind us, waving at the camera. More stood behind the camera, concern growing on their faces.

Riggle spun around to face me. "What are you doing?"

"I have a friend who's a cop. I told him how you wouldn't let me report getting roofied and almost murdered at your last party."

"Almost murdered?" said Stephanie.

"Or raped. If I hadn't puked on his shoes, who knows what could have happened in that alley."

"And I said I'd handle it," said Riggle. "The guy's not here. He was kicked out."

"Yeah, except he wasn't a client, was he? Rick Graves? He's what they call a cleaner."

"A cleaner?" said Stephanie. "Like with a maid service?"

"No, like with the mafia. He's contracted to clean up messes. Sometimes of the people variety." I sliced a finger across my throat. Behind me, someone gasped.

Stephanie thrust the mike in Riggle's face. "So what was a contract hitman doing at your party?"

"I have no idea what you're talking about. I don't know any Rick Graves."

"How'd he get into your private party?" I said. "Maybe one of your bosses gave him an invitation?"

"Maybe he got in the same way your reporter did," said Riggle. "You're just trying to throw false accusations at the organization because we couldn't get you a date."

I noted Riggle's clenched jaw and rigid posture. Knew I'd gotten him close to the line of no return. But I didn't want him to blow. Yet. I dropped my eyes to the ground. Shuffled my feet. Let him think he'd humiliated Ellie.

"Who are your bosses?" said Stephanie to Riggle. "We did

some digging and Platinum Partners doesn't even have a real address. We checked with the Better Business Bureau and the Chamber of Commerce. They have no information on Platinum. All you have is a website."

"We're very exclusive. We deal with businesswomen and men who have considerable assets and need to protect their privacy. Do you think these developers and CEOs care what the Better Business Bureau has to say about our service? Our record speaks for itself."

"Maybe they should care." Stephanie turned to me. "And what do you do, Ellie?"

My eyes drifted from the bar to the camera. Mark had just closed his laptop. No more stalling. "I'm a software app developer. Kind of interesting how—and I don't mind tooting my own horn, Stephanie—an excellent researcher such as I am couldn't find anything legitimate on Platinum. Although the dark web revealed a lot of interesting information. I've met a few black hats who love to dish dirt. Particularly their knowledge of illegal or underground activity."

Total bull on my part, but the flicker of astonishment on Riggle's face revealed he hadn't thought about the dark web.

I smiled at the camera. "Turns out Platinum Partners was created by a partnership between four Atlanta criminal organizations. They do the usual mobster things—drugs, prostitution, and gambling—but Platinum is their romance scam. It's called a badger game. And it's very lucrative."

"We have a high price because we throw amazing parties. And screen all our clients carefully," said Riggle. "That costs money."

"What's a badger game?" said Stephanie.

"The badger game is based on extortion. Everyone here is supposed to be a legitimate business person, right? Platinum's salted the parties with their own people. They only allow hookups between their people and the legitimate singles. They'll totally block you if you try to meet someone for real. Then, after love blossoms, the bogus lover is exposed. And the poor mark is blackmailed."

"Wow," said Stephanie. "That happens here?"

"No, it doesn't." Riggle wiped the sweat from his brow. Searched the heads around him. His staff had disappeared.

"It's simple and profitable to blackmail rich business types," I said. "They're easily embarrassed. And they don't want to involve the police. Usually. They'd rather it just go away. And will pay to have it do so."

"So who's fake and who is real?"

I grabbed Lex, who had conveniently sidled next to me. "This guy, Oliver, hit on me at the last party. And another guy named Brian. Neither one is the rich tech geek they claim to be. A few simple questions showed me that."

"Is your name even Oliver?" asked Stephanie.

"Uh," said Lex. "I... Riggle, what do I do, mate?"

"See what I mean?" I said.

"And I'm one of the jilted lovers," said Mark, speaking into the microphone on the stage. "Let me tell you what happened to me."

31

THE FALL

EVERYONE in the room turned to face Mark. I sidled away from the knot of people surrounding the reporter. Felt the handle of my satchel touch my hand. I grasped the bag and backed toward the bathroom.

The reporter and cameraman broke from the circle to approach the stage. Riggle pulled his phone from his pocket and began typing. Behind me, Lex had already disappeared into the bathroom hall.

"Hello, everyone," Mark's voice boomed. "Happy Valentine's Day. I first came to a Platinum Partners event four months or so ago. I met my future wife at my first event. Didn't start dating her until after the second party. I hope y'all get as much happiness as I did when I met her."

A smattering of applause worked through the room.

"So is Platinum Partners a scam or not?" called Stephanie.

Riggle's face changed colors like Dot's frogs. Pink to white to mottled red.

Hurry, Mark.

"I can prove to you that it is. And much worse." Mark's voice shifted. Tears wetted his eyes. "My fiancée, Penny was murdered. Made to look like an accident."

The room grew hushed.

I slipped into the ladies room with my satchel. Five minutes later, Ellie had disappeared. I was Elizabeth Ann again. The server waited for me outside the bathroom door. Knee propped, scrolling on her phone, tray beneath her arm.

"Hey, Luann." I handed her the satchel. "Dumpster, at another business if you can. Did Riggle get the envelope?"

"He has it. Don't think he's had time to look at it."

"Dot's got you covered?"

She smiled. "This job is easy and pays well."

"Get out front as soon as you can. There's a car waiting." I handed her my Burberry. "Thanks."

I exited the hall. Mark held the room spellbound, telling Penny's story.

Lex, now dressed as Carter, leaned against the wall. He'd changed into a bow tie and jacket. Hair swept back, glossy brown instead of blonde. Glasses gone.

"Riggle's disappeared into the kitchen. Probably took off," he said into his phone. "But his backup will arrive soon."

I moved toward the stage, tucking Elizabeth Ann's small purse under my arm. Stepping carefully to distinguish Elizabeth Ann's sway from Ellie's lumbering stride. Didn't glance at the vestibule, where a buzz of voices could be heard through the door.

"Most men would sensibly end the relationship. I'm not a sensible man, I suppose." Mark gazed down at me. There was a radiance about him that I'd not seen before. The quiet aloofness had disappeared, replaced by a charismatic passion.

I gave him a reassuring smile.

"I confronted Penny. She confessed everything. Including the fact that Platinum Partners was a sham and that she was a willing accomplice."

Mark held out his hand. I took it and stepped onto the stage. About fifty sets of eyes fell on me.

"After Penny came clean, they threatened her," Mark continued. "They demanded outrageous sums I couldn't cover. So I began embezzling for them in order to protect Penny. At their suggestion. Skimming from my own company. Some of you might be doing the same. I'm sorry if this puts you under investigation, but I believe you'll be protected if you confess. The blame should go to the perpetrators in charge of this organization."

Mark jerked his thumb toward the door. "The police are here with warrants. Not only was this on the news, but they're also here to arrest me. And take the management into custody."

A rush of whispers spread throughout the room. The front door banged against the wall. Two uniformed cops and two men in plainclothes entered.

Lex had moved to the bar, watching the police spread out. One uniform hurried into the kitchen. Another toward the bathrooms. The detectives covered the front entrance. Leaned against the wall to listen. Two of Platinum's shills moved toward the door and were stopped by a plainclothes detective.

The reporter, still holding the mike, motioned for Mark to continue.

"This woman is Elizabeth Ann. She was Penny's best friend. Elizabeth Ann's persisted in helping me discover the truth."

I stepped into Mark. He slipped an arm around my waist, and I allowed him to draw me closer.

Over the commotion of the guests, the microphone caught Mark's voice breaking. "Elizabeth Ann has also helped me to face up to my part in this crime. And I'm willing to give myself up. I've already turned in all the information to the FBI. Including the bank accounts where Platinum Partners had me deposit money."

I pressed my head against Mark's chest, tearing up. Wiped my eyes and grabbed the microphone. "I'm willing to help Mark Davis, no matter how long it takes, because he's a good man. A brave man. Penny was brave, too. Platinum Partners is run by the real criminals. They don't care whose lives they ruin."

More noise erupted from the entry hall. One of the detectives rushed out the door. The other moved toward the stage.

Mark held up a hand, motioning to the officer. "Can I just have one minute before I go with you?"

Taking my hand, he sank to one knee. Shouts erupted from the bar. The reporter moved in, catching Mark's voice on their microphone.

"Elizabeth Ann, this is horrible timing," said Mark. "But these last weeks have taught me that our time here is short. I'm in love with you. Will you marry me?"

My heart stuttered. I couldn't look at Mark. My gaze hadn't left Lex. He had gotten off his stool. A hand clenched his mouth, then dropped.

Mark squeezed my hand.

I mouthed, "Sorry."

Lex flinched.

I closed my eyes.

Better for him to think this than know your other plans, Fin.

Opening my eyes, I gazed down on Mark. "Someone needs to make up for what happened to Penny. I swear I'll spend the rest of my days trying to do that. You deserve it. You're a good man, Mark Davis. You're not a crook."

The crowd erupted. My ears rang. I didn't dare look at Lex, knowing those last words had spelled out my final answer.

Mark stood, gathered me into his body. Leaning over me, he kissed me on the mouth.

In the midst of the clapping and cheering, I'm not sure if the singles understood what had really happened. The detective motioned Mark from the stage. The crowd began jeering. Booing. Mark squeezed my hand and stepped off the stage.

I followed Mark outside, putting on the coat the server handed me. Two cars had parked in front of the restaurant. A door hung open on a black Mercedes. Mark's mother sat on the passenger seat, talking on the phone. Catching sight of Mark, she hopped out of the car. Pushed past the cop ushering him to the other car.

"Mark, what is going on?"

"How did you know I was here?" said Mark. His voice uneasy, confused.

I moved forward to embrace Melanie. I could feel her stiff body trembling beneath me. Not from the cold, though. I stepped away.

"Elizabeth Ann called me," said Melanie. "She announced you were going out for a special Valentine's Day event. And that I should come. That I'd want to be here. What did you do?"

Mark's victorious glow dimmed. I touched his arm. He slipped his hand into mine. Melanie's cold eyes took in the small gestures.

I licked my lips. This part was harder than I thought. "I'm so sorry, Mark. You didn't want your family to know about this. But I thought it was important for your mom to be here. I didn't want your parents seeing this on the news."

"Mark," said Melanie. "Why are you here with Elizabeth?"

"I guess you'll find out anyway." He took a deep breath. "Big night, Mother. Elizabeth Ann has agreed to marry me, and I've been arrested for embezzling. But she's sticking with me. Penny would have done the same, I know it."

"Embezzling?" She rocked back on her feet. Mark caught her before she fell. "Not possible."

"It's complicated, but I'm hopeful I'll beat the rap." The plain-clothes officer had sidled between us. Mark bent to kiss his mother on the cheek. "Elizabeth Ann can explain everything. I've got to go with the police."

"Police?" She shrieked and gripped Mark's arm. "You're not going with them. Do they even have a warrant? You need a lawyer. Don't go anywhere."

"Miss Melanie, he gave himself up." I reached to take her by the arm. She swung back, cold-cocking me with her elbow. I stumbled.

Mark broke free from his mother's grasp and grabbed my shoulder. "Are you all right?"

"I'm okay. Mark, you need to go. Now." I glanced behind me, saw the crowd spilling onto the sidewalk. The reporter and crew were behind them. "I can handle it from here."

The officer motioned Mark toward the car. Melanie grabbed his arm, sobbing his name. He patted her hand, broke free, and slipped into the back seat of the car. I backed from the curb. The car pulled away.

I took a deep breath. Rubbed my sore nose.

Melanie stood on the curb, face ashen and wet with tears. I almost felt sorry for her.

Almost.

I'd had my suspicions. Mark's reactions to his mother. His difficulty with relationships, which had nothing to do with his personality. Rick Graves had been in Penny's apartment. He must have been looking for her money or evidence of it existing. Now I knew, besides me, only Mark had known about that apartment. Platinum Partners wouldn't have sent their hit man to the victim's apartment a week after Penny was iced. If Penny owed them money, they would have shaken down Mark for it.

Penny's markers were made for Mark to pay him back for her mother's debts.

Melanie would have known when Mark had cashed in on his trust. I doubted she knew why. Mark didn't want her to know anything about Penny. Why he later skimmed from his company instead of the family. A one-time payment he could play off. For numerous blackmail payments he'd have to answer to his father.

But even a one-time withdrawal had made Melanie suspicious. She didn't like Penny and, granted, it was a hefty sum. Melanie hired Rick Graves to dig into the matter.

At least that was my best guess.

Besides Mark, Melanie was the only one who'd known I had been at Mark's house the night Rick Graves tried to run me off the road. Graves hadn't seen me slip from Mark's BMW. He was on the phone. Likely with Melanie. His stalking had taken a sudden malevolent turn for someone who, earlier that day, had wanted information—Penny's keys and my help to find the money. Malevolent, like his boss had just discovered another Penny getting cozy with her son. A boss who no longer cared as much about the information as getting rid of the new Penny.

I had invited Melanie to the party, hoping she'd see Mark's performance. Hoping it would shock her into some kind of confession we could get on video.

My conscience hoped I was wrong about Melanie. I wished the murder of Penny and attempt on me was all just gangster-related thuggery. It would be easier on Mark, even if it meant a witness protection relocation.

On our drive to the party, he'd told me he'd sent in his notice and quietly cleaned out his office. His company would find out on Monday.

Poor Mark.

Our reporter had moved toward the sidewalk. She'd seen Melanie's emotional display and wanted the reaction shot. I moved in with a half-hearted interception. A little reverse psychology for Melanie. "I'm sorry. I doubt Melanie wants to talk right now."

"Ma'am." Stephanie ignored me. "Did you want to say anything? We're the Consumer Fraud Investigation Team. Did you know your son embezzled money from his company because Platinum Partners was blackmailing him?"

Melanie stared at the reporter. "This is the club's fault?"

"We were right to suspect them, Miss Melanie," I said. "We were able to help Mark, just not in the way we originally thought."

"Help Mark?" Her nostrils flared. "How does this help Mark?"

"He's free from them now. By admitting his crime, he can help close Platinum Partners for good. The police will have his evidence. I'll be with him every step of the way."

"My son is going to jail? Because you talked him into it?" She turned to the camera. "There's no way my son is an embezzler. He has money. He doesn't need to steal. It's the fault of this woman and her friend. They're the reprobates."

The reporter thrust the microphone between us.

"Maybe we should talk about this somewhere else," I said.

"I don't need to speak to you, Elizabeth Ann. You may have fooled Mark, but you haven't fooled me. I know what you really are. This was all a scheme to sink your claws into my son. And his money."

I placed a hand on my chest. "I'm not interested in Mark's money."

"That's what your type always says." Melanie's laugh was brittle. "Penny was taking from his trust. And now I've found out she turned my son into a criminal."

"But Miss Melanie, it's not Penny's fault. You once told me you hired someone to investigate her. Surely they would have found this connection." My voice rose, filled with vindication and anguish. Using emotional bait to disguise the hook. "How could Rick Graves not suss out what was going on with Platinum Partners?"

"She's right," said Stephanie. "How could an investigator miss the criminal organization in disguise? Was Graves not qualified? Couldn't you have hired someone better?"

"I didn't hire him to investigate Platinum Partners, just Penny," she snapped. Caught the edge in her voice reverberating in the microphone. Took a beat to calm down. "I should've had him probe Platinum Partners. That was my mistake. But Penny Forbes was the real mystery. Our investigation couldn't find anything. I knew what that meant. My husband deals with criminals all the time. But my son didn't believe me, and look what happened. Who paid the price? My son. How is that justice?"

"Penny paid," I said quietly. "She was murdered."

Melanie hurled a venomous look at me. "She was a drug addict."

"No, she wasn't. That was the tip-off."

"There's always the first time." Melanie lifted her chin.

"Yes, when someone makes it look like an overdose," I said. "Too bad the body was cremated before an autopsy was done."

"I thought an autopsy was mandatory in an overdose," said Stephanie.

"I've had enough of your interview," said Melanie. "I need to see to my son."

"Don't you think you've done enough for Mark?" I said. "You had his fiancée murdered. If he had trusted you, he could've had his father take care of Platinum Partners and not get into this embezzlement nightmare. But he knew you and the judge would have tossed Penny away like dirty laundry."

"She was dirty laundry." Melanie's voice deepened. "You think he doesn't trust his own parents? I've been trying to protect him all along. The world is a terrible place. Mark's naïve. Women have always taken advantage of him. Made him forget his place. Who we are and what we represent."

"Mark's not naïve. He's gallant. And a grown man."

"He let Penny steal from us. And, it turns out, his company. Mark obviously needs protecting. Do you know what this could do to my husband's reputation?"

"Have you ever asked Mark what he needs?" I felt a hand on my arm and realized I was shaking. Checked myself. I'd lost my narrative. Gotten emotionally involved. But I needed more. Hoped I still had her hooked. "And is that why you hired Rick Graves to kill Penny? And attempt to kill me?"

Melanie blanched. But I'd let the line go slack. She pressed her lips together. Wouldn't bite.

The tug on my arm became an insistent pull. I stepped back. Lex stepped forward, his hand held out to Melanie.

"Let me assist you, Miss Melanie." His mannerisms made him somehow seem taller and larger than Oliver. "Carter Lexington. I met you at your country club. Penny's celebration of life?"

"With her," spat Melanie, glaring at me. "I'm leaving."

"Yes. An unfortunate turn of events. I see she hopped from me to Mark. But I'm here for Mark. Said I'd help him and I keep my promises." He turned a cold eye on me. "Funny how Mark spoke of timing in his proposal. Time was short? I think that's what he said."

I opened my mouth, then snapped it shut.

"Carter Lexington," said the reporter. "Can you tell us how you and Mark Davis decided to call our investigation team?"

"I believe we're done." Placing a hand on Melanie's back, he helped her move toward her car. The reporter and cameraman following, still peppering them with questions.

Time was indeed short. I glanced at my watch. Looked up and squinted down the street.

I'd taken too long. Let Melanie provoke me. Hadn't stayed on target. And lost.

One of the plainclothes detectives stood watching the proceedings. I peered at the cop. Jerked around. Hadn't he driven off with Mark?

"Carter," I called. "Wait. Just let me talk to you for a minute."

He opened the car door for Melanie, helping her inside. Ignoring me.

Who had Mark, then?

32

THE BUTTON

CARTER HAD GOTTEN into the car with Melanie. He'd keep her occupied. Waiting for me. I don't know how much Lex had heard or guessed. But his patter could last all day if needed. Jelly had parked down the street. In two minutes, the valet would bring Mark's car around. I would walk around the back of the car to enter on the street side. And when Jelly's vehicle approached, I'd step out, bounce over the hood, and stage a hit and run. On myself.

An old scam, but it almost always worked. Mark's car would block the sidewalk voyeurs' view. I had a cackle-bladder in my purse—a corn syrup and stage blood concoction—ready to blow when my head hit the ground in the fake accident.

From a block over, Bev readied an ambulance to take me away. The valet/waitress, Luann, would be on scene to help. The uniforms would exit from the alley and block the gawkers.

Lex believed Rick Graves was alive. He'd felt certain if Graves saw my staged accident and word got out that Elizabeth Ann had died, it would be a case of all's well that ends well. As he'd put it. Particularly because we'd have folded Platinum Partners by then.

Platinum's people would believe Mark was in jail. Investigated by the FBI. They'd steer away from him. Elizabeth Ann would be dead. Ellie had melted away. Carter Lexington, too. Oliver, they already knew as a con. He would have split like the other Platinum cupids.

That left Finley Goodhart and Lex Leopold. But we weren't in anyone's system. And we had some protection through Dot.

But Lex didn't know I was going to turn myself in for Graves's death. I'd planned on having Bev dump me at the nearest police station.

But who had just swooped in and taken Mark? That wasn't in anyone's plan.

I pushed past the crowd on the sidewalk. Moved toward the detective standing at the edge of the crowd. During my scene with Melanie, he had inched toward an alley entrance, where Mark's car had been parked.

"Hey," I said. "Where's your buddy? Did he take Mark Davis in the unmarked car?"

"That's police business, ma'am. You can wait for his call or wait at the station, but it'll be a while." The detective staying in character. Wondering why I was trying to break from the script.

I rolled my eyes. "Can you please just answer my question? I thought you had taken Mark to the police station. Was it the other guy?"

He shrugged. "There was already a driver."

He knew my role but didn't stick to his. Perfect. I popped into the alley. The uniforms leaned against Mark's car like they were guarding it. In reality, just smoking and waiting. At least they were in the right spot.

I returned to the plainclothes hire and lowered my voice. "If you can, call Jelly. Tell him to wait." Made a quick turn toward the restaurant. I had about a minute. Maybe a minute and a half.

The other detective was to follow the ambulance in Mark's car. We'd all meet at Dot's. Her garage would store Mark's BMW—I made her promise not to strip or sell it—and Mark would take a quickie Mexico vacay. Call the FBI from Cabo. But Lex and I would be free.

Or at least, Lex would.

Had the detectives switched roles? Or had I confused them? I needed to find the other guy. Lex would feel edgy, wondering about Melanie. Curious where I had gone. Suffering the steam from my not a crook line and Mark's proposal. I'd gone off script. Again. Withholding information. Should have told him my suspicions about Melanie. But I couldn't tell him about killing Graves because I'd promised Sue.

I needed to know Mark was safe before I took my hit.

A few of the patrons still milled on the sidewalk, excited by the drama, not seeing the whole picture. Most had figured the scam as legit and gone home to call their lawyers. A third had split because the con had folded.

I hurried inside the empty restaurant. That left...

Tony Riggle. Why hadn't he bounced?

"Hello," he said. "I don't think we were properly introduced earlier."

"I'm just looking for the police."

He pursed his lips. "Sorry, can't help you there."

"That's not true." A voice called from the partially open kitchen door. The door swung open. A man pushed through. He wore a sheriff's Stetson and khakis, not the navy uniform of Atlanta city police. Even at his age, he was still slim and toned, which worked with the proportions of his below-average height. But his voice resonated as someone much taller and bigger, his confidence larger than the city of Atlanta.

I stumbled backwards a step and caught my hip on a table.

"Watch yourself, Finley," said Sheriff Goodhart. "You never did look where you're going."

"I take it you two know each other," said Riggle.

"I'd say so," said my father. "What do you think, Finley?"

My heart had leaped up my throat, then shrunk to a pebble and splashed into my stomach. Ripples of fear spread through my torso, traveling down my legs, freezing my feet in place. Sealing my lips shut.

"Got yourself into trouble with this one, did you, Tony?" The sheriff glanced back at Riggle.

"It wasn't her." Riggle shook his head. "Another woman. But I think this one's dating one of our fish. Or at least working him. His deal was a total FUBAR situation. Claimed our girl, Penny knocked him, but he copped to the weight and still paid out. Then she overdosed, and he called murder. We were going to get one more payout tonight before we dropped him."

"You should have dropped him before the overdose." His hat shaded his face, but I felt the sheriff's eyes on me while he spoke to Riggle. "Got a little greedy, Tony?"

"We were going to close this enterprise soon, anyway. It'd gone on long enough."

"Going to and should have are two entirely different things."

"It wasn't an overdose." I swallowed back the surprise of hearing my thoughts leave my mouth. "And you know it."

"Do I?" said the sheriff.

"Your coroner does. He signed the death certificate. In the wrong county."

He swiped at the nonexistent lint on his sleeve. "John's drinking again. He gets confused."

"Is that what you told everyone about Mom?"

His chin tilted, lighting his face.

I steeled myself against the venom heating his eyes. "I think the FBI won't be amused to hear John Prince went on a bender and ended up signing a death certificate in the wrong county."

"The FBI?" He snorted. "Always a dreamer. And full of too much sass. Too smart for your own britches."

"Wonder why."

He was on me before my brain registered he'd moved. Hand around my throat, pushing me into the table. Felt it cutting into the backs of my thighs.

"Do not try me, girl." He jerked me a centimeter higher and dropped his hand.

I lost my balance and fell to the floor. Looked up, trying to see him through the red swarming my vision. "One day it's going to catch up with you, *Daddy*. But I'm not interested in your payback —today. Today's payback is for Penny. And Mark."

Pushed to my feet, my eyes now on Tony Riggle. He had an elbow on the bar, chin in hand. Smirking.

"This shop better be closed," I said. Hoping our guys had Mark somewhere safe. That the smirk was meant for the father-daughter showdown and not because Platinum had intercepted his fish.

"I know your fake story didn't air on the news. You got someone to feed the camera to our TV," said Tony.

"It's still taped. The TV was for your clients. They're not going to have anything to do with you anymore. Did you notice how many had their phones out? This is all over YouTube and Twitter. We don't need the news." I folded my arms. "Besides, Mark Davis did send the bank account information to the FBI. Did you forget his dad is a superior court judge?"

The sheriff turned toward Riggle. "A judge. What kind of idiot are you?"

"The money's overseas. They can't touch it."

I laughed. "That's what you think. You've lost everything."

The sheriff swung back to face me. "You realize what you've done?"

"Don't even think about it. Lay a hand on Mark, and you'll have the feds and every honest cop in Georgia on your ass." I narrowed my eyes. "Y'all won't be able to pee without someone watching. Tell your bosses that. And I don't mean the taxpayers."

"You think that'll stop us?" said Riggle.

The sheriff held his hand up. Riggle's eyes darted from the hand to me.

"Did you look at Ellie's envelope yet, Riggle?"

He patted his jacket. The smirk disappeared.

"Yeah, transcripts of your conversations with her that I'd taped. Plus your fingerprints. Those are with the FBI, too. I'm sure they'd take a plea if you give up someone good."

"You're messing with the wrong bull, girl." The sheriff pointed with his pinky and pointer. A reminder from my childhood. Showing me the horns. "Mark Davis can't protect you from this."

"I know that." I lifted my chin. The Georgia penal system awaited me. There was freedom in taking the punishment I deserved. "I've been hiding from you for years. I'm done hiding."

"You're both wrong."

Sheriff Goodhart dropped his fingers. I made a shaky pivot. Lex leaned against the wall, ankles crossed.

How long had he been standing there? I rubbed my temples. I needed him with Melanie. She could still confess. Plus, she might get away.

"Are you—" said the sheriff.

Lex skipped the introductions. "Mark Davis can protect her. Through marriage. She won't have to testify against him, and the judge can have the feds keep an eye on Finley. Which would be an even bigger hassle for you, Guv. I'd assume so, anyway."

Lex pulled something from his pocket, held it up. "I understand this now. And I accept it. Marrying Mark."

I squinted at the white paper, realized it was the napkin from the club. "That's not what I meant." I swiveled back to face the sheriff. "Ignore him. Back to Mark Davis. Do you know where he is right now?"

Under the hat, the sheriff's face was still imperceptible. Knew by his silence, he was thinking.

"Not headed to jail?" said Riggle. That smirk registered in his voice again.

"He's as safe there as anywhere," said Lex. "I think what Finley wants is your marker. Acknowledging that you're going to leave Mark alone."

"In exchange for what?" Riggle snorted. "My fingerprints?"

"I'm about tired of your mouth, boy. And your short-sightedness. You should've closed this down a long time ago." The sheriff swiveled around. Pulled the pistol from his holster.

And shot Riggle.

33

THE BLUECOAT

"FIN," called Lex.

"I'm fine." I needed Lex out of the restaurant. Away from the sheriff. The idiot had gone off script and was now a witness to murder. And the sheriff had counted on that when he shot Riggle. It gave him a reason to take out Lex.

The mental chess I had to play understanding a man like my father. It was no wonder I had become a small-time sociopath.

The sheriff sauntered across the restaurant to the front door. Lex darted around the tables, circling away from him and towards me. Found me squatting between two tables.

"Listen," I whispered. "He's not going to shoot me. Not here. But he might shoot you. It's better if you take off."

"You're winding me up, right? Bugger off, Fin. I'm not leaving you."

"Why didn't you just stay with Melanie?" I looked over my shoulder.

The sheriff had locked the front doors. Moseying across the floor toward the kitchen. I hoped no one was in the kitchen. He wouldn't think twice about killing them.

"I see. You can detour from our plan, leave whenever you

bleeding choose. People are counting on you, Finley. Do you forget who's running the bloody ambulance?"

Cripes, Bev. I didn't want the sheriff to see Bev.

"Where is Mark?" I whispered. "Your guy didn't drive that car."

"Lewis has him. Stop worrying about bloody Mark Davis for one bloody minute. You have a hit man ready to take you out. You've left him free to set you up. Why didn't you take the bloody fall when you were supposed to?"

"Because I was worried about Mark." I told myself to not think about the pain pinching Lex's face. Let out the breath I held. "And I don't have a hit man after me. Rick Graves is dead. I shot him. I promised Sue Marshall I wouldn't tell you."

"What?"

"And I'm not marrying Mark. I'm turning myself in for murder and taking Mark's mother down with me. She hired Rick Graves. She was the only one who knew I was at Mark's house on Sunday night. And she's the only one besides Mark and me who knew about Penny's money. I don't know how she knows, but she knows."

"Sod off, Fin."

"So you have to help Mark."

"You said you liked him. Do you love him?"

"Should it matter? His mother's a homicidal maniac." I leaned forward, watching the sheriff push through the swinging doors. "Go now."

"I should leave you." He grabbed my elbow and heaved me to standing. "Gormless bloody tosser that I am."

"Lex." The hold on my arm tightened, and he dragged me across the restaurant, my fake Manolos tripping and sliding on the wood floors. At the front door, he gripped my arm with one hand and fumbled with the lock with the other.

I placed a hand over his. Swallowed back the knot of grief welling in my throat. "Please, just go. He's my father. I'll be okay. Really."

A door creaked. Lex swiveled around. His eyes rounded. "Bugger."

"Lex." I grabbed his shirt, forced his gaze back to me. "I love you. Only you. My dad won't shoot me. But I'll die if he kills you. So leave."

Lex shook his head. "It's not your father, love."

I spun around.

Rick Graves stood in the hall to the bathroom. Stupid trench coat still swinging off his shoulders. Hands on his hips, showing off his holster.

Definitely not dead.

I backed into Lex. Held the little purse up, like a shield. Didn't even know why.

Graves grinned. He knew why.

"I heard the gunfire." He glanced at the bar, then back to me. "You didn't miss this time. But no weapon on you now, I see."

"Melanie can call this off. She's outside," I said. "Her son was arrested. She'll give me up to protect the son. Just call her."

He pulled the weapon from his holster, smooth as cream. "Funny, I just talked to Melanie about thirty minutes ago. Ducked in here when I saw you and Mark exit the building with the reporters."

I could hear Lex fumbling with the lock behind us. The creak of metal turning.

Graves racked the slide. "No ma'am, she hasn't changed her mind. In fact, I think you just ticked her off more. Don't think she'll mind the two-fer."

Lex's arm circled my waist. He would try to spin me around, take the bullets. I felt his weight adjusting. The catch in the door. The suctioned breeze swirling up from our feet.

"No," I said.

"Yes," said Lex.

He leaned. The door shoved open. I was flung around. My purse jerked from my hand. The shot pierced the air. And another.

I hit the tiled entryway. Felt Lex's body collapse on top of me. Another short pop.

My ears rang. But I could still hear. Outside, people screamed. Sirens, probably real ones this time, shrieked in the distance. I jerked up my head but could only see the bottom of the door in front of me. The dirty tile beneath us. Lex's weight pinned me to the floor. I tried to push with my hands. I couldn't move him.

Behind us there was movement. Heavy footsteps plodding forward. I braced myself to feel the hit. Almost wished Graves would hurry. Get it over with. I couldn't stand the trapped feeling, knowing what was crushing me to the floor.

A boot stepped over my head. Cowboy boot. The front door unlocked and opened. A rush of wind blew across my face. Dirt, bits of pine straw and leaves with it. I closed my eyes, breathed through my nose. Waited.

"You people, get back," said the sheriff. "Clear this area. You. Come here and guard this door. Don't let anyone in without my say-so. When Atlanta PD gets here, tell them the building is now secure. I'll unlock the door at that time. I don't want anyone coming in and disturbing the crime scene."

The door closed and locked. The boot nudged me. "Get up."

"I can't." I shuddered out a breath. Felt a tear leak. "I can't move."

"I'll roll him."

"Be careful. Don't hurt him." Red droplets sprinkled the tile. The sweet smell made me queasy. I squeezed my eyes shut. Felt the weight ease. I twisted to the side. Stared at Lex, lying on his stomach next to me. Reached to touch his face, but a hand gripped my armpit. Jerked me to my feet.

The ring on my necklace swung out and bounced against the zipper of my dress. The sheriff snagged the ring, examined it, and let it drop to my chest.

"You okay?" The sheriff's voice was gruff. "Who was that?"

I peered into the restaurant. Fought off the sickness wringing my stomach. Clanging between my ears. Rick Graves's body lay in the door of the bathroom hall. I backed into the wall. Let it hold my body upright. Breathed through my nose. Tried to lengthen the breaths.

"Mark's mother put a contract out on me."

The sheriff shook his head. "God almighty, Finley. What in the hell has happened to you?"

"Look in the mirror. Three bodies. You're not even sweating."

"I didn't shoot him." The sheriff toed Lex's leg.

"Don't touch him," I snapped. "Leave us alone."

"You're getting out before Atlanta PD shows up. I don't need a witness for this. Certainly not you."

I glanced outside. Pulled my thoughts together. Slipped the ring on my finger and slid it along the necklace. Pulling the sheriff's eyes with it. Zipping it back and forth while I talked. Like a pendulum.

"There's an ambulance right there. I know the driver. We were going to—never mind that. Just let me take him. I won't say a thing. You know I won't."

His gaze flicked from the necklace to my face. No reading. No telling if he felt any guilt at seeing my mother's wedding ring. If my stupid little trick worked.

Please work.

"You were always able to think fast on your feet. Too fast for your own good." He knocked on the door, cracked it. Spoke to Lex's fake detective. "Get a stretcher from that ambulance. Tell the driver to stay in the bus, put on the lights. The EMT can help you load him but don't bother with any measures. Get him out quick. I'll take care of the paperwork."

The door snicked shut.

The sheriff grabbed my chin. Brown eyes that matched mine bored into me. "I'm doing you a favor, girl."

I jerked away, tasting the humiliation. I'd eat crow if I could get Lex out. I couldn't look at him. Crimson splattered the floor, drenched his body. My purse was unrecognizable. My Burberry had been splashed with red and marked with dirt. I eased it off.

"Put that coat back on and dispose of it somewhere else," he said. All business. "Burn it. Do you know what to do with him? Ask them to take you to Grady. I can have a guy waiting to pick him up."

"No. I can deal with it."

"Suit yourself." The sheriff stepped over Lex. "I've got to fix this situation."

Took a deep breath, hating myself. But the sheriff had saved my life. Was letting us go. And I still needed help. "What I said earlier about the death certificate? You're going to hear about that from someone else. Someone who wants to work with you. I traded it for something important to me."

"Why're you telling me?"

"Because I need you to call something in for me. For real. A Buckhead address. In about twenty minutes."

I turned at the knock on the door. The fake detective with a stretcher. I unlocked the door, held it open.

The sheriff put his hands on his belt. Dipped his head. Walked into the restaurant.

Lex's man glanced at me, then at Lex. Didn't say anything. Another man pushed inside the door. Lewis. Or Bruce. I wasn't sure who was who.

Silently, they wheeled in the gurney. Rolled and hoisted Lex onto it. I held the door, and they rolled him out. The area had been cleared. The guests had been smart enough to be scared away. I laid my coat over Lex. Kissed his forehead. And stepped back. Watched them take him to the ambulance. Like two soldiers with their fallen lieutenant.

Bev leaned out the ambulance door. I shook my head, waved her off. They'd figure it out.

I still had Melanie to contend with. I wanted that confession.

34

THE STING

I FIGURED Melanie would be in their Buckhead home, anticipating Rick Graves's news. Eager to learn I wouldn't bother her family anymore. Waiting to hear from Mark. Probably had her lawyer putting together Mark's bail money.

This would go down easier if the judge weren't home. He would keep Melanie from talking. And she was nervy. Anxious to talk. The judge would spot the hook when I was ready for the sting. He'd lawyer her up, and I'd have no closure. No justice for Penny.

I had no opinion on the judge. Trusted Mark's instincts about his father. Maybe he cared more about the law or his position than his family. The sheriff was like that, in a different way.

Mark's feelings about his mother were different. He'd closed down every time her name was mentioned. Vague hints at his earlier failed attempts at relationships. The coolness. Biting remarks followed by defeatism in response to her helicoptering.

That was beyond prickly.

Mark's BMW was still parked in the alley. I located the keys stashed beneath the back left tire. Thankfully, found one of Mark's fleece jackets in the trunk. Tossed my coat and zipped his over my dirty dress.

The drive was short. But I had time to steel my nerves. My thoughts boxed away.

At my ring, Melanie opened the door. Expecting someone else. I moved quickly. Stepped into the foyer and pulled her into a hug. Patted her stiff back and rigid shoulders with murmurs about Mark before she could push me away. Dipped my hand into her pockets to nick her phone. Slid it into Mark's roomy coat. Evidence of her contact with Graves likely not yet deleted.

My phone was in the other pocket. An app already turned on, ready to record our voices. Just like I had done with Riggle.

I stepped back into the open doorway. She couldn't get out or shut me out without a fight. The eyes of the neighborhood would be on me even if they couldn't see her.

"What are you doing here? Why do you look...like that?"

Good, she was startled. I'd put her at a disadvantage.

"You should see the other guy," I said. "Actually, you really should. He's dead. Because of you."

"What are you talking about?" Her hands fluttered near her chest. "It's been a long night. Get out—"

"You hired Rick Graves to kill me. He wasn't very good at it. I'm still here. But there's been three attempts on his life. That I know of. And the last one was successful. True, he took a gamble in choosing his profession. But you paid to put him there. And the law says that's a big no-no."

"You killed him?"

"No. I didn't kill him." My heart lifted at that thought, then sank again. "Graves committed murder. He didn't get me, but he's still a killer. And I'm a witness."

"Get out. I don't want you anywhere near my family. What do you want? Money?" Her eyes flitted to a small chest in the foyer. Probably kept her checkbook in there. Making it easy for burglars.

"I don't want your money." I leaned against the doorframe. "But you want Mark's trust money back, right? That's why you sent Rick Graves to Penny's apartment. Had him try to find it. Or evidence of it. Then when he couldn't find the trust money, you wanted him to trap me there so I'd find the money for him. He was looking for bank statements instead of markers."

"That trust is part of Mark's inheritance from his grandfather. Our family money. His children's inheritance."

"Do you want Penny's money? Yes or no."

"It wasn't her money," she shrieked. "It's our money."

"I only know where Penny's money is hidden. Answer my question."

"You've got some nerve." She took a shaky step toward the chest of drawers. Sank on the dresser. Her fingers gripped the edge of the polished wood. "White trash. You cheap whore."

"Those names mean nothing to me," I said. "Listen, I want your marker. You're going to give me something. In return, I'll tell you where to find Penny's money. That's how this works."

"Do you think that just because Rick Graves is dead, you can order me around?" Her chuckle was forced, raw. "You don't know your place, missy."

I had her. "I'm offering Penny's money. That's my trade."

"Stop calling it *her* money." Melanie's voice rose. The knuckled grip on the chest had gone white, but her cheeks were mottled red.

"The trust money is gone. Do you know what Mark did with his trust? He paid off Penny's momma's accounts. Penny's mother's debts."

A nerve spasmed above Melanie's left eye. The little chest of drawers rattled beneath her.

"And do you know who Penny's mother is?" I continued. "A real-life crackhead. Although lately, I believe she's more into meth. Anyway, she's in prison. So the accounts started hassling Penny for the dough. Probably why she took the job with Platinum."

"Prison."

I smiled, careful to enunciate my final words. "Mark paid off loan sharks and drug dealers to help the grandmother of his future children."

At "grandmother," Melanie leaped off the dresser.

I spotted the open dresser drawer too late. The flash of a knife in her hand. Like a fancy stiletto. A letter opener, I reasoned. But fear had me backing out of the doorway.

She caught me on the brick porch, slashing at Mark's jacket.

Flipping sharp letter opener. Should have planned for this better.

I jumped back. Missed the edge of the porch. Fell down the stairs. Caught it on my palms. Skinned my knee. Flipped over and heard a crunch beneath me.

A phone. Dammit. I scuttled back from the stairs.

Melanie with a full head of steam. Lunging from the stairs. Waving the crazy sharp letter opener. Batshit crazy as only a rich Southern woman could get.

I pushed off the brick walk. Tried to pop up. Stupid fake Manolo heels wouldn't take my weight. Slammed back. Melanie on top of me. My skull bouncing against the brick. I reared up. Smashed my forehead into her nose. One of Lex's tricks. She howled. Hand flew to her face. Her pointy elbow caught me in the eye. And my head bounced against the brick. Again.

I squeezed my tearing eye shut. Reached for her throat with both hands. Melanie tore at my fingers and wrists with one hand. Dropped the knife. Went for my good eye with her fancy manicured claws. I released her throat. Jabbed a fist near her kidney. At her cringe, I pulled my elbow back and caught her under the chin. Pushed up with my core weight. She slid back.

"Cripes, woman. I'm half your age and lived on the streets. What are you thinking?" I snatched the knife and pulled my elbow back. Grabbed a fistful of silk blouse with my free hand. "Did you have Penny killed? Answer me, or we'll go another round."

"Yes!" she cried. Slung her arm up, trying to bat away the knife. "And I'd do it again. I'll do it to you now."

Blue lights flashed. A siren popped a short whoop. Headlights blared, lighting up Mark's BMW in the drive. A spotlight beamed on us. They'd heard us.

I tossed the knife. Pushed Melanie off. Rolled away. Got to my feet with my hands in the air. And walked toward the squad car.

Took them long enough. Probably thought our catfight hilarious.

Cops have a warped sense of humor.

I MADE MY STATEMENT. Handed over the phones. Promised to stay in touch and shoved the officer's card into my empty pocket. The blue lights faded. I hobbled on a broken Manolo to Mark's BMW.

Drove to Dot's. Opened the BMW's trunk. I lugged a bottle of fabric softener through her open door. Hoped to find everyone there.

But I didn't.

Elmore trotted up to the door to greet me. I found Dot on her throne, silk robe spilling over the sides. Feet up. Mark sat on the nearby couch, looking sick. I guessed someone had broken the news about Melanie.

Lewis and Bruce were examining the zoo. After discovering I didn't arrive bearing fries, Elmore pushed between them to press his nose against an aquarium.

"What you got?" said Dot.

"Penny's money."

I'd placed the jug in the trunk of Mark's car earlier that night. Taken it from Penny's that morning. Felt like a lifetime ago. I set the fabric softener on the counter and twisted the cap off.

Dot jerked her head at Lewis and Bruce. They took off. Elmore watched them leave, then returned to his aquarium vigil.

"Mark's not doing so good," said Dot. "But now that you're here, I think he feels better. Isn't that right, Mark?"

He attempted a smile.

"I'm really sorry about your mom," I said. "I didn't know another way to do it. Thought it'd be better if I let it get physical instead of legal."

"I still don't want to believe it." He slid lower on the couch, stared up at the ceiling. "My dad, either. This will get ugly. His wife hired a hit man. His son's an embezzler."

"Some families are real messed up like that," said Dot. "Kind of like Finley's, for instance."

I gave her a glare over my shoulder, then held the jug over the sink. Dumping the blue liquid. At the bottle's glug-glug, a baggie dropped into the sink. I fished it out and held up a dripping key.

"Penny's safety deposit box. I guess I'm the only one not mature enough to hide my money in a bank." I dried off the key and walked it to Mark. Placed it in his hand. Patted his cheek. "Penny wanted to pay you back for her mother's debts. That's why she made those markers."

"And I told Penny when a couple gets married, we're two halves that become whole. I'll invest some of it. When her mother gets out, she'll need it. I could support a halfway house to help her and women like her. And give the rest to Penny's rescue charity."

"All of it?" said Dot. "You're spending all that money on charity?"

"Dot," I said. "We did this for Penny, remember?"

"I mean, Mark, you'd make a good husband." Dot laughed. "Finley? Going to step up?"

I blinked back a tear. "I'd make a terrible wife, actually. Looks like I'm not the only one who thinks so."

35

THE TAKE

AFTER A SHOWER AND CHANGE, I called Bev to apologize and thank her. Drove out to Jelly's to do it in person. Jelly said he was real sorry he didn't get to run me over.

"Me, too," I said. "That would have been the highlight of my day. It went downhill and upside down from that point."

Jelly pointed to the pool tables behind me. A lone figure picked off balls with a house stick and cue. "Easy money there," he said. "Been drowning his sorrows all night. Almost closing time."

I sighed. "Might as well. Cinderella's already turned back into a pumpkin."

Dragged my tired feet across the room. And stopped. Felt the hostility rippling off him before I'd gotten within a couple yards. Possibly, this game would be too dangerous. Even for me.

But after the night I'd had, I could take one more gamble.

"Care to make a wager?" I said. "I bet I can take the black ball before you can."

Lex turned, leaned against the table. "I don't make wagers with known hustlers."

"Probably a good idea."

"Sometimes I have them. Despite what you may think."

"You're angry. It's a useless emotion, remember?"

He folded his arms. "I've every right to be angry."

"You do. I betrayed you. But I tried to explain on the napkin."

"Your note said, 'Sorry, but let me do this.' Bloody hell, Fin."

"I meant let me turn myself in, not get myself killed."

"So hard to tell what you mean, *love*, when you don't actually tell me what you mean."

"I had every intention of following the plan. Except for the turning myself in part." I fingered my necklace, pulled on the chain. "It's just that... Things went haywire, and I had to improvise."

"That's not what partners do. They should be honest with one another."

"I'm sorry." Dropped my necklace. Hugged my arms. "I'm really sorry. I'm a mess. I overthink. And I didn't trust you when I should have."

"But did you mean it?" He cocked his head. "Or were you just sending me off?"

"Mean what?"

"You know what."

I chewed my lip. Felt heat lick the back of my neck.

"Well?" he said.

"Yes, Lex. I love you. Only you."

"Not good enough." He shook his head. "I took a hit for you. Watched you engage yourself to another bloke. Dust me off. Lie to me. Leave me. Not to mention the countless times I've witnessed attempts on your life."

"Countless? I saved you from my sociopathic father. And when he realizes your blood is the same as that corn syrup leaking out of my purse, he's going to—"

"And when Sue Marshall finds out you double-crossed her, what's she going to do? We're in the same boat, you and me."

I sniffed. "Do you still want to be in my boat?"

"It's a rather rocky boat." Lex smirked. Unfolded his arms. "But I'm seaworthy. Grew up on an island, yeah? I believe you ought to come here. Take your consequences."

I took two steps and fell into him. My head thudded against his shoulder. "I don't have to turn myself in for murder. I'm so happy I don't have to go to prison. I can be with you." Circled my arms around his waist and squeezed.

He kissed my head. "Cheeky girl. As if I'd let you go to prison. I'd force you to marry Mark first."

"He wants to work with us." I pulled back. "Mark's a good hacker. And did you see how flexible he is? I think he's a natural. He'll be easy to turn out. He stayed so calm. Kept to the narrative."

"Unlike you."

"Do you fancy another partner?" I mocked Lex's accent, then sobered. "Mark needs us, Lex."

"I thought you were out of the grift."

"And you told me you'd seen the light. You'd use your skills to help people. Like we did for Penny."

"Helping people doesn't pay the bills, darling. And although you may be partial to tawdry motels and ratty castoffs, I, on the other hand—"

"We can still get paid." I ran my fingers up his arms and clasped my hand around the back of his neck. "Anyway, Mark's got plenty of money. Richie Rich. He moved it offshore a few days ago."

"Why didn't you say that at the start?" Lex bent me back against his arm. "We could do with another partner. I know a great little con that takes at least three."

I pulled his head down to mine. "Don't you ever stop talking?"

He did.

THANK YOU READER

This book would not have been written in the Winter of 2018 if not for my readers. After offering *Pig'N a Poke* to my subscribers as a free read, I had fans of Finley asking for more. How could I resist such sweet clamors? Her story had been banging around my head for quite some time, but I had too many other deadlines to give her any attention. With a free month after the release of *A View to a Chill*, I thought I might write another Finley Goodhart short story or short novella.

Nine weeks later, I had *The Cupid Caper*. Finley demanded a full character arc. Lex demanded a relationship arc. The themes of trust, faith, and redemption demanded complete treatment. And of course, I needed to wrap a long con into a whodunit. And so, my readers received a full Finley Goodhart novel.

I'm so glad!

I hope you enjoyed *The Cupid Caper*. I had a lot of fun writing it. I loved using Atlanta and its surroundings as a setting. All my books (so far) are set in Georgia, but Halo and Black Pine are imaginary, based loosely on places I know. Using real settings in *The Cupid Caper* were fun, particularly because it involved field trips to places like Oakland Cemetery. Come to Atlanta and try them out, too! Be sure to eat at Noodle, the Flying Biscuit, Chick-Fil-A, and have a coffee at Octane.

Just don't drive during rush hour. ;)

If you'd like to be alerted of my new releases, please sign up for my VIP Readers email group. You'll receive the prequel to *The Cupid Caper*, **PIG'N A POKE**, when you sign up plus a lot of other exclusive giveaways, news, and downloads!

Look for the signup button on my website: LarissaReinhart.com

And finally, you can help others by writing a review. Your five minutes of time is greatly appreciated by me and other readers!

Thank you!
Larissa

LARISSA'S GIFT TO YOU!

THE PIG'N A POKE
A Finley Goodhart Crime Caper prequel

When a winter storm traps ex-con Finley at the Pig'N a Poke roadhouse, she finds her criminal past useful in solving a murder.

Free for my VIP Readers!

Keep up with Larissa's latest releases, sales, and events (plus monthly giveaways and release drawings) by joining her email group — https://www.larissareinhart.com/larissasreaders — and receive *Pig'N A Poke* as a gift.

Note: Larissa will not share your email address and you can unsubscribe at any time.

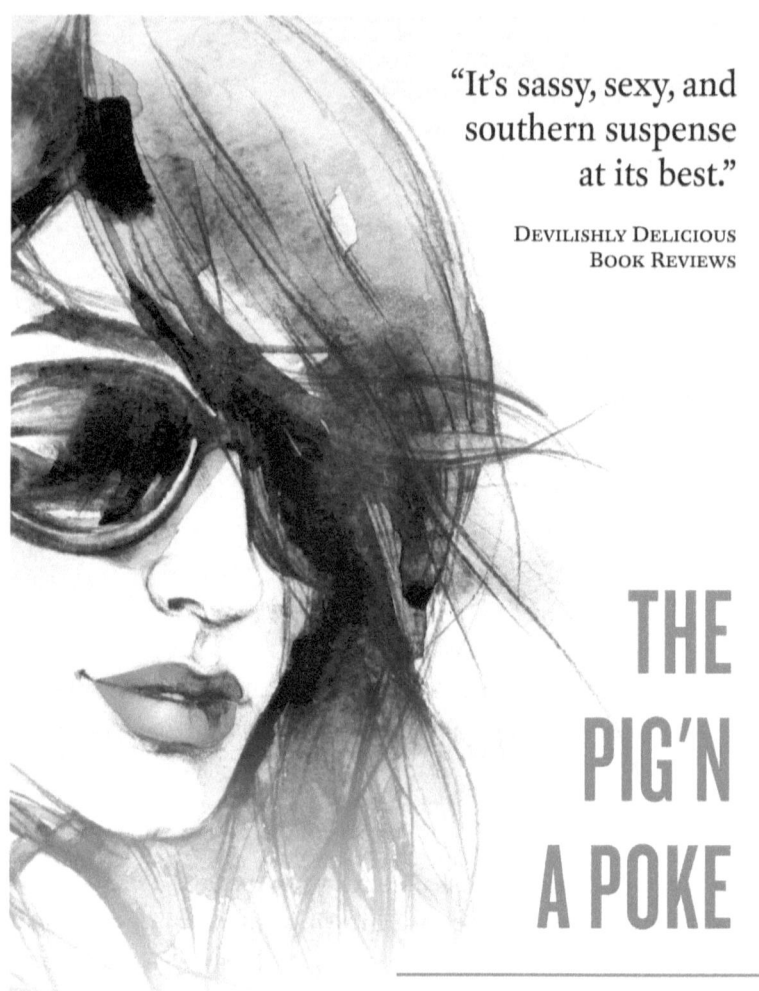

"It's sassy, sexy, and southern suspense at its best."

DEVILISHLY DELICIOUS
BOOK REVIEWS

THE PIG'N A POKE

A FINLEY GOODHART
CRIME CAPER SHORT

LARISSA REINHART

Wall Street Journal Bestselling Author

ALSO BY LARISSA REINHART

The Maizie Albright Star Detective series

15 MINUTES

16 MILLIMETERS

NC-17

A VIEW TO A CHILL

17.5 CARTRIDGES IN A PEAR TREE (novella)

18 CALIBER

18 1/2 DISGUISES

19 CRIMINALS

20 CARATS (novella)

"Child star and hilarious hot mess Maizie Albright trades Hollywood for the backwoods of Georgia and pure delight ensues. Maizie's my new favorite escape from reality." — **Gretchen Archer, USA Today bestselling author of the Davis Way Crime Caper series**

Ex-teen TV and reality star, Maizie Albright, returns home to Black Pine, Georgia, determined to start a new career as a private investigator, modeled after her childhood starring role as a "Julie Pinkerton, Teen Detective." Unfortunately, Maizie's chosen mentor, Wyatt Nash of Nash Security Solutions, is not a willing teacher and her learning curve includes becoming her own person after spending a life under the thumb of managers, directors, and producers, particularly her stage-monster mother.

> *"Ms. Reinhart has struck gold with these characters and written them into a fabulous and funny mystery story. Twists and turns, romantic tension, great dialogue full of humor and fast quips, along with some Southern flair had these pages absolutely flying."* — **Great Escapes**

A Cherry Tucker Mystery series

A CHRISTMAS QUICK SKETCH (prequel novella)

PORTRAIT OF A DEAD GUY

STILL LIFE IN BRUNSWICK STEW

HIJACK IN ABSTRACT

THE VIGILANTE VIGNETTE (Halloween novella)

DEATH IN PERSPECTIVE

THE BODY IN THE LANDSCAPE

A VIEW TO A CHILL

A COMPOSITION IN MURDER

A MOTHERLODE OF TROUBLE (Mother's Day novella)

Meet Cherry Tucker, big in mouth, small in stature, and able to sketch a portrait faster than kudzu climbs telephone poles! The Cherry Tucker Mystery series (Henery Press) begins with Portrait of a Dead Guy, a 2012 Daphne du Maurier finalist, a 2012 The Emily finalist, a 2011 Dixie Kane

Memorial winner, and a Woman's World Magazine book club pick for 2018!

"Reinhart manages to braid a complicated plot into a tight and funny tale. The reader grows to love Cherry and her quirky worldview, her sometimes misguided judgment, and the eccentric characters that populate the country of Halo, Georgia. Cozy fans will love Cherry Tucker mysteries." – Mary Marks, **New York Journal of Books**

Finley Goodhart Crime Capers

THE PIG'N A POKE (prequel, short story)

THE CUPID CAPER

THE PONY PREDICAMENT

THE HEIR AFFAIR

Ex-con Finley Goodhart finds her criminal past – and criminal ex-boyfriend – useful in catching crooks. Can she make up for her past by helping victims double-cross their swindler? More importantly, can she convince Lex that going straight is the best (and most challenging) hustle of all?

"Faced paced, bold, heartbreaking, this book has it all. It takes us deep into the world of hustlers, cons and dirty business. Yet it gives us glimpse of just how pure-hearted some of the worst con artist can be. Highly recommended for lovers of mystery and thrillers."

ABOUT THE AUTHOR

Wall Street Journal bestselling and international award-winning author, Larissa Reinhart writes humorous mysteries and romantic comedies including the critically acclaimed Maizie Albright Star Detective, Cherry Tucker Mystery, and Finley Goodhart Crime Caper series. Her works have been chosen as book club picks by *Woman's World Magazine* and *Hot Mystery Reviews*.

Larissa's family and dog, Biscuit, had been living in Japan, but once again call Georgia home. See them on HGTV's *House Hunters International* "Living for the Weekend in Nagoya" episode. Visit her website, LarissaReinhart.com, join her VIP Readers' Group, and get a free short Finley Goodhart story.

www.ingramcontent.com/pod-product-compliance
Lightning Source LLC
Chambersburg PA
CBHW020959120726
47905CB00009B/2764